Love Me

By

Michelle Lynn

Editor: S.G. Thomas
Cover photo: © Shutterstock.com
Cover Design: by Kerri Reaves

The author acknowledges the copyrighted or trademarked status and trademark owners of the following word marks mentioned in this work of fiction: Better Homes and Gardens Magazine, Ford Mustang, FJ Cruiser, Jeep Wrangler, Chevy Silverado, Mercedes, Adidas, Velcro, Skype, Brides Magazine

My Thanks

To my husband, who has been so patient during this process. Thank you for turning into our sole housekeeper, cook, and caretaker of two adorable kids while I sat in front of my laptop numerous days and nights. Your praise and reassurance on this journey gave me the strength to see it through. Most of all, thank you for being my happily ever after.

To my family and friends, who have patiently listened to me toss questions and ideas at them during this past year. I promise to stop the "What If" game, at least for a few weeks. On a serious note, your support and encouragement means the world to me. Thank you.

Last, but not even close to least, S.G. Thomas, my editor. Finding you was a blessing. Thank you for your dedication to Love Me Back, helping me see things in a different light, which in turn, gave me a stronger and more well-written novel.

Chapter 1 – 11 years old

"Madeline Dolores Jennings!" Bryan yells teasingly at me from the bottom of the hill.

"What do you want, Bryan Otto Edwards?"

"Hey, I'm just joking, Maddy." Bryan runs up the hill, throwing his arm around me. "You knew it had to be coming; I have been holding it in all day since Kenna slipped at lunch."

I hate the days my mom "works late". It entails me having to walk up the grassy hill from my grade school to my brother Jack's football practice with the other latchkey brothers and sisters of the football heroes of our small town. There are four of us that make the trek every day.

Mackenna Ross is my best friend and our polar opposite personalities only enhance our different qualities. She is free-spirited, whereas I am more conservative. She speaks her mind and I keep my thoughts to myself. We share a love for tennis, swimming, and the game MASH (mansion, apartment, shack or house), where we try to map out our perfect lives.

Our brothers are teammates but not the best of friends. In fact, they have been known to fight with each other on several occasions. The most recent battle is over a girl... Cindy Rydel. I don't see what is so intriguing about her, but I am not a seventeen year-old hormone-induced boy either. It doesn't matter to Kenna and me that they don't get along, so long as it doesn't keep us away from one another.

Jack glances up to the bleachers on his way to the field, giving me a wave as he checks to make sure that I made it safely across the hill from our school. I wave back and take my seat next to MacKenna. She already has her notebook out, wanting to go first. We keep all of our MASH games in a binder, marking stars next to the lives we want. I grab her notebook, flipping to the next blank page.

"Alright Kenna, four boys?" I ask.

"Let's do five today. I can't decide who to leave out, Jackson or Tyler," she says, tapping her lips with her finger.

"Fine, five," I reply. Mackenna never changes the cars she desires or where she wants to live, but the boys' list is forever rotating between the boys in our school.

"Ok, well my usual four boys and..." she pauses, glancing over to the field next to us where the latchkey boys are tossing a football around. "Bryan," she says, spitting it out so fast I barely catch what she said.

"What?" I scream at her. Two days ago, Bryan told her that her butt is big, and now she is picking him to be her future husband?

"Maddy! Shhh…it's my choice. Write it down," she says, pointing to the paper with her neon-green painted fingernail.

"Alright, but I don't understand you at all." I shake my head back and forth, writing it down and hoping that the rotation eliminates him. I love Mackenna but Bryan is a jerk; I would not let her marry him.

Luckily, Mackenna ends up married to Tyler, living in a shack in California with eight kids, and driving a Range Rover. I am happy Bryan was eliminated in the third round.

"Not my best life but I'll take it. I got my Range Rover." Mackenna shrugs her shoulders, moving her eyes toward the grassy area again but quickly turning back toward me. "Your turn, hand it over," she says, holding her hand out.

I dig through my bag and pull out my purple binder, handing it over to her.

"Maddy, this time you cannot put Trent down four times; you have to choose other boys." She starts writing MASH across the white sheet of paper.

"I only did that once, Kenna." I look over at Trent throwing the ball to Bryan. "Plus, I don't like him anymore," I say, trying to convince myself as much as Mackenna.

"I've heard that before," she says, tapping the pen on the paper.

I have known Trent my whole life. His brother, Doug, is Jack's best friend. We have been thrown together during our brothers' t-ball and football practices and games, as well as too many Cub Scout events to count. We would play together when we were little, but as we get older we tend to ignore each other, doing our own thing when forced to be around one another.

Mackenna is right though. If I am being honest with myself, I have had a crush on him my whole life. I have written "Mrs. Trent Basso" millions of times and scribbled over it a zillion more. Regardless of my current feelings toward Trent, he is always on my MASH list for a future husband.

Today I hate Trent because, during recess, Evan Graham said that Trent asked him to ask me if Mackenna liked him. I tried to act as though it didn't bother me, but I wanted to march over to Trent and kick him in the shin. I told Evan I would ask and get back to him tomorrow. I already knew her answer without having to ask her; she would never do that to me. I am so mad at Trent Basso today that I knock him down from his number one spot to my fourth option for future husband. Baby steps.

At the end of my MASH, I am married to Jimmy Schmidt, the class clown, and drive a minivan around Alaska with only one child. Not even close to my best life. I throw my binder on the bench in front of me, leaning back to enjoy the sunshine.

"Let's do it again," Mackenna says eagerly.

"No, I'm tired. Let's just relax." I don't open my eyes. I want to empty my mind and enjoy the peace, knowing it will end when Jack and I go home.

"You go ahead and relax; I am going to play some football." Mackenna walks down the bleachers over to Bryan, Trent, and the other boys.

I open one eye, peering down at her. I am jealous of her confidence. She just walks right up to the guys, grabs the football from Trent, and throws it to Bryan. The boys seem annoyed that she is interrupting their game but they let her join in. I see Trent trying to show her how to throw a football, but she just pushes him away and takes the ball again. I love that girl.

About fifteen minutes later, Mackenna comes running up the stairs and grabs her bag. Practice is over and the football team is making their way to the gates that enclose the field.

"Move your asses, Littles," Trent's brother Doug yells over to us. All the latchkey younger siblings are called "the Littles". MacKenna is 'Little Ross', Trent is 'Little Basso', Bryan is 'Little Edwards', and I'm 'Little Jennings'.

None of us say anything as we venture down to the end of the gates to meet our older siblings.

"Let's go Mad; we're going over to the Basso's for dinner," Jack says, motioning for me to hurry up.

"I'll be right there." I hold up my finger and give Mackenna a hug, even though I will probably talk to her in a couple of hours. I walk over to where Jack is already climbing into his Mustang, and see that Doug and Trent are already waiting for me. Doug pushes the front seat forward so I can climb in the back next to Trent.

"Hey, Maddy," Trent says, turning his head to stare out the window.

"Hi, Trent," I respond, staring out of my own window. That pretty much sums up our friendship lately. I have tried to figure out what happened to us but have come up with nothing.

We arrive at the Basso's ten minutes later. They live on the outskirts of town and have acres of land with horses. Their house has a wraparound porch with flower baskets hanging out of every opening. It looks like something out of a *Better Homes and Gardens* magazine. As the Mustang comes to a stop at the top of their gravel driveway, their yellow lab greets us the second we open the door.

I bend down, letting Dixon climb on me while I pet him with both of my hands. I stand up and Dixon follows me to the front porch and into the house. I know this house as well as my own, since I have probably eaten dinner here more than mine. As soon as we walk in, Trent goes up the stairs to his room, Jack and Doug head to the basement to play pool, and I venture into the kitchen.

"I was wondering when you guys were going to get here," Mrs. Basso says to me over her shoulder while she prepares dinner.

I sit on the stool at the breakfast bar, taking out my homework. "Hi, Mrs. Basso. Thank you for having us for dinner." I am grateful that I didn't have to make it myself tonight.

"Oh Maddy, you are always welcome. You know that." Mrs. Basso turns around, smiling at me. She is the epitome of the perfect mom. She works at the local library, always has dinner on the table for her husband and boys, and she volunteers for all of the school functions and fundraisers.

"I know," I say, and then begin to focus on my homework.

I am able to finish all of my homework while Mrs. Basso finishes dinner, humming to herself. She is always happy. I wonder what she knows that my mom doesn't.

"Dinner, boys!" Mrs. Basso calls, taking out her ponytail and shaking her golden blond hair back and forth. She is a beautiful woman and doesn't look her age at all.

Four boys come running in while I am setting out the plates and silverware.

"Hey, Madgirl. Long time no see," Trent's older brother, Gabe, says as he messes with my hair.

"Hi, Gabe," I softly say. Gabe is fourteen and is a freshman at the high school. He doesn't have to wait for Doug at practices because he is old enough to come home by himself.

"Where's dad?" Doug asks, while stealing a roll out of the basket and devouring it. I can't imagine how much food they must go through in this house with three boys.

I wonder why Mrs. Basso stays at home when her husband isn't around. Not like my mom, who is gone as soon as my dad leaves town for a couple of days. They couldn't be more different.

We eat the chicken and rice with broccoli, while the three older boys fight over the food. Trent is quiet, never looking up from his plate. I don't know what I did to make him hate me so much? After dinner, Jack says that he wants to play one more game, so I go into the family room to watch television. Trent and Gabe are already in there. I decide to sit down on the opposite end of the couch as Trent.

A couple of minutes later, Gabe leaves, mumbling something about homework.

I take this as my chance to find out what Trent's problem is and why he is so set on ignoring me lately.

"So, you like Kenna?" I ask, not turning my head from the television.

"I don't know," he says with a shrug.

"You don't know? Well, why did you ask Evan to ask me to ask her then?" I ask, looking at him out of the corner of my eye to try and read his expression.

He sighs and says, "I wanted to see what you would say."

"What do you mean? If you like her, go ahead and ask her out," I say, even though my heart is screaming at me to say something else.

"I don't like Kenna." He moves closer to me on the couch. I am totally confused by this boy.

"Then why did you have Evan ask me that?" I repeat, turning to face him on the couch. We have been friends since we were in diapers. Why is everything so awkward now?

"I wanted to see if you would be jealous," he says quietly, taking my hand and entwining our fingers.

"Did you get the reaction you wanted?" I ask, not removing my hand with his.

"No, I thought you liked me. Am I wrong?" He is staring at me now, his crystal blue eyes boring into mine. I couldn't look away if I tried.

"You are right, I do like you." I bite my lower lip, unsure of what happens now.

"I like you too," Trent whispers and turns around to watch television, never letting go of my hand.

Chapter 2 – Present Day 25 years old

The plane dips down and both of my hands clutch the armrests. I have never liked flying but I am extra on edge this trip. I don't want to go back home but I have no choice. My brother has decided to finally marry his college sweetheart, Lindsey Jacobson.

Don't get me wrong. I love Lindsey and I couldn't ask for a better sister-in-law. The problem is that they planned a week-long wedding extravaganza and, like every other wedding of the Bigs and Littles over the years, everyone is involved. Therefore, I'm not only spending a week with Jack and Lindsey and their wedding party, but I'll also be seeing Bryan, Mackenna, and, from what I heard last night, Trent.

A hand squeezes mine gently. "It's alright sweetie, just some turbulence," Ian Fisher, my best friend, says quietly.

"I know. I hate flying," I say. Ian and I became best friends our senior year of college when we worked together at the rec center. We both lusted over the same guy but unfortunately for me, the object of our mutual affection swung Ian's way, not mine.

I made Ian take a week off work to come with me, and since he already knows most of the people, it will make things easier. I need him there with me to face everyone again.

"It's going to be fine Maddy, just relax." Ian looks at me, squeezes my hand, and then goes back to reading his magazine. We both know he isn't talking about the flight, and we also both know that things won't be fine.

The plane lands five minutes early. I am torn with wanting to get off or not, but I know I have to. Ian and I make our way to baggage claim and he stops on the way to get one of the luggage carts.

"Why do we need that?" I ask sharply.

"For our bags. I can't carry them all," he snaps back to me.

"How many bags to do you have?" I met him at the gate this morning so both of us had already checked our luggage.

"I don't know," he says, tilting his head down to look at me.

"Oh God, you probably have more than me," I gripe.

"Probably. Now help me pull this through," Ian says, yanking at the cart corral.

"Here, let me help," a deep voice says from behind us.

I see the tanned forearm easily guide the cart out of the corral. My eyes roam upward, taking in a firm bicep, strong shoulders, and when my eyes reach the face attached to all of the above, I gasp.

"Hey Madgirl, long time no see," Gabe Basso says, smirking at me.

"Gabe," I say stunned. I'm not ready to face him so soon.

"I know, I caught a break at work in order to get here early." His eyes leave mine, focusing on Ian. "Hi, I'm Gabe," he says, extending his hand out toward Ian.

Ian looks as dumbfounded as I probably do, but puts his hand out to shake Gabe's.

"Sorry, Ian this is Gabe Basso. Gabe, this is Ian Fisher." I motion my finger back and forth between the two of them.

"Nice to meet you," Ian says.

Gabe nods his head to him. "What baggage claim are you guys at?" he asks.

"Five, you?" Ian takes charge of the conversation, since apparently I have been struck mute. If I am this bad in front of Gabe, how will I make it through everyone else?

Gabe's eyes shift to me and I see the concern in his eyes. "Six," he answers. "Is anyone picking you guys up?" he asks, still looking at me. I can't believe how much he looks like Trent, or more accurately, how much Trent looks like him.

"I rented a car. I didn't want to rely on anyone for rides the whole week," I say, divulging more information than necessary.

"Do you mind if I hitch a ride? I was going to catch a cab, but since you guys are here...." he says, his sentence trailing off.

"Sure, no problem," I say with a shrug.

The three of us walk over to our respective baggage claims. I can see Gabe's has already started moving, but ours is still quiet. A minute later, Gabe jogs over to us, holding a garment bag in his hand.

Although it's only June, Gabe is already tan, which I assume has to do with living in Florida instead of the Midwest. I'd heard that Gabe moved down there after college with a couple of buddies, going in together on some real estate deals. I also heard that he's doing pretty well for himself, especially for only being twenty-eight.

My bag is the first to come off, and I hope that's a sign that this week won't be too bad. Ian is waiting next to his cart; he has pulled off two bags already and is going for a third. His matching plaid faux designer-print luggage is a set of five and I assume he brought every piece.

"How much luggage did he bring?" Gabe asks, motioning his head toward Ian.

"I have no idea, but I bet he comes home with even more than he brought," I say, smiling.

"I guess he'll be prepared for whatever is going on. From what Doug told me, it's going to be quite a week."

"Yeah, I haven't heard much of anything," I respond, raising my shoulders and looking down at my feet.

"Knowing Jack, I'm sure he's planned a fun time."

"That's my brother, party planner extraordinaire," I say, smiling back up at him, noticing how perfect and white his teeth are.

"I'm looking forward to it; it has been a killer summer. All of our houses are booked for the season and we have been working like crazy getting everything ready. It was all I could do to get the time off," he explains. "How about you, Maddy? What's the decorating business like?"

"Hard to get into. I do most of my work for free, just to get my foot in the door. I tried to work as an assistant for another decorator, but they just want to boss you around and do their personal errands," I confess. I have actually thought about switching careers lately, but I don't want to go back to school.

"Yeah, I have heard that. I had a friend who graduated in fashion design and she had a hard time too."

"What happened? Did she finally break through?" I cross my fingers, praying his answer is 'yes'. I could use some hope to continue with my dream.

"Unfortunately, no. She ended up getting married to some investment banker she met and now lives in Connecticut with two kids," he says, giving me a lopsided smile.

"Oh," I murmur, deflated. I knew going into design that few people were able to really succeed in it, but since it's my passion, I went for it anyway.

"But," he says, nudging his shoulder with mine, "she wasn't half as talented as you, Madeline Jennings." He smiles down at me sweetly.

"Thank you," I grin back, "but you have never seen my work."

"Yes, I have," he answers. Before I can question him further, we see Ian coming over with his cart overflowing with luggage.

"About time, Ian." I turn around, towing my suitcase behind me. Suddenly, I feel my suitcase jerk to a stop behind me.

Gabe is there grabbing it. "You might as well take advantage of the cart," he says, taking the suitcase from my hands and placing it on the cart. Ian huffs as though it is too much to push, but Gabe and I both chuckle as we walk to the rental car counter.

As soon as we get there, the young boy behind the counter motions for me to step forward so I walk over to him. I am surprised to see Gabe step up next to me.

"Can I help you?" the young kid asks.

"Reservation for Madeline Jennings." I place my ID and credit card on the counter.

"Okay, we have you down for a compact this week." The kid moves to take my ID and credit card, but a hand quickly covers them both.

"Can we upgrade to an SUV?" Gabe asks.

"What?" I ask, raising my eyebrows at him.

"His luggage isn't going to fit in a compact," he says, pointing to an exhausted Ian who is making his way over to the rental car place with all of the luggage in tow.

"We will have to strap it to the roof. I can't afford to upgrade," I admit, nodding to the young man to continue with the previously agreed upon transaction.

"First of all, I don't think a compact has a rack you can strap luggage to," he says, laughing. "Second, I would never make you pay. Let me get an SUV, and we can share it all week. We will be going to the same places anyway," he adds, awaiting my answer.

I bite my bottom lip, contemplating my options. "I can't let you do that, Gabe. Not to mention, the reason I'm getting a rental car is so that I don't have to rely on anyone this week."

He pulls out his wallet, handing the kid his ID and credit card. "Go ahead and book us an SUV and put both of our names on it." He grabs my credit card and hands it back to me. "You can keep the truck and come get me when we are doing something," he says with finality.

Did I miss something? Since when is he in charge of me? The problem is, I knew Ian's luggage might be a problem. I guess I will just go ahead with Gabe's plan and then drop the truck off later for him to use. I don't need or want his charity.

We lug all of Ian's bags onto the shuttle van that will take us to the rental car lot. When we arrive, Gabe makes me pick out the SUV we are going to use. Of course, Gabe doesn't just get a regular SUV; he has to get a full-sized one. I pick a nice blue Chevy Tahoe, but it is huge and I don't really want to drive it. After living in New York for the past two years, I've gotten used to not driving, and to go from taxi cabs to this monster of a truck is too much for me to take. When Gabe tries to give me the keys, I tell him to keep them.

Gabe raises his eyebrows, but begins loading the SUV with luggage. When the last bag is in the back, I am astonished to see that it is jam-packed with luggage. *Does he always have to be right?*

We head down the freeway toward our town, which is about an hour outside of Chicago. I can't stop nibbling on my lower lip. I don't know what to expect when I get there. I have heard Gabe's phone buzz a few times with text messages, and I wonder who they are from.

By the time we pass the sign "Welcome to Belcrest: population 1,531", my lip is raw and I am starting to sweat. I can't believe I am back in the one place I swore I would never return.

"Holy shit. You weren't kidding when you said you came from a small town," Ian remarks from the backseat.

"Belcrest is small but mighty. Right, Madgirl?" Gabe playfully nudges me with his elbow. That is how the football team has always been described, 'small but mighty'. We've never had as many guys as the other teams, but we were still state champions five years in a row when my brother and Gabe played. By the time I graduated, the run ended.

I remain quiet, nervous about seeing everyone. We pull up to Gabe's house, which still has the same white porch with hanging flower baskets. I get out, stretching my legs and Mrs. Basso comes walking out with a chocolate lab behind her. Dixon passed away when we were in high school and they got a new pup, Kisses, which was affectionately named by Mrs. Basso. She said she was outnumbered for years and it was time she had a girl around the house. Since all of the boys were pretty much out of the house by then, there wasn't really a fight.

"Gabe, it's so good to have you home," she says, embracing him in a tight hug.

"It's good to be home, Mom," he responds, squeezing her back. I know he has always had a close relationship to his family, unlike me. "Anyone else here yet?" he asks.

I freeze, not wanting to know whether or not Trent is here.

"Doug is out back with your dad," she says and then turns towards me, doing a double take. She looks back and forth between Gabe and me, though whether she is confused or upset, I can't really tell.

"Madeline?" she asks curtly.

"Hello, Mrs. Basso," I say.

"I assumed you would be in town this week," she says, coming over to give me a brief hug. Cold compared to how she used to hug me.

"Why are you guys driving together?" she asks, seeming irritated.

"We ran into each other at the airport and thought we would share a rental car this week." Gabe tosses the keys in my direction.

Catching them, I hear Ian clear his throat behind me.

"Oh, I'm sorry. Mrs. Basso this is my friend, Ian. Ian this is Gabe's mom, Mrs. Basso," I motion back and forth.

She eyes him up and down. "Please, call me Wendy," she says, extending her hand.

"Nice to meet you…Wendy," Ian says, shaking her hand.

"Alright then, let's go," I say to Ian. "Nice to see you again, Mrs. Basso. Gabe, let me know if you want the car." I turn around before either one of them can say anything, heading back to the driver's side of the blue monster.

"Wait, Maddy!" Gabe calls, jogging over to me.

"What's up?" I say, trying to keep the impatience out of my voice.

"I don't have your number. Give me your phone," he demands.

I dig it out of my purse and hand it to him. He programs his number and then calls himself. After he hands it back to me, I see that he stored himself as the 'Hot Basso Brother'.

"Nice," I smirk up to him.

"It's not my fault my brothers got stuck at the shallow end of the gene pool." He holds his hands out, waiting for me to disagree. I don't.

We pull out of the driveway from the place that I once considered my home, and I want to cry for all that has happened between me and the Bassos. I promised myself that I wouldn't let myself get dragged into it again. I see Mrs. Basso giving Gabe the third-degree, probably about why he would show up with me, and I watch him shaking his head back and forth.

"She's a trip," Ian says. "What is her problem with you?"

"She used to be nice. I was like a daughter to her," I say, staring at the road ahead of me.

"What happened?" he asks.

I don't answer. I don't want to talk about it. I can't tell him that I took something from her that I could never replace.

Chapter 3 – 12 years old

Trent and I "went out" for about two weeks before we broke up. Fortunately, we were able to maintain our friendship, even with Trent "going out" with Candice Montgomery, Katie Pierce, Amanda Schmidt, and Jenny Roberts. Needless to say, Trent was a lot like Mackenna and had difficulty making up his mind.

Over the course of the year, Trent, Bryan, Mackenna, and I became a close-knit group. We usually got together with the Bigs and watched movies, played video games, or went bowling. We had turned into the best of friends.

There were some days I talked more to Trent than I did to Mackenna. When Jack's football team went to play in the state championship, we traveled to the game with the Bassos. We were able to convince Trent's parents to take Bryan and Mackenna with us. We piled in the Basso's conversion van with games and snacks, not realizing that our destination was only a few hours away.

We were staying in a hotel with a pool, which we were beyond excited about. After we arrived, we threw our bags in our rooms and immediately changed into our swimsuits.

"Mackenna Ross, what are you wearing?" I ask when she struts down the hall in a bikini top and towel wrapped around her waist.

"Well Mad, it's called a bikini," she says sarcastically.

"I know that, but why are you wearing it?" She looks gorgeous. I stare down at my one-piece pink swimsuit.

"Duh, I am going swimming," she says, putting her hands on her hips.

Suddenly, I am not so excited to go swimming. Mackenna can tell I am upset.

"I have another one if you want to borrow it?" She tries to comfort me and puts her hand on my shoulder. "But I think you look amazing."

"Thanks, Kenna, but I would never be able to hold that top up," I say, pointing to her chest. Kenna matured early compared to the other girls our age.

"They aren't that great Mad, believe me," she says softly.

"I know, but you look gorgeous Kenna," I respond, hooking my arm through hers. "Let's go show the boys how to dive."

She smiles back. It's funny that we are both self-conscious about the same thing, but for entirely different reasons.

As we draw closer to the pool, the smell of chlorine fills the air, making my body itch to get in the water. The boys are already here, and I am surprised to see that, in addition to the Littles, a lot of the

Bigs are here too. As we approach, all of the splashing ceases and all eyes are fixated on Mackenna's chest. I look over at her and she suddenly turns back around, bringing the towel from her waist across her chest and sits down on one of the chairs facing the window.

I sit next to her, putting my hand on hers. "Kenna, let's go in the water. Don't let these boys get you upset."

She shrugs her shoulders and I see her eyes watering.

"Come on, Kenna, we are diving for pennies," Bryan calls over to us. He is always making sure she is okay.

I wave my hand so that he knows we need a minute, but when I turn around, Mackenna is standing up and removing her towel.

I take off my cover-up and the only person I see looking at me is Trent as I enter the water. Go figure. When I am fully submerged in the water, Trent comes up to me, asking me if I want to go first. I think that is his way of making me feel better that no one is looking at me.

After a half hour of diving for pennies, Trent and Bryan start jumping off the diving board, doing cannonballs and flips while Kenna and I rate them. She and I start arguing about the score of one of Trent's cannonballs. I gave him a ten, but she insists it wasn't a full cannonball since he had a leg out. I am about to splash her, when I suddenly feel someone under me and my body starts rising out of the water. I look at MacKenna and see that she is emerging from the water too. All of the boys start screaming, "Chicken fight!"

I look down and see that I am on top of Gabe's shoulders and Kenna is on top of his friend Paul. Gabe is holding my knees and walking toward them.

"What am I supposed to do?" I look toward Trent and Bryan for advice. They are sitting on the edge of the pool with scowls on their faces.

"Knock her off Paul's shoulders," Gabe yells up to me.

Before I know it, Kenna is grabbing my hands and twisting them backward. I fall to the side but Gabe is able to keep me up. Since she and I are laughing more than actually pushing each other, Paul tries to take Gabe out by his legs. Even though Gabe holds his own, I feel myself slipping off his shoulders. He manages to grab my thighs, bringing my legs tighter around him. *When did he become so strong?*

I see Kenna start grabbing at Paul's head, trying to stay upright, so I put my hands on both her shoulders and lightly push her back into the pool. Everyone starts laughing and cheering. Kenna pops up and I am happy to see her smiling as well.

Gabe goes underwater, effectively removing me from his shoulders and then puts his hand up to give him high five. "Way to go, Madgirl!"

"Thanks, couldn't have done it without you," I say, slapping his hand back.

All of the parents come walking into the pool area with boxes of pizzas a few minutes later. We all hop out and grab our towels. Kenna and I get our pizza and go over to sit with Bryan and Trent, but they are ignoring us while they talk with the other boys. Eventually, Kenna and I finish our pizza and go back to her room.

I don't know what had made the boys so upset, but they seemed to be over it the next day. We went to the football game and Jack's team won State for the third year in a row. It was even more exciting since Gabe and Paul were both part of the team as well, and they were the only two freshmen playing on varsity. I knew Bryan and Trent secretly thought the streak would continue until they played and that one day, they would be the state champions like their brothers.

When we arrive home, the town is completely decorated for the win, complete with "congratulations" signs in every window. The guys are like movie stars in our small town. The mayor even put on a parade the next weekend and a huge potluck party in the school gym.

I love our small town and everything that it represents. That's why, the summer before I was set to enter junior high, I was devastated when my parents told me we were moving out of state. My dad had gotten a new job in Michigan and we were moving there at the end of the summer. When I told Mackenna, we cried together for two hours.

This is the happiest I've seen my parents in years so I have hope that maybe this move will fix their marriage. If it is going to make my family better, then it will be worth leaving my friends. Even if it makes me miserable in the process.

The day of my move, Trent, Bryan, and Mackenna sit on the driveway with me, watching as my stuff is loaded in the moving van.

Bryan puts his arm around Mackenna as she cries, but I stay firm, not letting the boys see me cry. Trent is quiet and keeps to himself.

Doug, Gabe, and a few of their teammates throw a ball back and forth with my brother in the front yard. Jack doesn't care; he is leaving for college in a couple of weeks. Since almost all of his friends are attending State, he will see them soon enough. Not me though. I am saying good-bye to my friends forever. I am moving six hours away, but it may as well be clear across the country.

After the van is packed up, we all watch it pull away from my now empty house. I think of the new family moving in and if they have a girl my age. Will she take my place with my friends? Will they forget all about me?

"Jack, Maddy...it's time to go," my dad announces.

Bryan walks over first, embracing me. He squeezes me tight. "I'll miss you, Maddy. Good luck in Michigan," he says in my ear.

Next is Mackenna. "I don't know what I am going to do without you. Take this, but don't open it until you get in the car. I made it for you last night." She hands me a piece of paper. She throws her arms around me, knocking me backward in the process. I giggle a little. "I love you, Maddy. Write me and call me every day. You hear me? Every day, Maddy," she says between sobs.

I can barely breathe at this point. It is all I can do to tell her, "I promise, Kenna. I love you, too."

She turns, walking away from me and Bryan leads her down the driveway a bit while consoling her. I stand there, wiping my eyes and I see Trent. We both know it is his turn to say good-bye, but we can't do it so we stand there staring at each other.

This boy has turned into my best friend over the past year and I don't think I will ever find someone like him again. I don't even want to. Suddenly, big arms surround me and I look up to see Doug hugging me.

"See you later, Maddy. You will have a great time in Michigan," he says and pulls away.

"Thank you, Doug," I say as he walks toward my brother again.

"Bye, Madgirl," Gabe says, hugging me. It's so tight that my ribs start to slightly ache.

"Take care of him, okay Gabe?" I tell him. He knows who I am talking about.

"I will, I promise. He's going to miss you like crazy though," he whispers in my ear. "We will see you soon." He gives me another tight squeeze before he steps back.

That leaves me and Trent, and I really do not want to leave him. He starts walking toward me and I lower my head, watching the tears fall as they leave dark spots on the concrete.

"Maddy, I don't want to say good-bye," he says and I see the tears in his eyes.

"I don't want to either," I say, shaking my head back and forth.

He wraps his arms around my waist and I wrap mine around his neck. We can't get close enough to each other, and neither of us wants to let go.

"I'm going to miss you. There will be boys in Michigan that will go crazy over you, but I want you to remember that no boy will ever love you like me," he whispers in my ear.

I melt into him, burying my head in his neck. He finally grew taller than me this past year. I can't say anything, even though I feel the same way about him. But for some reason, I can't seem to open my mouth.

He inches away from me and puts his lips on mine. We stay that way for a couple of seconds until we hear the Bigs whistling, and then he pulls me into one more embrace.

"I love you, Maddy," he says.

"I love you too," I whisper back.

Chapter 4 – Present Day

Ian and I make our way back toward town. I am dreading going back to my mom's house, but I know that I don't have a choice. If I don't stay with her, she will throw a fit. Sometimes it feels as though I am the mother and she is my child. I don't understand how my brother can live near her; I can barely handle her bi-monthly telephone calls.

We round the bend where the town begins and I see the cemetery. I look over but can't see the tombstone from the street, which I am thankful for. I know I will have to visit while I am here, but today is not the day. I fear if I go now, I will leave this town faster than I did the last time.

We pass the high school and grade school, noticing the hill that I walked up so many times with the other Littles. I forgot how many memories every inch of this town holds. The town square is exactly how I remember, with the same white gazebo in the middle of it. I am sure Jack and Lindsey will have wedding pictures taken there, just like everyone who marries here. We pass the library on our right, as we head out of downtown Belcrest. I remember all of the days after school that Trent and I would hide out from everyone there.

I knew this was going to be bad when Jack told me he was getting married here, but what choice do I have? He is my brother and has been by my side my whole life. Even when people I love have abandoned me, he always stuck by me. It is time for me to be there for him.

We pull down my street and I automatically feel like I'm going to throw up. Ian must notice because he reaches over, putting a hand on my leg. I look over at him and he smiles, letting me know he is there for me. I never told Ian the whole story of why I hate this town now. He never pushes me for details, always waiting until I am ready to tell him. That's one of the reasons why I love him.

My house is the same brown, ranch-style brick that I remember. I assume Jack is keeping up the landscaping for her. Appearances are everything in this town.

There are no cars in the driveway so I don't pull all the way up, instead stopping at the walkway to the house. I don't get the warm welcome Gabe does; no one is coming out to see me. I put the car in park and put my hands in my lap, sighing. I look at the house and more memories flood my mind, all of them bad. They are the reason I hate this town, the reason I ran away from it.

Ian is already out of the car, banging on the back door and telling me to unlock it. I shake off my thoughts, looking for the unlock button. After I click it, the back door opens and Ian starts pulling out the bags.

"It's like a band-aid, Maddy. You've just gotta tear it off," he says from the back.

"I'm fine, Ian, but thank you." Lying to people has become second nature lately.

"Let's go, it's hot. Please tell me your mom has air conditioning. I think my hair is already falling," Ian complains. There is no way his hair could fall with all of the gel, mousse, and hair spray he has in it, but I don't bother telling him this.

"Of course we have air conditioning. I know you aren't used to the country, but we do have modern conveniences," I say, reaching around to grab my one bag.

"I'm just saying. It's hard looking this good, Madeline." He has three bags hanging from his arms and pulling one behind him, and is out of breath by the time we reach my doorstep. He only uses my full name when he is agitated with me.

I ring the doorbell since I don't have a key anymore. No one answers. I should have known she wouldn't be home when I got here. I told her three times when I would be arriving. God knows what is more important than me this time. I search the front steps, looking for the fake rock she has used for years to hide the key. Bingo! I grab the key, inserting it in the lock and open the door.

"Wow," Ian says behind me.

I am speechless, unable to believe my eyes. The house has been completely remodeled from floor to ceiling. All of our furniture has been replaced with new modern furniture. The light oak tables are now glass. Our plaid couch is now a soft gray sofa with yellow armchairs on either side.

"Go," Ian pushes me into the house, "it's like 103 degrees out here."

I fumble my way into the house that is now unrecognizable to me, and drop my bags by the door. I love my mom for doing this. It helps keep the bad memories at bay, but I assure myself it wasn't done for my benefit. I wonder where she got the money; being in the designing world, I know these pieces cost a small fortune and aren't something an office assistant can afford.

"Your house is beautiful," Ian says, shutting the front door and looking around the house, I assume for a vent to cool down. It's hard to believe that Wisconsin summers can get so hot.

"This isn't my house," I say flatly, "not the one I grew up in."

"I see where you get your style," he says.

"I can assure you this is not my mother's doing. She must have hired someone. She has always been partial to more of a country theme," I respond, still in awe over the changes to the interior of the house. Every aspect has been redone. Even the pictures from when Jack and I were little are now in modern frames.

"Whoever did it, it's really nice," he says.

I put Ian in Jack's old room, which actually looks pretty much the same. His football trophies line the bookshelves with ribbons hanging below. The only difference I notice is that the twin-sized bed has been replaced with a queen. I am surprised the bedding has been washed, ready for Ian. I assumed I would be taking care of that when I got here.

I am happy to see my room has been redone. My daybed is gone, replaced by a queen as well. The walls are thankfully not still purple, but now a light blue with a chic new bedspread. All of my old furniture is gone and white furniture is now in its place. I throw myself on the bed, closing my eyes. Even with all new furniture, I can still feel the fear when I close my eyes and I am instantly transported back to that night. I open them quickly, not wanting to remember.

Peeking in on Ian, I see him unpacking so I head downstairs. The kitchen has been-remodeled as well with the most up-to-date stainless-steel appliances. The nice black high top table sits in the corner with a bowl full of fresh fruit on it. If there weren't pictures of Jack and I on the walls, I would think I was in someone else's house. I open the fridge for a bottle of water and it is filled with food, so I open the freezer and find the same. I don't know who is responsible for all of this, but I wish they would have been around when I was younger.

Just as I grab a bottle of water, I hear the door open.

"Maddy," she yells, "I assume that's your blue car in the driveway."

I walk out to the foyer and am shocked once again. My mom is wearing a navy blue pants suit and heels. Her chestnut brown hair is cut short and stylish. Her make-up is subtle and complimentary. She looks beautiful, just like the house.

"Yeah, I will go ahead and move it right now." I walk over to get the keys from my purse.

"That's okay, I just parked behind it," she says.

Who is this lady and what did she do with my mom?

"Um…sure," I hesitate. Before I can think whether to give her a hug or not, she is embracing me.

"It's so good to see you, Maddy. I've missed you so much." Her hug is tight, but I don't respond. I have never been hugged by my mom like this before.

"Hi, Mom." It's all I can think to say. She pulls back, grabbing my hands and looking at me. I see the anguish in her eyes, which is another reason I have stayed away. I don't want sympathy either.

"You are beautiful, honey. New York agrees with you," she says, smiling at me and I wish I had this mom when I was growing up. "So, where is this guy you brought home?"

"He is upstairs unpacking in Jack's old room," I answer, opening my water bottle.

"I don't need to tell you that bringing a guy to the wedding is just going to complicate the situation, Maddy." Her heels click on the dark hardwood floors as she goes into the kitchen.

There's my mom. Oh, how I missed her for those five minutes.

"It's not like that mom, he's just a friend." I follow behind her.

"I've heard that before," she says, smirking at me over her shoulder.

"Mom, let's just say I am not his type."

"Oh Maddy, you are everyone's type," she compliments me.

Okay, I like this new mom.

"Believe me, not Ian's."

"Did I hear my name?" Ian asks, entering the room. He changed his clothes to plaid shorts and a tight v-neck shirt with a pair of converse shoes. *Did he restyle his hair?*

"Yes, I was just telling my mom that I am not your type," I say, smiling at him.

"Don't get me wrong, Mrs. Jennings. I love your daughter, but I prefer broader shoulders."

My mom looks at me, raising both her eyebrows and turns back to Ian.

"Maybe you would have preferred her brother?" my mom asks, laughing.

"After looking at pictures, I am a little disappointed he plays for the opposing team," he joins in, laughing with my mom. "Oh Mrs. Jennings, I think that we are going to get along fabulously," Ian says, taking a swig of my water bottle. I give him a look telling him he is a traitor.

"Please, call me Barb," she says.

"Barb?" I question.

"Yes Barb, that is my name." She looks at me, knowing what I am implying. I decide to let it go for now. "I am making a stir fry for dinner. Will you two be sticking around?"

"You're cooking?" I question her again.

She ignores my question, starting to cut up chicken. "Your brother and Lindsey are coming by," she says with her back to me.

"We can stay; I don't have many other plans anyway. I think Ian saw most of the town on the drive from the Basso's house to here." Before I can take the words back, my mom has swung her head around and I see her mouth is now set in a straight tense line.

"Why would you be at the Basso's?" she asks, her tone curt.

"We ran into Gabe at the airport; that's his rental car outside. We are sharing it for the week," I say quickly.

"How is Gabe?" Her voice turns pleasant and she turns back around, focusing once again on the chicken. *What was that? Is she suffering from multiple personality disorder now?*

I notice Ian's eyes narrow, confused as to what is going on. I am just as confused at her responses.

"Fine, I guess." I shrug my shoulders at Ian.

"He always has had a good head on his shoulders," she says and then continues, "handsome, too. Too bad Ian, but I don't think he plays on your team either." She looks at him sympathetically.

"Oh Barb, I am pretty sure he prefers the pencil sharpener instead of the pencil," Ian says jokingly, taking a swig of my water bottle again.

My mom bends over in a fit of laughter. "Ian, I love you already," she says.

I smile at him. He always wins people over.

It is close to six when Jack and Lindsey arrive. Jack looks the same, with dark hair and emerald green eyes. He is over six foot and has maintained his muscle-toned body pretty well. Lindsey's curly blond hair has gotten longer since the last time I saw her. She barely wears any make-up, but doesn't need to with her natural good looks. She is cute and adorable, and they make a great couple. I am so happy that my brother found the perfect life partner.

"Hi, everyone," Lindsey says cheerfully, giving Ian and me a hug. She and Jack had met Ian last winter when they came to visit me in New York. "It's good to see you guys."

"You too, Lindsey. You look relaxed considering you're promising yourself to this guy in a week," I laugh, gesturing to Jack.

"That's why I am so relaxed; your brother has magic hands." She walks over to Jack, snuggling into his arms.

"You tell her baby," he says sweetly, kissing her head.

"Barb, let me help you." Lindsey walks over to my mom, grabbing vegetables to cut up.

"Thank you, Lindsey." My mom puts her arm around her shoulders and pulls her close.

Lindsey looks up to my mom, smiling back at her.

"So, are you guys ready for the week? This is no vacation, you know." Jack takes a big gulp of his water.

"What's the plan, brother?" I ask.

He looks at Lindsey, they smile at each other, and then he turns back to us. "Softball game tonight, dress fitting tomorrow, Great Adventures on Wednesday, BBQ and B-ball on Thursday, Bachelor and Bachelorette parties on Friday, and the wedding is Saturday," he says, smirking at me.

"Jesus, Jack. Do I have to go to everything?"

"Yes, you are a bridesmaid." He turns to Ian, "As her date, you are expected to be there too."

"I wouldn't miss it for the world." Ian's lips form a huge smile and I stick my tongue out at him. "It will be fun, Maddy."

I raise my eyebrows and sulk down into my seat. "Who all is involved in these plans?" I ask Jack. He knows specifically what I'm asking.

"All the groomsmen and bridesmaids, along with a couple of others," he answers, pausing because he obviously doesn't want to tell me.

"For heaven's sakes, Jack, just say it," I yell at him.

"Trent got in last week, Maddy." He looks guilt-stricken.

My heart jumps in my throat.

Chapter 5 – 15 years old

I never heard from Bryan again after my move. Trent and I wrote a few letters back and forth; Mackenna and I wrote every day and called every week. Soon the letters and calls got further apart and eventually stopped altogether. I made new friends in Michigan and I assumed a new girl took my spot. When Jack came home he would fill me on tidbits he heard from the Bigs, but other than that, Bryan, Trent and Mackenna were out of my life.

My parents' marriage was great right after the move. We all drove Jack up to college and my mom and dad seemed to bond over sending their oldest off to college. They started having date nights and my dad stopped traveling so much. When my dad did have to travel, my mom didn't go out like she used to before. That didn't change the fact that she never made me dinner and I had a mile-long list of responsibilities around the house. Just knowing that my parents were happy and staying together was enough for me.

I missed Jack so much and was always eager to spend time with him when he would return home for holidays. I cried when I found out that he had decided to go down to Florida for his spring break this year instead of coming home.

Not that I blamed him, but that seemed to be when our parents' relationship took another turn for the worse. My mom started drinking and going out a lot more. My dad was rarely home during the week and made excuses to go out on the weekend. This left me alone most of the time, which I started to prefer.

The last straw was when Jack announced he wasn't coming home for the summer. He was going to stay at the Basso's and work at some dairy farm in the town next to Belcrest. My parents both lost it. Unfortunately, Jack was an adult and, since he had a scholarship to State, my parents had nothing to hold over his head to make him come home.

After I finished my freshmen year, my parents sat me down and told me they were getting a divorce. I can't say I was surprised that they couldn't make it work. I'm sure it was hard when both of them were probably seeing other people.

I was surprised when my mom told me I would be moving with her back to Belcrest, while my dad stayed in Michigan. They assured me I would see him often and we would still get together for holidays. I still missed my friends in Belcrest, but I was nervous to go back after three years away. I had changed so much and I was sure they had too. Thanks to my full-fledged hormones, I was dying to see how Trent looked now.

Two months later, my mom and I pull up to a small three bedroom, ranch-style house a few blocks from downtown Belcrest. The outside looks like it's been here since the town originated. The grass is overgrown with patches of dandelions. The shrubs are so long they cover the walkway. Paint is chipped on the side and the brick seems stained. I can't even imagine what the inside looks like.

"I know it looks a little rough on the outside but just wait," my mother says, pushing a branch aside as she walks to the front door.

I look around the neighborhood; the other houses are kept up really well. Their yards are all mowed and the landscaping looks nice. I wish one of those was ours.

Before I have time to think about it or go inside, I hear a girl's voice screaming down the street. "Maddy!"

I turn and see a red head hanging out the window of a black truck. When it stops in front of my house, she hops out, running toward me.

"Maddy, I am so happy you're back," she says, her arms wrapping around me. She pulls away, putting her hands on my shoulders. "Why didn't you call me or write me? Why did I have to find out from Trent, who found out from Gabe, who found out from Doug?" she exclaims.

Trent knows I am back.

"Hey, Mackenna! I see some things don't change." I smile, nodding my head toward the guy in the black truck.

Mackenna has grown up to become a gorgeous teenage girl; not like I ever thought she wouldn't. Her red hair is long and wavy, making her green eyes stand out. She is slim and petite and her breasts have gotten even bigger.

"Oh yeah. Do you remember Billy Cummings?" She waves at him in the truck and he waves back.

"Didn't he used to be...awkward and play that wizards card game?" I question skeptically.

"Oh Mad, the boys you remember have turned into men. Just you wait and see."

I can't help but picture Trent. I wonder how tall he is, how his chest looks, his eyes, his hair. "I am sure everyone is different than what I remember," I say.

"Believe me, they are. So, I will meet you outside the office tomorrow morning before first class, okay?" She is already walking back to Billy's truck.

"Um...okay," I yell toward her.

"You'll see. Maddy. We are going to have so much fun. I'm never letting you leave me again." She climbs into the truck and it speeds away with her waving out the window.

The next morning my mom drops me off at Belcrest High School. I decided to wear a yellow sundress with a pair of flip-flops. I didn't want to look too underdressed or overdressed. I haven't been through these halls since Jack's graduation, and I'm nervous because I'm not very familiar with this school. I stop at the main office to pick up my schedule and am thankful the town is so small.

"Hi, Maddy Jennings. I haven't seen you in years. Welcome back to Belcrest." The lady behind the desk hands me my schedule. I know her from somewhere, but I can't remember her name. "Oh, there's Mackenna Ross waiting for you. You two were always together."

"Thank you Ms....,"

"Ms. Gilbert. Peter's mother," she fills in for me.

"Thank you, Ms. Gilbert."

"Have a good day dear."

The door shuts behind me and my ears fill with the sounds of a noisy high school hallway. Mackenna is dressed in a pair of plaid shorts with a cute tank top and flats. She looks adorable, as always.

"I love the dress," she says, hugging me tight. "Sorry, I still can't believe you're back."

"I know. I can't believe it myself."

"The boys are going to flip out."

"I thought they knew."

"They do, but wait until they see you." She snatches my schedule from my hands. "Let me see if my connections worked."

"Connections?"

"I have connections in the office. I was hoping to have a lot of classes with you. Yeah, we have first and seventh period together and most importantly, we have the same lunch." She hooks her arm through mine. "This guy who had the locker next to me always uses his girlfriend's, so I asked him if he would switch with you and he agreed after some persuasion."

"I don't even want to know, Kenna, but thank you," I say, looking around the hall. Some of the people look familiar, but it's hard to place names with faces.

By the time lunch rolls around, I'm feeling pretty good. Everything is starting to become familiar again. It helps that our school isn't that big. A few students remember me and come up to welcome me back. Kenna walks me to every class and always comes back to her locker to meet me in between. I don't know what I would have done without her. After three years, she is still my best friend.

Kenna and I walk into the lunchroom and panic strikes me. It is loud and students are scrambling to their seats at every table. I am thankful to have Kenna by my side again. We stand in line for our food and, needless to say, the pickings are slim. I choose a cheese pizza with a side salad and water. Kenna has the same thing, except she chooses a coke.

I follow her to a table in the back, hearing whisperings from those wondering who I am. Mostly I hear the words, "sister of Jack Jennings". In Belcrest, you are always associated with who you're related to. She sits me down at a table with two other girls and introduces me to Chloe Rodgers and Jenny Hunt. They seem friendly enough. I recognize Jenny, but not Chloe. Mackenna explains that Chloe moved to Belcrest last year.

"So, are you happy to be back to this hick town?" Jenny asks.

"Yeah, I guess," I say, shrugging. "I missed everyone."

"Like who?" Chloe snaps.

I don't know how to take her question, but before I can answer, I am picked up from behind and swung around in a circle.

"Look at Little Jennings, all grown up with tits and ass." Bryan Edwards puts me down, grabbing my ass. He has grown up into every teenage girl's dream. He has long dark hair and wide hazel eyes. You can tell he works hard on his body by the way his cargo shorts fit and his polo shirt hugs his shoulders.

I slap him on the shoulder. "Little Edwards is all grown up too, but still nothing between the legs, huh?"

"I can assure you that I am very grown up there too," he laughs. "I've missed you, girl," he says, hugging me again.

"Missed you, too." I pull away and see Trent standing behind him.

He is staring at me intently, but not making a move. My brown eyes meet his blue irises and all those years apart seem to fade away. If I thought Bryan had grown up, it was because I hadn't seen Trent yet. His honey blond hair is shaved short and his tanned skin seems to glow. He's wearing jeans that hang off his hips with a red t-shirt that is snug around his biceps, but falls down over his taut stomach. I hope I'm not drooling, but my imagination just hadn't done him justice.

A smirk crosses his handsome face as he notices me checking him out in the exact same way he is checking me out. "Maddy," is all he says, walking towards me.

"Hey, Trent." I don't know who touches who first, but suddenly I am wrapped in his arms and the smell of him overwhelms me.

"And there they are, together again. Just like old times," Bryan yells over to everyone, clapping his hands. I am surprised I didn't notice earlier how quiet the lunchroom had gotten.

"Hm, hm." I hear a girl clearing her voice behind me.

Trent pulls away and walks behind me, kissing Chloe on the cheek before sitting down next to her.

The rest of lunch goes by in a blur, mostly because I can't keep my eyes off of Trent and Chloe holding hands. She is practically sitting in his lap at one point. Every time she turns her head away, I find his eyes on me. Bryan seems to want to recall every story involving the four of us, which I am sure bores everyone else to tears.

On the way back to our lockers after lunch, Mackenna turns to me. "Don't mind Chloe. She and Trent have only been together a month. I think hearing that you were coming back scared her a little."

"She's just marking her territory, that's all," Bryan chimes in after her.

"Who said I was interested in her territory?" I ask them back. They both grin at me.

"I think she's more worried about someone wanting to leave her territory and occupy yours," Bryan says.

"Whatever, Edwards," I say.

"I am just saying, she might have heard the stories of Trent Basso and Madeline Jennings, but seeing it in action is a whole other story." He shakes his head, leaving us at our lockers and walks down the hall.

"Stories?" I question Mackenna.

"Come on, Maddy. You and Trent are Belcrest's Romeo and Juliet," she says, shutting her locker and walking away.

I stand there in awe. I never imagined that people would talk about Trent and me. I was naïve to think that no one noticed what was between the two of us all those years.

Chapter 6 – Present Day Softball Game

Gabe texts me, asking me to pick him up for the softball game. I don't quite understand why since I am sure Doug or Trent could take him, but because he is paying, I'm not going to tell him no. When my brother got wind of the arrangement, he smiled at me as though he knew something I didn't. Then he insisted on me driving him and Lindsey as well. I'm sure Gabe won't mind and if he did, it's his own fault for renting such a big vehicle.

The four of us pile into the blue monster. My mom decides to stay home, making me wonder yet again where my real mom has gone. Ian won't shut up on the way over to the Basso's, asking Jack everything about our town. I keep rolling my eyes since Jack makes Belcrest sound like Mayberry. Everyone is *not* nice and not everyone is your friend here. They can turn on a dime when you need them the most.

I pull up to the Basso's and honk the horn. I am not about to run the risk of another run-in with Mrs. Basso. Once today was enough.

"What's wrong with you, Maddy? You don't just honk your horn." Jack hops out of the truck, jogging up to the front porch.

"Whatever," I roll my eyes for the thousandth time this trip already.

Jack doesn't even make it to the front step before Gabe opens the door wearing athletic shorts and a t-shirt, slinging a bat bag over his shoulder. I see him motioning to someone behind him, but I don't see who it is. My breath finally releases when I see it is Doug that comes out, the door shutting behind him. I get out, toss Gabe the keys, and get in the back with Lindsey. He looks at me curiously, but takes the keys and jumps in the driver's seat.

When Jack and Doug get in the third row, Doug rubs my head in greeting and I introduce him to Ian. Doug waves 'hello' and I see him raise his eyebrow inquisitively at Jack.

The parking lot at the ball field is overflowing with cars. The teams are warming up, wearing their designated bar-sponsored jerseys, while their girlfriends and families fill the bleachers and gossip with one another. I hook my arm around Lindsey, walking ahead of the pack. I feel bad that I am leaving Ian behind, but Gabe seems to be keeping him company.

I take my seat in the bleachers with Lindsey on one side and Ian on the other. I sip my much-needed beer, watching the boys warm up. Their team, sponsored by Gentry's Bar and Grill, is a mixture of Bigs and Littles. I know more people were added to the roster with the out-of-town guys coming in for the wedding.

"There's my girl," a man's voice says from behind me. I know who it is before I turn around.

"Bryan Edwards. I most definitely am *not* your girl. In fact, maybe I should tell your wife what you said," I say smiling, as I walk down the bleachers to hug him.

"Please don't tell her. You know how she feels about you," he says with a laugh and kisses me on the cheek.

"She loves me," I remind him, hitting him in the shoulder.

"Yes I do, she's my bestest friend," Mackenna interjects, waddling over to me.

"How have you gotten bigger in just a month?" I hug her cautiously.

"I can't stop growing since I popped," she says, rubbing her stomach.

"You're even more gorgeous when you're pregnant," I assure her.

"I agree. She's the most beautiful pregnant woman I have ever seen." Bryan puts his arm around her, bringing her close to his chest.

"What about when I'm not pregnant?" Kenna asks indignantly.

"*And* when you're not pregnant. Christ Kenna, you know what I meant," Bryan says, flustered.

"I know babe, no worries." Kenna gives him a quick kiss on the cheek.

"Straight men just don't know how to talk to the ladies," Ian says, coming down to join us. "You look marvelous girl," he says, giving Mackenna a hug. "I can give you some lessons, Bryan," he jokes while shaking Bryan's hand.

"I might have to take you up on that, man," Bryan says, returning the handshake.

Bryan and Mackenna join us on the bench.

"How come you aren't playing Edwards?" I ask.

"Gave up my usual spot for Basso," Bryan says, not looking back at me.

"Gabe?" I clarify.

"Trent," he corrects. Mackenna hits him in the arm, giving me that sorrowful look again.

"He's late. Like usual," I sigh.

"It's not late, Maddy, the game hasn't started." I don't even need to turn around to recognize that voice; it is permanently etched in my head. I will myself not to look. I can't see him, not yet. I need more time. The others freeze, staring at the two of us.

"Practice is over, Trent. The game is about to start." I point with my finger toward the field.

"Always the dictator, right Maddy?" he sarcastically spouts.

"Give me a break, Trent. Just go play," I say.

Trent looks at the field where the team is staring over at us, waiting for him. He climbs the bleachers toward me, coming close as though he is going to kiss me, but at the last second he moves his mouth toward my ear. "Every home run is for you. Stick around after the game, we need to talk." Then he turns around, walking through the gate to the dugout.

"Hi, Trent. Nice to see you too," Ian screams out to him.

"How you doing, Ian? Keeping my girl safe I hope." He waves his hand, not bothering to turn around.

I want to scream at him that I am *not* his girl, but I just roll my eyes again instead. I am not going to make a scene. I see Jack looking at me from the field, concern in his eyes. I wave him off, reassuring him that I can handle it. Next to him, Gabe is talking to Trent and looking over at me every few seconds. The conversation looks heated, but I have seen them fight numerous times before and they usually end with fists. Since no one is swinging, I figure that I'm seeing something that isn't there.

Gentry's is behind eight to ten by the seventh inning and Gabe is up to bat. I start cheering for him and he looks up at me and winks. He takes a practice swing, then sets up his stance. Gabe has always been good-looking; some would say he's the most attractive Basso brother. They all share the same honey blond color of hair and crystal blue eyes, but Gabe has more muscle than his brothers. Trent is a little taller and Doug looks more like their mother, while Gabe and Trent favor their dad.

He swings and connects with the first pitch, and we all start screaming from the stands when it goes over the fence. Gabe's home run brings in two more runs, which puts Gentry's in the lead. The stands are going wild, shouting Gabe's name.

He walks over to the fence near us. "It's been a pleasure, ladies," he says with a bow, "and gentlemen too." Then he turns around, walking back to the dugout.

I actually spit my beer out when he says that and everyone starts laughing. I feel Trent's eyes on me, but I don't turn toward him. I can't give in and I know why he is looking. I'm sure I resemble the girl he used to love, but she isn't here anymore.

I am thankful that Trent never hits a home run; I don't want him drawing attention to us. We are all supposed to go to Gentry's after the game. Trent asks if I will ride with him, but I am hesitant. Everyone waves us off except for Gabe, who sticks around to see if I want a ride. Reluctantly, I agree to go with Trent, and Gabe heads toward the blue machine to drive Ian and the others.

Trent comes over and opens the passenger door of his black Mercedes. Sliding onto the leather seats, the familiar scent of his cologne fills my nostrils. Seconds later, I watch him ease into his seat, his long legs and muscular build forming to the black leather. He smiles, looking at me while he starts the car. I can't help but smile back.

"Trent, I--"

He rests his hand on my leg. "Maddy, I want to talk to you, but not right now. Let's just have fun like old times." I look into those blue eyes and see the boy I loved, and I want nothing more than to enjoy our time together with none of the drama.

"Alright," I nod my head in agreement.

"So, how's New York?" he asks, driving slowly out of the gravel parking lot.

"The same...nothing new," I respond, shrugging my shoulders.

"I miss it, especially the people," he says with a wink.

"Yeah?' I question.

"Why would that surprise you?"

"Why wouldn't it? Believe me, the people *you* cared for in New York have moved on to their next celebrity."

I see the disappointment in his face, but that doesn't change things.

We make it to the bar and the blue machine is already there, along with all the other players' cars. Ben Gentry, one of the Bigs, rehabilitated an old feed barn by the railroad tracks. The bar fills the downstairs and basement with family dining on the top level. High oak tables encircle the room, and there's a bar that runs down the length of one side. Every type of alcohol imaginable lines the mirrored wall behind the bar, even though this town is more partial to beer.

I don't know how Gentry managed it, but all of the football team's state championship trophies are encased in a glass cabinet high above the seating, along with numerous awards that the Belcrest Spartans have won over the years. There are even some of the players' individual trophies.

Trent leads me down to the basement, where there is a sign claiming that this area is reserved for a private party. No doubt my brother arranged this; he is known to be Belcrest's unofficial party planner. The basement is a typical bar scene. Pool tables and dart boards are set up, with small tables lining the walls. There are two bars, one against the back wall and a smaller one up front. Everyone is lined up in front of the bar in the back, waiting to be served. Jack is passing out pitchers to everyone, so I make my way over to Ian and Kenna.

I take a pitcher out of Jack's hands and a cup out of Ian's and pour myself a beer. I down half of it and take a seat.

"It must have been quite the trip," Ian jokes.

"Like always," I respond, tipping my beer back again.

"You didn't have to go with him," Kenna sneers. I know what she thinks, but she has never understood the connection between Trent and me.

"I know, Kenna, but sooner or later we have to face each other again," I answer as calmly as possible. I understand she wants to protect me, but what am I supposed to do, ignore him?

Trent catches up with me a little while later after being cornered by some other Littles, no doubt asking him about his wonderful life. He stays by my side the whole night, touching the small of my back and putting his arm around the back of my chair.

We play in a pool tournament, but are knocked out by Bryan and Mackenna in the third round. My cheeks hurt from laughing so hard. I had forgotten how Trent makes me laugh and feel like a million bucks. Wasn't that the problem though? He could make anyone feel like they were special...until he left.

The night winds down and a slow song starts to play on the jukebox. Mostly couples are left so the dance floor is full. Bryan is lovingly rocking Mackenna back and forth, while Jack spins Lindsey around, dipping her. I sit quietly in the corner with Ian, finishing my beer and observing the happy couples.

"Come on," Gabe whispers in my ear. He grabs my hand, leading me out to the dance floor.

Wrapping his other hand around my waist, he pulls me closer and dances around the room with me.

"Are you having fun tonight?" he asks.

"I actually am."

"You sound surprised. Did you think you weren't going to have fun coming back to Belcrest?"

"I don't know what I thought," I say with a shrug.

I can smell a hint of Gabe's cologne mixed with his sweat. It is oddly appealing. One of his strong hands is holding me firm against him, and he has the other tucked close between our chests. His breathing is even-paced and his heart rate is steady.

I look up into his blue eyes and notice him peering down at me. Butterflies seem to be dancing in my stomach at a much faster pace than the music that's playing. We stare at each other for a couple of minutes while the room fades away. He inches closer to me, and I lick my lips in anticipation. Just then, someone taps his shoulder and we are catapulted back to reality.

"Can I cut in, *Bro*?" Trent is behind him and his eyes are tightly drawn, glaring at Gabe.

Gabe looks at me and then back to Trent. The anguish in his eyes is evident. "Of course, brother," he says, releasing my body. I suddenly feel cold all over. I watch Gabe make his way back to the table and sit with Ian. I can't explain it, but I don't want him to go. I turn back to Trent, who is smiling down at me and wrapping his arms around my waist. Without even thinking about it, I automatically put my arms around his neck. It feels comfortable...like home. I stare over his shoulder at Ian and Gabe. Ian is flailing his arms while telling some story, but Gabe's eyes are set on me.

Trent moves me across the dance floor, saying sweet things in my ear. The kind of things that used to make me melt, but I am preoccupied with thoughts of what almost happened. It is impossible for me to focus on Trent when all I can think about is how much I want to kiss his brother.

Chapter 7 - 16 years old

Maybe Mackenna was right about Trent and me. We couldn't stay away from each other, but we couldn't stay together either. Trent broke up with Chloe the day after I returned to school. Although we didn't start dating right away, Chloe never sat at our lunch table again. We began our friendship exactly where it had left off three years earlier, and soon the four of us were joined at the hip.

Freedom came when I turned sixteen. I passed my driver's test on the first try and my dad, who still felt guilty about the divorce and the move, bought me a car. I decided on a red Jeep Wrangler. My dad wanted to get me a car, but I had my heart set on the Jeep.

Mackenna didn't turn sixteen for a couple more months so I became her chauffeur. Bryan's parents bought him a brand new FJ Cruiser. Trent inherited Gabe's Chevy Silverado. Gabe had put custom rims with big mud tires and a muffler that you could hear five miles away. It was Gabe's most prized possession, so we were all stunned when Gabe agreed to let Trent drive it while he was away at college.

Trent and Bryan didn't follow in their older brothers' footsteps. They joined the soccer team, and both started on varsity their sophomore year. At first, I thought Trent was wasting his arm. Everyone assumed he would be the all-state quarterback when we were younger, but when I saw his first soccer game, I knew that was the sport he was born to play. He was the lead scorer for the team; the other teams couldn't keep up with him. With Bryan making saves at goalie, they were unstoppable.

Mackenna and I would go to their games on Saturday afternoons, and then we'd all go to the Basso's afterward to hang out. Sometimes we would go to my house, but since my mom was never home and there was never any food in the fridge, we all preferred Trent's house.

Trent and I flirted, but nothing went any further until the middle of our junior year. The Belcrest soccer team won the state championship, and Trent and Bryan's parents agreed to watch Kenna and me so our parents didn't have to go to the away game. Not that my mom would have gone anyway.

We shared a room that adjoined the Basso's. Jack, Doug, Gabe, and some other Bigs met us at the stadium to watch the boys play. We were all sitting down, cuddling together under blankets and waiting for the boys to come out on the field, when a young kid walked up to us asking for Madeline. The kid couldn't have been older than middle school.

Everyone turns around to look at me and I just shrug my shoulders. "That's me. Who are you?" I ask, skeptically.

The kid looks at our big group and starts stuttering.
"Um...Tr...Tr...," he stutters.

"It's alright kid, calm down. What do you want with Maddy?"
Gabe stands up, putting his hand on the kid's shoulder.

"Um...," he takes a deep breath, "Trent Basso wants to talk to
her."

"Okay, we can do that," Gabe motions over to me to come over.

"Where is he at?" I ask the young kid.

"Fo...Fo...follow me," he says and heads down the stairs.

"Do you want me to go with you?" Gabe asks me.

"No, I'll be back soon. I'm sure it's nothing," I reassure
everyone.

I descend the stairs behind the boy and see Trent bent over in the
breezeway that leads out to the field. I notice that the rest of the team
is already out on the field warming up. He is dressed in his blue
shorts with his shirt tucked in, along with his shin guards and
matching blue cleats. He looks incredible in his uniform. I rush over
to him.

"What's the matter, Trent?" I bend over to look at his face.

"I don't know, Mad. I can't stop shaking and I feel nauseous.
This has never happened to me before." He sits up, putting his head
in his hands.

I feel his forehead. He doesn't feel feverish but he is sweating.
"You feel okay," I inform him.

"What if I mess up? You know how good that other team is?
Scouts have already come to see their star player and he is only a

sophomore," he says, confessing the real reason that he doesn't feel good.

"Are you kidding me, Trent?" I get in front of him, putting my hands on each shoulder. "Trent Basso is afraid he won't play well?"

He looks at me as if he wants to agree.

"Trent, you are the best soccer player I have ever seen. You are better than that kid. You were born to play forward. That team won't be able to keep up with you," I say, pointing out to the field.

"I don't know, Maddy. I took a chance leaving football behind to pursue soccer. What if it was a mistake and I can't bring the championship back home?" he asks, shaking his head back and forth.

"Trent, don't think like that. I am so sure you can and WILL bring the championship back to Belcrest, I am willing to make a bet."

"A bet?" He raises his eyebrow at me.

"Anything you want," I say.

"You are that confident?"

"I am that confident in you," I say assuredly, pointing my finger into his chest.

"If I win the championship, I want us to go out on a real date, just me and you. No Kenna and Bryan."

"And here I thought you were going to ask to feel me up," I say with a laugh.

"I am confident enough that after the date I might get that too," he winks.

"We'll see. Now go out there and kick some ass, Trent Basso," I hug him. When I step back, he pulls me harder against him.

"Thanks, Maddy, you are the best." He looks down at me and it is obvious that we both feel the pull between us. Bending down, his lips graze mine. I taste the orange Gatorade that he must have just consumed. His tongue licks my bottom lip, begging to enter. I open my mouth and meet his tongue before allowing it in. He moans into my mouth and I fall into him more. His hands come around to the back of my head, holding my lips against his, while my fingers grasp his jersey.

"Oh Jesus, you guys pick *now* to make out?" Bryan calls out to us.

I pull away fast but Trent grabs my waist. "See you after the game. Every goal is for you." He gives me a short kiss on the lips.

I lean against the wall, trying to catch my breath.

"Maddy?" Trent stops at the opening of the field.

I raise my head.

"What if I lose? What do you want?" he asks.

"You won't," I say.

Trent smiles and runs out to the field.

I was right. Trent led the team in scoring, bringing the championship back to Belcrest. The final score was six to three. After the game, we all head-back to the hotel to celebrate. We eat pizza and discuss the highlights of the game. Trent grins from ear to ear, and I am ecstatic for him.

The adults soon grow tired and want to relax, but they allow us to go down to the pool area to soak in the hot tub. We use the boys as an excuse, since they need to relax their muscles. Mackenna and I go into our room and change into our swimsuits. We both wear our bikinis and I can't help but think about how different it is this time.

We walk into the pool area with our cover-ups on. Some of the boys are already in the pool and others are in the hot tub. Kenna and I are used to being the only girls since it has been like that most of our life, but I am unreasonably nervous to take off my cover-up.

Trent and Bryan are in the hot tub, so we make our way to a table near them. Kenna takes off her cover-up, sauntering into the hot tub and showing off her black and white bikini. A couple of the boys look but don't make a big deal of it, so I have high hopes that they won't pay much more attention to me.

I take off my white linen cover-up, displaying my pink and blue polka-dot bikini. Looking over at the hot tub, Kenna is staring at me with a huge smile on her face and Trent's mouth is open in awe.

"Man, what a difference from last time," one of the other players screams from the pool.

"Shut the fuck up," Jack yells back at him.

"Sorry, Jack," he apologizes to my brother.

I look toward the pool and I notice the other boys gawking and my brother scowling. I rush into the hot tub, sitting next to Kenna and hiding under the bubbles.

"It's like they've never seen breasts before," Bryan exclaims, making me turn even redder.

"Let's not talk about it," I request to him.

"Yeah, let's talk about how next Saturday you two are on your own," Trent points from Mackenna to Bryan.

"Why?" Kenna looks over to me and I shrug, even though I know where Trent is going with this.

"'Cause we won the championship," he says, matter-of-factly.

"Is there some special celebration I don't know about?" Bryan asks.

Trent scoots closer to me, putting his arm behind me. "You could say that, right Maddy?" He grazes my shoulder with his fingers and my body is suddenly covered in goose bumps, despite the ninety-five degree water.

Mackenna and Bryan stare at me confused.

"Oh, for heaven's sake, Trent and I are going on a date. From what I gather it is next Saturday," I divulge the secret.

"Finally." They both shake their heads back and forth and we all start laughing.

The next Saturday, I wait outside of my house for Trent to pick me up. I don't want him to come in since my mom is getting ready for one of her 'dates'. He pulls up at six-thirty, parks the car, and comes walking up the driveway. He is wearing jeans and a dark Henley thermal with his Adidas soccer shoes. I always love the way his jeans hang low on his hips. I walk up to meet him.

"You look beautiful, like always," he leans in, giving me a kiss on my cheek.

"Thank you," I look down at my jeans and sweater, not thinking much of it.

"You ready?" He takes my hand, leading me to the house.

"Yeah, let's go." I start pulling his arm toward the truck.

"Hey," he says, bringing me closer and putting a hand on my face. "I have to talk to your mom before taking you out. It's only right." He looks into my eyes, trying to reassure me.

"You don't understand, Trent. She's getting ready for a date. It's fine, she doesn't care," I plead.

"I do, Mad. Come on." He starts walking up the path to the front door.

I reluctantly follow him. I open the door to my house, thankful that I cleaned it today. I call up to my mom in her room but she doesn't answer. I leave Trent in the living room and run upstairs to get her.

She is blow-drying her long blond hair. She turns the dryer off. "What do you want? I thought you left," she snaps at me. I cross my fingers, hoping Trent can't hear her.

"Trent Basso is here to take me out on a date and is asking to talk to you first," I whisper to her.

"Isn't he Mr. Proper? Just like his daddy," she says loudly, putting liquid black eyeliner and five coats of mascara on.

"Please Mom, it will just take a second," I beg.

"Alright, give me a minute. I have to get dressed," she says, shooing me out of the bathroom.

I go downstairs to wait with Trent for my mom. Trent has never seen her like this. He is used to the 'Jack's mom' version, which was toned down significantly more than 'Madeline's mom' now. My mom frequents bars out of Belcrest city limits, meaning a lot of people in town don't know about her extracurricular activities, which makes me happy.

My mom strolls down the stairs fifteen minutes later and my head falls when I see what she is wearing. Her skirt is barely covering her ass, she has red high heels on, and she's wearing a tight black blouse that shows her bra. Her bleached blond hair is damaged and stringy. I bite my lower lip in anticipation of what is to come.

Trent gives me a despairing look and turns to my mom.

"Hi, Mrs. Jennings. I just wanted to let you know I am taking Madeline out for the night," he says confidently, holding his hand out for her to shake.

Thankfully, she shakes it back. "It's *Ms.* Jennings now," she corrects him. "Have fun, you two," she nods her head toward both of us.

"I will have her home by midnight, Ms. Jennings," Trent assures her, not knowing that she could care less.

"Okay, but I won't," she giggles and then straightens up quickly. "I just mean I won't be here to wait up for her." *Did she just tell two hormone-crazed teenagers that they had the house to themselves tonight?*

"Well, we should get going," I say, pulling on Trent.

"It was nice seeing you again, Ms. Jennings." Trent waves goodbye as I drag him to the door.

"You too, Trent. Give your dad my best…and your mom," she adds.

Finally we are out of the house and my body relaxes. I can't get to Trent's truck and away from my mom fast enough. He opens my door, helping me to get in and then walks around to his side. After he climbs in, he takes my hand in his, squeezing it tight. He always has subtle ways of telling me that he understands and is there for me. The tears in my eyes are in danger of spilling over and that is the last thing I want on our first date.

"So, where are you taking me? If you expect to cop a feel, your date better be good," I joke, attempting to change the mood.

"After what I have planned, you might give up the whole package," Trent says, smirking at me.

"Uh-huh. Tell me, what is going to make me want to strip my clothes off and scream for you to take me?"

"It's a surprise," he says and finally starts backing the truck out of the driveway.

Twenty minutes later, Trent pulls up to a pumpkin farm.

"Why didn't we just go to Ghords Pumpkin Farm in Belcrest?" I ask.

"I didn't want us to be bothered. I knew if we went there, we would end up hanging out with our friends." He gets out of the truck and I wait for him to come around the truck.

He grabs my hand, leading me toward the haunted hayride.

"Oh no, you don't," I say, trying to pull away from him.

"Come on," he urges, tugging me back toward him.

"Trent..." I sigh at him. He knows I hate anything scary. Sitting on a barrel of hay in the pitch dark waiting for people to jump out at me is not my idea of fun.

"I won't let go of you." He puts his hand up, placing his other like it is on a Bible.

"Promise?" I ask him.

"Promise," he responds.

"And you won't try to scare me either?"

"Promise. Now come on." He puts his arm around my waist, bringing us closer together. I love his smell of cotton and soap, and I begrudgingly follow him.

Trent knows I don't live on the edge like he does. I have never enjoyed scary movies or roller coasters. Even the high dive at the park district pool is too much for me. I like to feel in control and those things make me feel anything but.

Trent has pushed, or in his words "persuaded", me to do all of these things our whole lives. I have gone along willingly, as long as he was there beside me. He held me tight during the horror movies, held my hand on the "Screaming Eagle" when we went to Great Adventures, and always waited at the bottom of the pool when I jumped off the high dive. I may have been terrified, but with Trent there to hug me afterward, it made the fear I felt worth it.

I walk up the wooden steps to find a bale of hay, thinking that I must have a death wish. I tuck myself in one of the corners close to the tractor in the front. Trent sits next to me, squeezing my hand to reassure me. I smile up at him, despite the apprehension I'm feeling. How could I not? Those eyes alone could melt away any fear.

The trailer is full of high school kids from a nearby school. I don't know any of them and they don't know us, so it seems that Trent's plan worked.

I jerk forward when the tractor starts to move and my heart starts beating faster. Trent automatically pulls me closer to him. As all of the people come at us from behind the trees, I clinch him harder and he pulls me so close that before long, I find myself in his lap. His arms are firmly wrapped around my waist and my face is tucked in his neck.

"I assume this is why you wanted to take me on a haunted hay ride?" I ask, lifting one eyebrow at him.

"Maybe," he says, shrugging his shoulders.

"Uh, huh. For that, you owe me some apple cider." I slap him on his muscular shoulder as I dart in front of him to get off this hell on wheels.

He catches up to me quickly, wrapping both of his arms around my waist again, pulling me back to him. "I will buy you whatever you want, as long as you ride me again," he says jokingly.

I push him away with my hand. "I don't recall the bet being anything other than a date," I remind him, laughing.

"Hey, I can hope, can't I?"

We sit down on a hill with our apple cider and kettle corn.

"So, tell me why you quit football and went for soccer." Since I wasn't around when he made his decision, I've been curious to know.

"I don't know. I played my freshman year and it just wasn't there," he looks down, sipping his cider.

"What wasn't there?"

"My arm. I didn't have it."

"Okay, I am so confused. Didn't have what?"

"The Basso arm." He tosses some kettle corn up in the air, catching it in his mouth.

I knew what he meant. Doug and Gabe had both been quarterbacks for the Belcrest football team, earning them scholarships to state. It was a running joke that, between the three Basso brothers, there would be a Basso starting quarterback for ten years straight at State. The joke ended when Trent switched to soccer.

"Maybe you needed more time?"

"It wasn't there for me. I always had the speed so they moved me to running back, but I hated it. That winter, my friend asked me to play on his indoor soccer team. I fell in love with it and was surprised to find that I was pretty good at it too."

"*Pretty* good?" He was definitely selling himself short.

He flushes red, shrugging his shoulders.

"I bet you still have the arm," I say, leaning back on my elbows and extending my legs.

"I don't throw anymore, Maddy." He picks at some grass, tossing it aside.

"Come on, you choose the bet," I coax him.

"That's tempting," he raises his eyebrows, cocking his head to the side while deciding my fate. "Alright, if I can throw this piece of popcorn in your mouth, you have to kiss me."

I start to lick my lips in anticipation; I know he will get it my mouth. "Do you want me to stand up or lie down?"

"Stay just the way you are. You look comfortable." He stands a good distance away from me, preparing to toss the popcorn toward my mouth.

"Come on, hot shot," I urge him on.

"Hot shot?" he asks, smirking.

"Well, if the shoe fits…"

"Open up, Maddy."

I open my mouth as big as it can go. I might want this kiss more than he does at this point. He throws the kernel and it lands smack dab on the middle of my tongue.

A smile spreads across my face, not only because I get to kiss Trent again, but because I knew he could do it. He has the infamous Basso arm, and he also has something that his brothers don't. Trent has the speed of a cheetah.

"You ready to pay up, Jennings?" he questions, cocking his head.

"I'm ready, Basso. Remember, only a kiss. Keep those hands to yourself," I joke while Trent leans down, crawling up my body until his lips touch mine briefly. I close my eyes in expectation and his kiss becomes firmer and more urgent. Our lips open and he grazes his tongue across my bottom lip. We groan into each other's mouths as our tongues mingle together. A while later, Trent slowly stops the kiss, lingering over my lips and looking at me with those amazing eyes. I lie on the grass hill, my body covered in goose bumps, longing for another bet.

Chapter 8 – Dress Fitting

The cell phone beeps, waking me up from a surprisingly blissful sleep in my new bed. Reaching for my phone, I am in awe once again of my newly decorated bedroom. My phone reads seven-thirty in the morning, making me wonder who on earth is interrupting my 'vacation' on the first day.

Gabe: Good morning, Madgirl! Hope you had a good night's sleep. I will be there at nine.

Me: Nine?

Gabe: What? No good morning?

> *Yes, nine. Dress fitting today.*

Me: Why would you be going to the dress fitting?

Gabe: Tux fitting at the same place. All groomsmen and bridesmaids going together.

Maddy: I can meet you there, no worries.

Gabe: I hate to be the bearer of bad news but I have the truck from last night.

Shit. I forgot Trent drove Ian and me home last night. Thank God Ian was with us.

Gabe: I am assuming you just realized you have no option here. So see you at nine.

Uh…

Maddy: Okay

I roll over for another half-hour of sleep, only to be interrupted by a knock on my door.

"Go away, this is my vacation," I yell, throwing my pillow at the door.

"Madeline? It's mom," she says from the other side of the door.

"Come on in," I say, sitting up against my headboard.

My mom walks in smiling, while she looks around my room. "Do you like it?" she asks.

"Mom, I love it. It wasn't necessary though," I say, hoping she doesn't hear the lie in my voice.

"Yes it was, Maddy." She sits on the edge of my bed.

"Thank you, Mom. How did you afford all of it?" I ask, playing with my comforter.

"As much as I wish I could say I did all of this for you, I couldn't have afforded it. It was a gift from someone." She stares down at the ground. Since she can't face me, I know it is some new guy in her life, probably a married man who is cheating on his family. Although it makes it bearable for me to stay here this week, I don't want my mom to owe anyone, much less a male who I am sure has already called in his payback.

"Whoever did this, please thank them for me. It made coming home a lot easier," I confess.

"Well, I better head off to work, so have fun at the dress fitting. Will I see you tonight for dinner?"

"Sure." She is going to make dinner again. "Um…Mom?" She turns around in the doorway. "Thank you."

She nods her head, shutting the door behind her. She knows what I am grateful for, and it isn't just the redecoration of the house.

After the door clicks shut, I lie in my bed staring up at the white ceiling and thinking about last night. Gabe enters my mind and chills run through my body. It's always been about Trent. He was the Basso I was meant to be with, or so I thought once upon a time. From the way Trent acted last night, I know he wants us to rekindle what we had, but how many chances are we supposed to give this fated love?

Thinking of fate, I jump from my bed and look through my new dresser drawers, finding nothing. Running over to my closet, I fling the doors open in a panic. All I find is a closet full of my old clothes, things I will never wear again. Bending down, I crawl on my hands and knees, searching for it and praying no one threw it away. Accepting defeat, I push myself back up and lean against my bed. I knew I should have taken those things with me, but I left in such a hurry.

Looking into my closet, I see an outline of the missing box in the top right hand corner. Standing on my tippy-toes, I reach with my hand as far as I can get it. My fingers find the bottom edge, enabling me to scoot it closer to me until I can pull it down. The flowery box covered with stickers is lighter than I remember.

Walking over to the bed, I sit Indian-style, hesitant to open my very own version of Pandora's Box. Before I can second guess myself, I rip it off.

I can't stop the smile from forming on my face. My MASH notebook is on top. Mackenna and I had filled many more, but this is the only one I kept. It was from my last year with her, before I moved to Michigan.

Flipping through the pages, Trent's name fills every page. Mrs. Trent Basso is written on the cover, the back, and probably every page in between. Picking up the notebook, I notice the piece of loose-leaf paper under it. It has been folded and refolded thousands of times. I pick it up, holding it against my heart. My eyes close and I remember that day in the driveway when Mackenna handed it to me, before we drove away to our new home in Michigan. I wondered then, as I do now, if fate truly does exist? Or is it all coincidence and luck of the draw?

A half-hour later, Gabe rings my doorbell. Because I took a trip down memory lane, I'm running late and my hair is still wet. I barely had time to throw on some capris and a t-shirt and, wearing my favorite flip-flops, I pulled my hair back in a ponytail as I headed toward the door.

"I guess you don't want to impress *this* Basso brother." Ian smirks at me from the kitchen doorway as I walk by him.

I flip him off while snatching the granola bar from his hand and open the door.

"Hey, Madgirl." Gabe looks me up and down. I can't tell if he is disgusted or pleased. "Hi, Ian." He waves, walking into the house.

"Good morning, Gabe," I state. He is wearing a pair of khaki shorts with a tight-fitting blue tee and a pair of sneakers. The shorts show off his long, muscular tanned legs. I shake my head to clear it, knowing that I should not be checking out Gabe like this.

"You heading over with us, Ian?" Gabe asks him, making himself comfortable at the kitchen table and not even paying attention to the remodeled house. I figure that either he doesn't care or has already been over since it was done.

Ian looks down at his pajama pants, shaking his head. "No, since I agreed to take this as my vacation to help out my girl, I am taking at least one day to lie around."

"Must be nice." I glare over at him, humorously. "I get to go try on some hideous bridesmaid dress and listen to people tell me that I can wear it again sometime."

"Don't sound so bitter, it's your brother's wedding. Now go put on your happy face and be that cheerful bridesmaid I know you can be." Ian smacks me on my ass, walking out of the room.

"Whatever, Sleeping Beauty. Please, enjoy your day of leisure," I call out to him. I'm really only teasing him. I couldn't be more grateful that he's here with me. He deserves some relaxation time, especially dealing with my drama.

"Don't hate, Madeline Jennings. It isn't becoming of you," Ian calls back from upstairs.

"Let's just go get this over with," Gabe says, hopping off the stool and putting his hand on the small of my back, leading me to the door.

He doesn't remove his hand until I am safely in the passenger seat of the Blue Monster. Once in the car, my heart starts beating faster and my breathing becomes erratic. Why is Gabe having this effect on me? I don't know what has happened in the last twenty-four hours, but somehow he has weaseled his way into my thoughts and I can't seem to shake them.

"So, I want to talk to you about the dance," he says, glancing over at me. My face pales and I probably look like I am coming down with something.

"Gabe, its fine. Just a dance with your little sister, right?" I ask, trying to play this off. One Basso brother has torn my heart to shreds on numerous occasions. I'm not going to let another one finish the job.

"Little sister?" he questions, looking confused.

"I know you and Doug have always thought of me as Little Jennings," I say.

"Well...yeah...when we were younger," he confirms. "But now..." He is interrupted by the ringing of his cell phone.

"Hello?" he answers, giving me an apologetic smile and then pauses to listen.

"I will be back next Monday; can't this wait until then?"

"Absolutely not," he angrily says to whoever is on the other end.

"Listen. I am here for a good friend's wedding. There are events planned all week long and I don't have time for this right now. We can discuss this on Monday night when I get back."

Monday night? I assume it isn't business then. Girlfriend?

"I don't know how much clearer I can make this for you," he says, his tone curt.

We turn down the street toward the dress shop. He parks in one of the diagonal parking spots that line the street of the downtown area.

"I have somewhere I have to be right now. It's Monday night or never...you decide," he says.

"That's what I thought." He hangs up the phone with no goodbye.

I have never seen Gabe act like this to someone so I can't imagine what or who it is that would cause such a personality change.

"Sorry about that." He smiles over to me, but gives me no explanation. Not that he owes me one.

"It's okay," I smile back, "let's get this thing over with." I can't get out of the car and away from Gabe fast enough. I leap out of the car, walking toward the dress shop.

"Hey, hold up." Gabe grabs my elbow, bringing me back to him before I can open the door. "Is something the matter?" His face is etched with concern.

"No, I just want to get this dress fitting done," I lie.

He looks at me for a long moment, eventually accepting defeat and letting go of my elbow.

The dress shop is small and quaint and is connected to the tuxedo shop by a little walkway. I notice all of the guys already standing around dressed in the tuxedos; we are obviously late.

"What the hell, Basso?" Jack calls out to Gabe. "Maddy, the girls are waiting for you in the dressing room." He points me in the right direction.

Gabe and I raise our eyebrows at each other, as if we are schoolchildren who just got in trouble but don't really care.

"Finally, Maddy." Lindsey comes out from the dressing rooms, urgently waving her hands at me to meet her.

"Are we really that late?" I ask, checking my watch, only to realize that I was in such a hurry I forgot to put it on.

"We only have an hour before the next bridal party arrives."

"Are you serious?" I ask in disbelief. They couldn't spread out the whole two weddings that happen in this town a year?

"Yes, Maddy. This is the best wedding shop in the county. A lot of girls come here from all over," she says. "Now, go in there and try on the dress." She pushes me into the fitting room.

"Alright, alright. When did you become so bossy?" I joke, stopping myself short of running into the mirror from her push.

I cringe, looking at the emerald green satin gown hanging in front of me. There are beads sewn on the top half, falling into an A frame over the stomach and hips. It would be a beautiful dress for someone else. I look at my pale post-winter New York skin, wondering if there's anywhere I can get a spray tan before Saturday.

"Let's go, Maddy," Lindsey knocks on the door impatiently.

"Just a minute, Linds," I yell through the door.

Five minutes later, I walk out of the room in the seemingly Irish bridesmaid's dress. All of the other girls are sitting down looking bored and annoyed. I am pretty sure that they are annoyed by me, the groom's little sister who is ruining the dress fitting by showing up late and taking forever. I notice instantly that I am the only one in a green dress. The other girls are each in a different color.

"Oh, you look beautiful, like I knew you would. Green is definitely your color, Maddy," Lindsey gushes at me.

"How come we are all in different colors?" I ask her. This is my first time being a bridesmaid, and Mackenna's elopement in Jamaica didn't really count since all I needed was a sundress.

"It's a rainbow wedding. Every bridesmaid wears a different color," she says, her smile indicating how excited she is.

"Oh, I've never heard of that. Interesting." I know that it doesn't really matter what I want; this is her day and her wedding. I just wish I could trade my Irish prom dress for the blue one. Maybe then I could actually wear it again one day.

"Go up on the pedestal so Marge can do the last minute alterations," she says, pushing me forward again. You would think she was my naturally born sister the way she treats me, but I secretly love it. Lindsey doesn't have any sisters either so we were both equally excited when we found out we would be sister-in-laws.

"Jeez, Linds, calm down," I say, walking grudgingly up to the pedestal so Marge, the shop seamstress, can molest my body.

"Hey, don't be talking to my fiancé like that. She is technically going to be your older sister in a couple days." Jack's deep voice carries over the store as he and his groomsmen come into view behind me.

Great. Now I am going to have the boys witness my humiliation of being poked and prodded.

"Wow, Little Jennings," one of the Bigs says. "Talk about an ugly duckling turning into a swan."

"She was always a swan," Gabe whispers. I pretend that I don't hear him, but the smile that forms across my face might give me away. My eyes meet his in the mirror and he instantly looks down.

"Whatever. Now she's a smokin' hot swan," the guy bellows.

"That's my sister, Edwards." Jack hits Bryan's older brother.

"It doesn't change the fact," he says, shaking his head.

"Enough boys, get out." Lindsey looks directly at Jack, pointing toward the door.

"Sorry Linds, but I gotta stay. It's like she's on display for all of us to observe and appreciate." Edwards sits down, making himself comfortable. It is hard to believe he is Bryan's brother.

"Listen, Shawn Edwards. I know your mom and dad and they wouldn't approve of you disrespecting a girl like this. I suggest you go with your friends." Marge looks him square in the eye.

"Alright, alright Marge. Calm down." He stands up, pressing his hands down the front of the legs of his pants. "Maddy, we can catch up later. If I'm lucky, I will be escorting you down the aisle at your brother's funeral on Saturday," he says, winking at me through the mirror.

"Enough, Shawn!" All the girls scream, as well as Jack.

"Okay, okay. I'm leaving," he backs up, still checking me out in the mirror.

I roll my eyes in disgust and then look toward Gabe, who I notice is staring at me once again.

"Let's go, Edwards." Jack grabs the back of his neck, leading him toward the exit of the shop. "Linds, we will meet up after at Taps?"

"Yeah, baby. I still have to try on my dress and you cannot be here for that," she says, looking lovingly at Jack. He and the rest of the guys walk out, but not before Gabe winks over at me. *What has gotten into him?*

After Marge finishes poking a zillion little holes in my skin, I can finally take off the dress. I hear loud "oohhs" and "ahhs" from the fitting room and I assume Lindsey has on her wedding dress.

Walking toward her, I see Lindsey in a Cinderella-style dress. It's form fitting through the top and flares out at the waist into layers of tulle and satin. She looks beyond gorgeous; she should be a model in a bridal magazine.

And it isn't just her dress. Lindsey's smile is ecstatic, lighting up her whole face; her enthusiasm to be marrying my brother is written all over it. A sudden desire sweeps through me to someday have that same look, the one that says that if her life ended tomorrow, she would die happy.

It is a short walk over to Taps after we finish with the dresses. I assume we will have lunch and then I can go home and lounge.

"So, are you with Gabe?" One of the bridesmaids comes up alongside me as we are walking.

I think her name is Caroline and she was Lindsey's college roommate. "Um…no," I say, looking her way. I think she was wearing the orange dress. She is shorter than me by a couple of inches, has strawberry-blonde hair, and is attractive in that make-up model kind of way.

"You guys drove together so I figured I'd ask," she says, shrugging her shoulders "So you don't mind if I go after him?" she asks.

"No, I don't mind. Thanks for asking though," I say. A part of me wants to answer differently, but it's not my place.

"Great, thanks." She excitedly skips over to some other girl, gesturing my way. Taps is a bar and grill that has been in town for decades. It has few windows so it is dark inside, with heavy oak tables and black, leather-covered booths, making it cozy and quaint.

We see the boys in the back waiting for us. Caroline scoots in next to Gabe. I sit a couple seats down from them since I really do not want to see them flirting. Trying to divert my eyes from them, I fail to realize whom I sat down next to.

"Hey, beautiful. It's been so long, Maddy," Shawn Edwards says, leaning into me.

"You just saw me last year at your brother's wedding," I remind him. I know why he didn't notice me then. He was with a tall blond with huge breasts, his usual type.

"Oh, yeah! Sorry about that. You still with Little Basso?" he asks, moving closer to me than I would like.

"I guess it was hard to see past your date's breasts," I say to him, avoiding the question.

He laughs and says, "Funny and hot, what a great combination." Then, leaning closer to my ear, he whispers, "I can't wait to find out your other attributes."

"You will be waiting a long time, Shawn."

"So you are still seeing Little Basso?" he asks, hopeful.

"No, I'm not."

"Then why don't you give an Edwards a chance? Your friend seems deliriously happy with my brother and I share the same genes with him." He puts his arm around my chair, leaning so far over that I can feel his breath on my neck.

"Shawn, my brother would kill you if you touched one hair on my head." I move forward, eyeing my brother down at the end of the table.

"Who says he has to know?" He puts his hand on my knee.

"Shawn, I suggest you take your hand off my leg before I stab it," I threaten, picking up my fork and aiming it toward his hand.

"Man, you've got the Jennings temper, huh?"

"You think Jack's bad, you should see my girl when she gets mad." I could place that raspy voice anywhere. It has given me goose bumps my whole life.

Shawn quickly pulls his hand off, and I look to my savior in time to see the smirk on his face. He knows I'm not his girl but right now he can say whatever he wants.

"Hey guys, sorry I'm late." Trent asks the girl next to me to scoot over, which she does after looking him up and down. Probably imagining him naked.

"Hey, Trent," most of the table calls out in unison. He waves to everyone, saying hello in return.

"So, Edwards. Mind moving your arm off my girl's chair now?"

"According to Little Jennings, she isn't your girl anymore, soccer stud. That means she's fair game." As if to emphasize his point, Shawn doesn't drop his arm from the back of my chair.

"Listen boys, I'm not a piece of land so no one is staking their claim." I look at them both, and then notice that Gabe is attentively watching what is going on. I can't decipher from his face whether he is angry or amused.

"Just because you are some soccer superstar, it doesn't mean you will always get the girl," Shawn says over to Trent.

"It's not because of my *soccer* skills that she's my girl, believe me," Trent returns.

I look at Trent in disgust. "I haven't been your girl in over a year." I glance to Shawn and back to Trent. "If you don't both stop, I will be leaving,"

"Well, we don't want that," Shawn says, finally removing his arm.

Eventually the waitress comes around, taking everyone's orders. Shawn's attention veers toward the blonde, thank goodness. Unfortunately, she is interested in Trent and Trent is never one to turn attention away.

Therefore, I sit at lunch watching Caroline hang all over Gabe and the waitress hang all over Trent. Neither Basso seems to mind, and Shawn is looking better every minute.

I did my duty as a bridesmaid and I am beyond ready to go home. Ian might be going crazy there by himself and I might go crazy if I stay here a moment longer. Since Gabe is obviously occupied, I walk over to him, asking him for the keys.

"I will drive you back home." Gabe scoots his chair back, getting ready to stand up.

"No, I am sure Trent or Doug can drive you home. Just let me know when you want the car and I can bring it over." I stop him from getting up by putting my hand on his shoulder. This whole car-sharing thing is really starting to get on my nerves.

"It's no problem, and I need the car later on anyway. This way you don't have to be bothered. See you guys tomorrow," he says, standing and waving to everyone while throwing some money on the table.

"Gabe, I am sure someone else can take Madeline home," Caroline whines next to him.

"Yeah, I'll take her," Trent chimes in, moving the waitress off the arm of his chair.

"I can take her since *my* hands aren't all over someone's ass," Shawn chimes in, smirking at Trent.

"We don't want any fights so I will take her. It's not a problem," Gabe says diplomatically.

"I'm sure it isn't a problem, *brother*," Trent murmurs.

We both ignore Trent's comment. Why does he think he can express feelings on who takes me home after ignoring me the whole lunch and concentrating instead on the waitress? Gabe leads me out of Taps and we walk to the Blue Monster together.

Chapter 9 – 17 years – Senior year

It was the state soccer championship again and thanks to Trent, Belcrest made it to the finals another year. We all traveled up to Madison together and, since we were all looking at colleges to attend the next year, our parents agreed to let us stay with Gabe at the house he shares with four other football players.

The bright yellow two-story house appears more suited for a family home than a group of college guys. There are two worn-out plaid couches on each side of the cement front porch. The screen door squeaks when we enter announcing our arrival, but no one comes out to greet us. It is surprisingly clean except for some soda cans and magazines sprawled across the coffee table. Mismatched couches, chairs, and tables fill the living room that is covered in a dark shag carpet. The house smells of sweat and beer, which is already making me nauseous.

Bryan and Trent each flop down on a couch, making themselves at home, while Kenna and I have a look around. "Hey if it isn't

Ricky, Lucy, Ethel, and Fred," Gabe calls as he jogs down the stairs. He's shirtless with a pair of faded jeans that hang low on his hips.

People began referring to the four of us as the "I Love Lucy" gang after Trent and I started dating last year. This past summer, Trent and I decided to end things. I couldn't explain it if I tried; we were just better at being friends. Trent started dating Chloe again but that only lasted a month. And since Trent and I are still close, a lot of girls have had a hard time dealing with it. Our relationship has caused a lot of fights, all of which have led to break-ups.

I am not naïve though. I have heard on more than one occasion how Trent hooks up with girls from the neighboring towns when he goes out with the guys from his indoor soccer team. At first I was jealous, but when I have needed him, he has always been there for me and that's all that matters.

"Put on a fucking shirt, man," Bryan says, nodding his head toward Kenna.

"You afraid your girl will be thinking of me while she's under you? Can't change genetics, Edwards." Gabe gestures his hands toward his body, while putting on the shirt he is holding. I suddenly and unexpectedly feel disappointment that his body is covered. I don't remember him being so lean and muscular.

"Anyway, didn't you hear Lucy and Ricky are taking a break, *AGAIN?*" Kenna speaks up and I turn, giving her a traitorous look.

"Surprise, surprise. You guys are off more than you are on," Gabe says, rolling his eyes before walking into the kitchen. "You guys want something to drink?"

"Beer?" Trent asks. He knows it's a long shot, but figures Gabe might give in.

"I'll tell you what. You win state tomorrow and you guys can have a beer."

Trent and Bryan look over at each other, grinning wide, while Kenna and I roll our eyes. The four of us aren't huge drinkers. Yes, we have attended some parties over the years in high school, but none of us have gotten out of control and we always make sure someone is the designated driver.

"So, where's the place to be tonight?" Bryan asks Gabe.

"Nowhere. You both have a huge game tomorrow, so you're staying in," he says, pointing to the two of them. "But the girls can come with me if they want." He gives me a smirk.

"No, thank you," Mackenna sneers.

"What about you, Madgirl? You want to have a night out with a real man?" he asks jokingly, never once looking toward Trent.

My eyes drift to Trent, who seems unfazed by his brother's bold request. He raises his shoulders indifferently, which only manages to piss me off.

"Sure," I agree, my eyes never leaving Trent's face.

Trent shakes his head back and forth.

The five of us go to dinner at some pizza place and then return to the house. Gabe takes the keys to Trent's truck; I'm assuming to make sure that the guys don't go anywhere. I am sure Mrs. Basso gave Gabe strict instructions not to let Trent and Bryan party before tomorrow.

Starting to feel guilty about going out tonight, I mention my apprehension to Mackenna.

"You should go," she urges me. "He goes out with other people, you deserve the same."

"I know, but he has the game tomorrow and I shouldn't make him upset."

"Mad, he doesn't seem upset. Just go...have fun. You know Gabe will take good care of you," she says, pushing me to go.

"I know he will, and Trent doesn't seem to really care." I lower my voice, fiddling with my phone.

"Is that what's bothering you? The fact that Trent doesn't care if you go out with his older and hotter brother?" she questions, concern in her eyes.

"No, why would you even think that?" I come back, fast and sharp.

"I will never understand you two. You won't be together, but you want the other one to act like it's the end of the world if you are with someone else," she shakes her head in disgust.

"I just don't want to ruin his chances at State tomorrow," I lie.

"Trent will be fine, Maddy. Bryan and I are here," she reminds me, resting her hand on my arm. "He isn't your responsibility."

"I know...I know." I feel the tears pricking in my eyes, but I quickly shake them off.

An hour later, I come downstairs after showering and getting ready. I have no idea where we are going since I can't get in a bar. I am wearing a pair of dark jeans that hug my hips, with a long-sleeved black shirt that is a little tight around my chest. I have always dressed pretty conservatively, never showing cleavage or a thong like other girls. To be truthful, I don't even own a thong.

Sometimes I wonder if that is the problem with Trent and me. He always goes after girls who wear cleavage-baring shirts and jeans so low that when they sit down, you can see their butt crack. Or what Kenna and I refer to as a "coin slot". He also seems to favor blonde-haired girls, whereas mine is a dark chestnut.

I come down the stairs to find the four of them watching some prank show on television. Trent and Bryan are sporting their running pants with t-shirts, and Mackenna is already in her pajamas. I guess it's safe to say that they aren't going to sneak out tonight.

"Wow, you look awesome Maddy," Kenna says, most likely complimenting herself since she did my make-up.

"Let's go." Gabe motions with his hand toward the door.

I look over at Trent one more time, but he never takes his eyes off the television or says anything to me.

"Go Maddy, have fun," Kenna urges, pushing me toward the door. "Don't even think about him," she whispers in my ear while hugging me goodbye.

"Take care of him. Make sure he goes to bed at a good time, okay?" I whisper back.

"You are hopeless," she says and turns to Gabe.

"Now, take care of our girl, Gabe Basso. Otherwise you will have me to answer to."

"You scare me a little, Ross," he responds with a laugh, and then immediately ushers me out the door.

I am surprised when Gabe climbs into Trent's truck.

"I hope you don't mind, but I told a couple friends that I would pick them up on the way," he divulges while pulling away from the curb.

"Of course not. Where are we going?" I sheepishly ask. I don't remember ever being alone with Gabe before now; usually someone is always around. It feels awkward and uncomfortable.

"A buddy of mine's house. Just a small get together, nothing major," he assures me.

"Okay," I respond. All of sudden, I am having second thoughts about this. I won't know anyone but Gabe, and I don't want him to feel like my babysitter.

Five silent minutes go by and we pull up to a huge fifteen-story building that reads "Terrace Hall" on the outside. I assume this is one of many dormitories here. Before I can ask him, two huge guys come running up to the truck, hopping into the quad cab in the back.

"About fucking time, Basso. What took so long?" the bigger of the two shouts over the music.

"How about some manners, Smith?" Gabe motions toward me with his head.

"Oops, sorry. Grady Smith," he says and puts his hand over the seat for me to shake.

"Maddy," I shake his hand back. It is softer and weaker than I expected.

"Pleasure, Maddy. This is Rich Taylor," he says, pointing to the quieter, smaller guy next to him.

I turn around so I can face him. "Nice to meet you, Rich." I smile and he smiles back, but responds only with a nod of his head.

"So Maddy, what year are you?" Grady asks me.

"She's not. She's my brother's girl from high school," Gabe states, pulling the truck away from the curb.

"You brought jail bait?" Grady looks me up and down. "And hot jail bait at that."

"I'm not jail bait," I remark, looking back at him. "I turned eighteen last month."

"You did?" Gabe asks me, surprised. I nod in response.

"Now I have to be extra careful with you tonight," he says casually, his eyes never leaving the road ahead.

"That's for sure. You should just take her home now, Basso. I won't go after it because I like you so much, but I guarantee you that Cooper won't be so obliging," Grady says from the back seat.

"It?" I ask him, raising my eyebrow.

"Your ass," he deadpans.

"Oh…thanks for the clarification. Maybe my *ass* wouldn't want to be with you or this Cooper guy," I state. Gabe starts laughing and I hear Rich chuckle behind me.

"Honey, if I turn on my charm, you would be escorting me back to my dorm before one o'clock," Grady scoffs, leaning close to my ear so I can feel his breath on my neck.

"More like running from you come midnight," I return sarcastically, moving closer to the window and away from him.

Gabe full-out belly laughs, Rich chuckles, and I am stunned to see Grady laughing as well. I think I just made a new friend.

"Oh Maddy, we are going to get along just fine." He leans back into his seat, remaining silent for the rest of the trip.

There are co-eds everywhere when we pull up. If this is what Gabe calls a "get together", then I would hate to see a full-fledged party. This is three times bigger than any party in Belcrest.

Rich and Grady get out, walking into the house. Gabe comes around the truck, taking my hand and following the two. "Stay by me, okay? Don't drink anything unless I give it to you."

"Okay," I answer, starting to feel a little paranoid.

If I thought that the outside was crowded, the inside is ten times worse.

"Here," Gabe says, handing me a bottle of beer. I don't like beer, but I am not about to ask for something else. He twists the tops off and takes a long pull on his.

"Hey man, new girl already?" A long lean guy comes up next to Gabe. His eyes and hair match and are both a dark brown, almost black. He has a dimple in his right cheek when he smiles and has the sexy look of someone who forgot to shave this morning. He isn't as muscular as Gabe or the other two guys, but you can tell he is strong.

"What's up, Coop? No, this is my brother's girl," he nods his head toward me while shaking the guy's hand.

"I'm *not* your brother's girl," I remind him.

"They may have broken up," he says to this other guy, "but they are one of those couples who break up, get back together, and will probably get married one day."

"Cooper Sears." He puts his hand out for me to shake.

"Maddy." I take his hand and he brings mine up to his mouth, kissing it.

"Hello, Maddy. Welcome to my place." He doesn't let go of my hand.

"Well, I have some people I want to introduce Maddy to, so we'll see you around, Coop." Gabe puts his hand on my elbow, pulling me closer to him.

"You just got here, there's plenty of time for that. Come on, Maddy. Let's go downstairs where it's quieter," he says, tugging on my hand.

"Cooper, I am warning you once. Leave her alone." Gabe pulls me back.

"It's fine, Gabe, we can all go down to the basement." I move my elbow out of his grip. I actually wouldn't mind some alone time with Cooper.

"I have to find someone first. Maddy, this isn't high school," he whispers in my ear.

"I can handle myself but thank you for your concern, Gabe," I say, and start walking with Cooper.

"Cooper," Gabe yells over the crowd. "I will be down there in five minutes. And Madgirl?" I look over to him. "Remember what I told you."

I nod my head. I appreciate his interest in my safety but I am a big girl. I follow Cooper Sears down the stairs. His name alone sounds sexy. There is a tattoo on his forearm and another peeking out from under his short-sleeved shirt on the other arm. I am curious to know what they are. The basement is decked out with a pool table, some arcade games, and a poker table in the corner, where a girl is sitting in only her bra and underwear. On the floor nearby is a pile of clothes.

"Nice, Coop." A guy looks me up and down, as though I am there for his viewing pleasure.

Cooper gives him a high five, winking in his direction. We sit together on a black leather couch and he asks me about Belcrest, saying he came down with Gabe a few years ago and couldn't believe the town is so small. He is from Chicago and makes it clear to me that he is from the city, not the suburbs, stating that there is a big difference between the two.

I find out that he was the kicker of the football team before he graduated last year. I fail to divulge who my brother is, since I am sure he would know him, only being three years apart and both playing on the football team. I don't want to be Little Jennings in his eyes.

He caresses my leg and arm as we talk, but doesn't take it any further. Gabe never returns so I assume he is okay with me and

Cooper together. I haven't talked to a guy like this except for Trent. Since I was never really interested in anyone else, I never hooked up like Trent did after we broke up.

The poker game heats up when a girl has to take off her bra, and one of the guys has to remove his underwear. I give her props for being so forthcoming. I would never have the guts to do that. Everyone in the room starts talking louder and people from upstairs start coming down to watch the people stripping their clothes off. The guys are gawking at the girl and the girls are drooling over the guy.

"Let's go into my room. It's quieter." Cooper entwines his fingers in mine, leading me through a door at the right.

I sit on the edge of the bed, starting to realize that I am out of my league here. I want to kiss Cooper, but I have only really kissed Trent. I don't want to come off like some naïve high school girl, even if I really am.

"I think I should find Gabe." I stand up, walking toward the door.

"He's fine, probably making out with some chick. You know him." He comes closer, putting his arm around my waist and kissing my neck.

"Really, Cooper, it's been great talking with you. Thanks for having me over," I say, turning myself away from him. Instead of letting me go, he clutches me harder.

"Any of those girls out there would love to be in here with me but I picked you," he softly speaks in my ear, sucking on my earlobe.

"Please Cooper, I don't want to do this," I start pleading to him.

"You know you want to, just let yourself enjoy this." He makes his way down my neck while his hands roam my body.

I freeze, not knowing how to react. This has never happened to me before. In Belcrest, I am either Little Jennings, Jack's sister, or Trent's girl. No one ever asks me out or hits on me. I know I have to get out of this situation fast.

"I am sure Gabe is looking for me. Let's go find him and then we can come back down here once he knows I am okay," I say, trying to trick him so I can get out of the room.

"No can do. I told you Gabe is fine. He's a big boy." His lips are coming dangerously close to mine and I keep scooting back, but he puts his hand on the back of my neck and holds me in place while his face inches closer. The face I found stunningly gorgeous five minutes ago now resembles a pervert.

Right when I feel his lips against mine, I hear someone trying to open the door. It is locked, even though I don't remember him locking it as we came in.

"Cooper, open this fucking door," Gabe screams from the outside, banging with his fists.

"Go away, Basso, we are having a killer time in here." He never takes his hands off me, but thankfully his mouth moves so he could yell toward the door.

"I am giving you one warning, Sears. Open this door or I am busting it open," Gabe shouts as he continues pounding against the door.

"Give it your best try, Basso," Cooper yells back, having no intention of letting me out. "Now, where were we Maddy?" His lips are suddenly on mine, and he forces his tongue through my lips and down my throat. My arms are limp at my side, as though all of my energy is drained. His hand grabs my breast and he moans in my mouth, while I feel bile rising in my throat.

The sound of wood splintering fills the room as Gabe breaks through the door. Everyone from downstairs huddles around the doorframe, speechless.

"I gave you fair warning." Gabe tugs my arm, bringing me to his side and then pulls me behind him.

"What are you going to do? You think you're so noble. Mr. Quarterback, captain of the football team, and scholar on the dean's list. You are just like me, a ladies man. I see you with all those girls, tossing them aside just like I do. I think the problem here is that maybe you want this girl, but let me warn you, she is just a tease. Her legs are zippered shut," he says, pointing toward me.

Before anyone can react, Gabe hits him square in the jaw. "That one's from me." He then hits him in the stomach. "That one's for her." He follows this with an upper cut in his chin. "And that's for her brother; I think you might know him." Gabe steps away, knowing he has the ace in the hole. "Jack Jennings," Gabe divulges. Cooper's face goes white.

He doesn't come after Gabe for retaliation. Gabe grabs my hand, leading me through the crowd toward the stairs when a blonde girl stops him.

"Where are you going Gabe?" she whines, putting her hand on his chest.

"Leaving," he says shortly, pushing past her.

"Don't come back, Gabe. I won't be here when you do," she sneers.

Gabe ignores her, tugging me up the stairs.

"Grady, Rich. I assume you are good," he asks them on the way out.

"Don't worry about us, we'll get home," Rich quietly says.

"I told you Cooper was going to get to her," Grady yells loudly.

Gabe doesn't respond, just walks us both out of the house and past the oblivious co-eds standing around the lawn. My eyes follow him as he moves around the front of the truck and into the seat next to me.

Tears begin to form, but I curse them to stop. That is the last thing I want to do. I am sure Gabe is mad at himself for even suggesting that I come tonight. He says nothing as he starts the truck, pulling away from the party. I notice his knuckles are red and swollen, and I am thankful that he doesn't have a game this week.

"I'm sorry," I whisper, looking down in my lap.

"It's not your fault. Cooper's an ass," he says, but I can still hear the anger in his voice.

"I should have listened to you," I admit.

"Yeah, you should have, but it's over," he says, his voice calming a bit.

"Are you going to tell my brother?" I ask, finally finding the courage to look up.

"Hell no, your brother would kill him," he chuckles, probably thinking about Jack beating up Cooper. "Just knowing Cooper will be scared shitless of your brother for the next month or so is enough payback."

"Thank you," I say sincerely.

"No thanks required, Madgirl. But I have to say, my brother must have his hands full with you around."

"Why?"

"You're a good-looking girl and obviously naïve to how attractive you are. I assume you get yourself in bad situations often, since you see only the good in everyone."

"Gabe, your brother has been the only guy to even ask me out. I don't know if it's the fact that I am Jack's little sister or 'Trent's girl'," I say, using air quotes for emphasis, "but it gets really annoying sometimes."

"I can see that."

"So is Cooper telling the truth?"

He raises an eyebrow at me.

"That you are like him, make out with girls and then toss them aside for someone else the next night."

"No. Yes. I don't know. College is different, Maddy. Everyone just wants to have fun, no strings attached. You will see next year. Too bad I will be gone by then." He looks genuinely upset that we won't be able to attend the same school again.

"I don't think that whole casual hooking up thing is for me," I confess.

"You're probably right. That's why my brother always keeps you close."

"What do you mean?"

"Nothing, let's go in."

I hadn't realized we were at the house already.

"Tell me, Gabe. What are you talking about?" I grab his arm, stopping him from leaving the car.

"I just wonder if he knows you are the one he wants to settle down with in the future, but he wants to enjoy what's out there before he will commit to you."

"Or maybe we aren't supposed to be together and that's why it never works out. I don't really think I'm his type."

"Believe me, Mad, you are every guy's type."

There is something stirring in his eyes when he says that, but I can't put my finger on what it is.

"Thanks for that, Gabe, and I am so sorry for tonight."

"Don't mention it. I just wish I could have shown you a better time." He reaches over to remove my hand from his arm, but it lingers in his hand while chills spread through my body. "You better get in there to your boy before he comes out to get you," he motions to the front window with his head.

Trent is peering out of the window, looking directly at us. When he sees me turn my head in his direction, he quickly moves away.

I lean over and kiss Gabe on the cheek, and then run into the house before I do something I will regret. Bryan and Kenna are wrapped in each other's arms, lying on an air mattress in the living room, and Trent is feigning sleep on the couch.

I go into the bathroom and change into my pajamas. Afterward, I lie down on the empty couch, trying to turn off thoughts of Cooper, Trent, and the things that Gabe said.

"Did you have fun?" I hear Trent whisper.

"Yeah, it was okay." I prop myself up on my elbows to face him.

"I missed you," Trent says, staring at the ceiling.

"You should be asleep; it's a big game tomorrow," I say, trying to detour the conversation.

"Will you lay with me?"

"Trent, we aren't a couple. We really shouldn't."

"Come on, Mad, we are friends. I won't touch you anywhere you don't want me to. I just need you next to me right now," he confesses.

"Okay." I get up, hoping this will help him get the sleep that he needs.

"Come here, girl." A huge smile spreads across his face and he lifts the corner of the blanket for me. I snuggle on the narrow couch next to him with my back to his front, and he swings an arm around my waist, nuzzling his face in my neck.

After five minutes of quiet silence, my eyelids start to close.

"I love you, Madeline Jennings," Trent whispers in my ear.

I ignore him, pretending to be asleep. That is a line I am unable to cross. Trent wants me when he can't have me, but he doesn't want me when he can.

Chapter 10 – Present Day

Gabe and I are making our way out to the Blue Monster when Trent comes jogging over to us.

"Maddy, wait up," he yells over to me.

"What's up, Trent?" I turn around and Gabe follows my lead.

"Can I talk to you for a second?" he asks.

I look at Gabe and then back to Trent. "Sure," I say.

"Privately, Maddy. No offense, Gabe."

"Umm…alright," I say hesitantly.

"I can take her home, Gabe. Go ahead and do what you have to do," he tells Gabe.

"You okay with that Maddy?" Gabe asks me.

"Why wouldn't she be?" Trent demands angrily.

"Do you really want me to list the reasons?" Gabe spats at Trent.

"Stop it, guys." I ask Trent to give me a second and then walk over toward Gabe.

"Thank you for your concern, but Trent can take me home. I know you said you had stuff to do, so please, go ahead and do it." I place my hand on his shoulder, trying to reassure him that it will be fine.

"Maddy, you don't have to go with him. I can stay while you talk and then I will take you home," he offers pleadingly.

"Go Gabe, it's fine. I assume you will be picking me up tomorrow for Great Adventures?" I try to divert his attention to something else, hoping he will let this go. The last thing I need is for them to start fighting.

A smile forms on his lips. "Well, of course. I'll come get you at nine."

"Why does everything have to be so early?" I whine.

"Rest up tonight, Madgirl, we've got a big day tomorrow," he says with a laugh.

By the time I make my way toward Trent, he is resting his back against the wall with one foot propped up behind him, looking completely annoyed.

"Madgirl?" Gabe yells. I turn around. "You have my number. Call me if you need *anything*."

"I will, Gabe. Thanks," I say, waving goodbye to him.

"About time. I swear you wouldn't guess he was my brother, the way he goes after my girl all the time," Trent says, irritated.

"Trent, I am not your girl anymore. You need to stop saying that," I snap at him.

"You are more *my* girl than *his* girl."

"I'm not anyone's girl!" I scream. A couple of people stop to look our way, but at this point I don't care. "You sure didn't seem to care if I was your girl back at Taps when Blondie was practically giving you a lap dance."

"Mad, you know I have to make the fans happy."

"Do you really think a blonde bimbo would ruin your career if you told her she couldn't sit on your lap? Give me a break, Trent."

"I really don't want to argue, Maddy," Trent pleads while he leads us toward the river.

"I don't want to either. What did you want to talk about?" I ask, trying to stay on point. No reason for us to keep reliving the past.

"May I?" He looks down at my hand.

"No."

"Come on, Maddy. I need to touch you when I talk to you."

"You lost that right, Trent. My patience is starting to wear thin so spill it."

"Fine," he says, stopping us at a bench on the river's edge. "Will you at least sit down?"

I sit down, obliging him.

"I miss you." His blue eyes meet mine and I see the truth in his words.

"I know. You've told me that numerous times over the past year," I say curtly.

"I'm sorry I never saw it before. I know I took you for granted," he apologizes.

"I don't really want to talk about *us*, Trent. It is hard enough being back here, let alone dealing with our drama."

"Okay, I'm sorry Maddy. I should have realized I am probably making it hard on you..." He takes my hand without permission, but I don't fight him. I can't. He knows why it is so hard for me to be home. He has always been the one to comfort me through my nightmares.

"Thanks, Trent," I say, squeezing his hand.

"How about we do something fun?" he asks with a smirk.

"I was just going to lounge around at home," I say.

"Not today," he says, pulling me up to my feet, leading me over to his Mercedes.

"Where are you taking me?" I ask.

"It's a surprise." He winks at me, opening the door to his car.

I see he is heading out of town, but to do most things, you have to leave the city limits of Belcrest. The air conditioning cools my body, as I shift in the comfortable black leather. I tilt my head back, inhaling a deep breath. My eyes start drifting down slowly. I open them up, but they drift back down until eventually I don't have the strength to hold them up.

My eyes open when I hear horns honking and traffic sounds found only in a city. *Milwaukee?* Then I see Watertower Place. *He brought me to Chicago?*

"Why are we in Chicago?" I ask Trent angrily.

"Oh good, you finally woke up," he says. "You must have been tired. You were asleep before we hit the freeway."

"Sorry, I didn't get much sleep last night. Again Trent, why are we in Chicago?"

"I have to show you something." He pulls into an underground parking garage.

I see him swipe a card through the slot and the yellow gate opens. He parks in front of a sign that is marked "Resident Only".

When the car stops, I get out. He meets me at the back of his expensive car and grabs my hand, but I pull it away. He remains quiet, although I see the look of annoyance that crosses his face. He walks us over to the elevator and hits the button.

The elevator stops at the thirty-sixth floor and I follow him down to the end of the hall. He enters his key and I am astonished when he opens the door to a completely empty condo. There isn't a couch or table, not a rug or even paint on the walls. It is a dream, a blank canvas. I walk over to the windows that overlook the lake and, just to the right, you can see the Navy Pier Ferris wheel. It is a breathtaking view.

"Trent, this is magnificent. What a great place," I exclaim.

"I thought so too. I wasn't going to buy anything since I am always moving around, but I couldn't help myself."

"Do you mind if I look around?" I motion toward the hallway.

"Not at all." He puts his hand out, welcoming me to explore.

There are two small empty bedrooms down the hall, with a bathroom separating each of them. The master bedroom is located at the end of the hall, and consists of a king-size bed, matching dressers, and two nightstands.

I veer to the left and find the master bathroom. There is a jacuzzi tub with a view of the lake. The hair products Trent and I both prefer fill the shelves of the see-through shower, which has showerheads facing one another on either side. On the opposite wall, there are marbled double vanities with separate mirrors. Trent's favorite toothpaste and cologne occupy the counter.

Trent's clothes are neatly placed in the walk-in closet. His suits and button-down shirts are hung with precision, according to color. Pants, sweaters, and shirts are stacked in the shelves built from ceiling to floor. His shoes are aligned at the bottom in the shoe racks, mostly consisting of soccer cleats. The whole right-hand side of the closet is bare, except for one dress hanging. The dress I wore the last night I was with him.

"It's an amazing condo, Trent," I say, walking out of the closet quickly and trying to forget what I saw.

"As you can see, I am in desperate need of a decorator. Know anyone?" A smile creeps across his face.

"Don't, Trent," I warn him, narrowing my eyes.

"Don't what? Ask the best decorator I know to decorate my place?" He sits on the edge of the bed and I briefly wonder how much it would cost me to have a taxi drive me home.

"Don't use the excuse of me decorating your condo to get me back in your life." I turn around, pretending to be looking at the items on his dresser in an effort to avoid looking him in the eye.

"I am not going to deny I want you back. I think I have made my intentions clear. Regardless, I do need you to help me decorate this place. I thought we could go shopping today."

"I have dinner with my mom tonight," I respond, keeping my back turned and picking up one of his watches.

"Cancel. God knows she has cancelled on you your whole life," he says with bitterness.

"She seems different since I came back. I don't know what the change is but I like it," I say, turning around to face him. I can't tell him not to talk about my mom like that; he lived that night with me. "Can we not talk about her right now?" I ask.

"Will you cancel on her?"

"I have Ian there too," I remind him.

"Perfect. Your mom can spend the evening with a man she can't have. Come on, Maddy."

I bite my lip, contemplating what to do. "Okay, but I have to be home no later than nine o'clock tonight, got it?"

"Got it."

"No hand-holding, no hugging, and no kissing."

"Promise," he says, placing his hands behind his back as though they will stay there.

"Alright," I agree begrudgingly.

"What are we waiting for then?" He starts to walk out of the room but I don't follow. He turns around at the doorway and looks at me questioningly.

"We have to measure before we go. Since you kidnapped me, I'm without a tape measure and pad of paper." I stand there, knowing he doesn't have that in his condo, but to my surprise he doesn't flinch.

He walks over to his dresser, opens the bottom drawer, and I gasp when I see it's filled with all of my things that I left in our apartment back in New York. My pajamas are on one side, laundered and folded. A couple of my interior design magazines, my idea book for our place in New York, along with pencils, note pads, and a few tape measures. My ponytail holders, nail polish, and a small bottle of perfume lie in the drawer.

"I couldn't get rid of these things, but I didn't want to give them back to you. I guess I was hoping you would come looking for them," Trent says sheepishly, looking at me.

"Gosh. I don't even know what to say." I bend down, digging through my things. I grab one of my tape measures and a pad. "Let's get started," I say, quickly shutting the drawer from my past.

We go room to room, measuring windows and floors. We start laughing when I release the tape measure and it springs back to Trent, popping him and making him drop it. I forgot how easy he makes me laugh.

Once we finish, we head out to Michigan Avenue. Five stores and three arguments later, Trent finally agrees with me on a couch. He wants to sink into it and I want a specific color and texture. We compromise on a nice steel-colored, deep-set couch with a couple of fabric-decorated chairs. Trent doesn't give much more input after the couch, except when it comes to the beds.

He convinces me to lie with him on each mattress in the store, and we laugh our way through the stiff-as-a-board beds. Trent never crosses the line, until he has to pull me out of one of the sink-hole beds with both of his hands. He raises me up with such force that I end up in his arms.

"Sorry," I say, stepping back.

"Don't ever be sorry for running into me. I quite enjoyed it," he says, winking. It's definitely time to get out of here. I've already gotten all of the furniture I'm going to buy at typical furniture stores, and it's too late to hit the antique stores and flea markets today for the unique items that will suit him.

"You hungry?" he asks, interrupting my thoughts.

"Starving actually," I admit, putting my hand over my stomach.

"I have just the place." He smiles at me when I let him take my hand, leading me out of the store.

"It better be casual. Look at me," I remark.

"You look gorgeous, like always," he says without looking back at me.

"You've always been a sweet talker, Trent Basso," I laugh.

"Did you say Trent Basso?" A dark-haired guy stops us in the street.

Oh great, here we go again.

"Oh shit man, I am a huge fan. I have been following you since college," the guy remarks, hitting the blonde guy next to him in disbelief.

"Thanks, that means a lot to me," Trent says, putting his other hand out to shake the guy's hand, but keeping his other hand firmly in mine.

"I can't believe you are playing for Chicago. How we got you, I have no idea," the blonde chimes in now.

Pretty soon, I will be pushed aside while he chats with strangers.

"It's great to be with Chicago; I love the city," Trent says, obviously well coached in what to say to fans.

"How come you aren't in Europe?" the dark-haired guy asks. *Now that they mention it, he should be playing in Europe right now.*

"A good buddy of mine is getting married. Listen guys, I would love to chat but my girl here is hungry," he says, squeezing my hand. Both guys look me up and down, giving me an uneasy feeling.

"Sure thing, man," the blonde says, giving him a smirk that seems to say that he doesn't want to be responsible for the almighty Trent Basso not getting laid.

"Hope to see you at some games." Trent shakes both of their hands and we turn and head in the other direction.

"Sorry about that, Maddy. It's been nice here so far; not a lot of people recognize me yet." He truly looks remorseful that he was recognized.

"It's okay. None of my business anymore," I tell him, not missing the disappointment in his eyes caused by my words.

Five minutes later, he walks me into a diner where we gorge ourselves on malts, burgers, and fries. I know I shouldn't consume all of these calories since I have to fit into my bridesmaid's dress in a few days, but it feels like old times. After Trent's games, we would always go out for greasy food and stuff ourselves until we couldn't eat one more bite, then lie around watching movies. Those were some of our best times together.

Now here we are, joking about Mackenna giving birth and how Bryan will probably drive to the hospital without her. It scares me that we can pick up where we left off, like last year never happened. From all appearances, anyone would think that we still were the perfect couple.

Once we finish dinner, we walk back to his condo to get his car. Trent drives me home, holding my hand the whole way back.

"Thank you, Maddy," Trent says as I open the Mercedes door.

"You're welcome. I had a lot of fun," I confess.

"I'm glad," he says, smiling.

"Good night, Trent," I say, one leg out of the car.

"Hey Mad," he says and I turn to face him. "I won't be at Great Adventures tomorrow; I have something I have to do for the team. Can I take you to dinner tomorrow night?"

"I don't know, Trent," I answer. Today was great, but it was nice just getting to a place where we could be in the same room together.

"Please Maddy, there is something I have to tell you," he says, pleading with me.

"Alright Trent, but a late dinner. Is eight okay?" I ask. I know we will be out late at Great Adventures and I need to spend some time with my mom.

"Sure, I will pick you up at eight tomorrow night," he says. I close the door and watch him drive away, wondering if I am making a huge mistake.

Chapter 11 – 18 years old Senior Prom

Trent's soccer team won the state championship and that night, he asked me to date him again. He took me out on the porch at Gabe's house, telling me how stupid he was for letting me go last summer, and that he wanted his Lucy back. In the back of my mind, I knew it had something to do with me going to the party with Gabe the night before, but I still couldn't resist him. I had high hopes we could make it work this time around.

It is now spring and we have been dating for six months, the longest stretch we've been together. We are even more inseparable than Kenna and Bryan. With my mom gone almost every night, I spend most of my time at the Basso's. Since Jack is living in Chicago with Doug and a couple other guys, the Bassos are my family. Luckily, Mr. and Mrs. Basso have never minded having me around, especially after Gabe moved out.

My mom and I continue to drift further apart. She is rarely home and when she is, a male companion is always with her. I sneak out on those nights, driving over to Trent's, meeting him in an old barn that they have on their property. It's mostly used as a garage now for fixing up cars, but there are still some hay bales lying in a loft where Trent and I like to hang out together, talking about the future.

Trent wants to become a famous soccer player like David Beckham and I dream of becoming a designer, although not one that remodels the homes of the rich and famous. No, I'd rather see the faces of middle-class families when I design something that they could have never imagined themselves.

We picture Mackenna and Bryan living next to us and raising our kids all together. We would have it all: love, kids, and careers. And unlike our parents, we would get out of this town. No longer would I have to endure the stares of those who knew I was the daughter of the woman who slept with some of the married men in town. We could have a fresh start, far away from here.

Of course, we do more than talk but, other than heavy make-out sessions and Trent's roaming hands up my shirt, we do nothing more. We are both worried about the possibilities of a pregnancy and the surety that it would change our future in a drastic way. Not that holding off isn't hard. Trent has begged me more than a couple of times to go on the pill, but I haven't wanted to go to the doctor by myself, and I am definitely not going to ask my mother.

Prom is next month and I have decided that I am going to surprise him, even though I know that sex on prom night is very cliché. Mackenna accompanied me to the doctor last month, since it takes a month for the pill to kick in before it's effective.

Mrs. Basso takes me dress shopping since my mother apparently has more important things to do. Fortunately, I have a credit card my dad gave me in case of emergencies. Trent's mom takes me to Marge's, the only dress shop in town, which is filled with girls and their mothers scrambling to find dresses. I imagine every girl in a thirty-mile radius comes to buy her prom dress here.

"Thank you for bringing me, Mrs. Basso," I say sincerely.

"Oh sweetie, don't thank me. It's my pleasure. Having three boys, I never get to do these girly things." She puts her arm around me, pulling me closer and kissing me on the temple. "Now let's find you the perfect dress."

"It's so crowded, I hope there's one here." I am skeptical that we will find the right one. Mackenna's dad took her to Chicago to get hers.

"Maddy, you would look beautiful in anything, but I am certain your dress is here," she assures me.

I walk over to the first row, spotting a lilac dress that comes up around the neck like a halter-top. I have this feeling about it so I take it to the dressing room.

"Oh Maddy. You look gorgeous, honey," Mrs. Basso flushes when I walk out of the dressing room.

The dress has a rhinestone edging that meets between my breasts where it is cinched together. It flows out across my stomach, all the way down to my ankles. The dress suits my body shape and I instantly fall in love with it.

"I think this is it, Mrs. Basso," I exclaim, looking at myself in the mirror. A couple of girls are looking at me from the side, most likely waiting for me to put it down but I am keeping it.

"Are you sure you don't want to look around, sweetie?" she asks, clearly disappointed that our girls' time is being cut short.

"I'm positive, this is it." I turn around to face her.

"I guess that when you know, you know. Let's get it and go get our nails done, my treat." She grabs both of my hands and brings them out to my sides. "You look so beautiful, Maddy, and I am sure my son will pass out when he sees you."

"I hope so."

"I know so," she says and we both smile.

Prom night arrives in the blink of an eye. I get ready at Mackenna's so she can do my make-up and hair. Her dress is tight and short while mine is flowing and long. Trent loves my hair down so I decide to wear it that way, even though Kenna wants me to put it up like her. I don't let her put too much make-up on me either. I want to look natural. Tonight is the night I am losing my innocence, so to speak, and I don't want to look like my mother.

Trent and Bryan come to pick us up with their parents in tow to take pictures. We can hear all of the parents chatting together, along with the clanking of bottles and glasses. Their laughter fills the downstairs, and I try to push away the twinge of pain I feel caused by the absence of mine.

Mackenna and I make our way down the stairs and when we turn the corner into the family room, everyone quiets down. My face instantly becomes pink and I bite my bottom lip as I wonder what Trent is thinking. Bryan walks right up to Mackenna, hugging her and whispering something in her ear. Whatever he says makes her giggle, and she playfully slaps him on his shoulder.

Trent's expression is unreadable as he stares at me from across the room, his mom and dad on either side of him. I have never seen him speechless like this. I start walking toward him, but he quickly puts his hand up, telling me to stay where I am. He slowly walks over to me and when he reaches me, I notice his hands are shaking.

"You look beautiful, Madeline Jennings," he softly speaks. "I can't believe you are my girl." He takes out the corsage he bought me, wrapping it around my wrist. It's beautiful, with white roses and lilac ribbon running through it.

I catch the scent of his cologne mixed with his soap when I grab his lapel to pin on the boutonniere. He smiles down at me as I pin it into place.

"Thanks for not pricking me," he jokes.

Mrs. Basso insists on an ungodly number of photos and Mr. Basso stands by my side during the picture containing Trent, his parents, and me. He is a quiet man who keeps to himself so when he speaks to me, I am taken by surprise.

"I hope I am not overstepping my boundaries. I have always thought of you as my daughter, Maddy. You look incredibly beautiful tonight and are a remarkable young lady. Have fun tonight but not too much fun," he says, winking, and I feel a teardrop fall from my eye.

"Thank you, Mr. Basso." I crush into him, wrapping my arms around his neck. He seems taken by surprise at first, but then squeezes me tight. Mrs. Basso grins at the two of us.

We pile into Bryan's dad's silver BMW, waving goodbye to our parents who are still standing on the lawn. It is a forty-minute drive to the swanky hotel where the prom is being held in Milwaukee.

The Hollywood-themed room is decorated in black, silver, and white with hues of blue. There are twinkling lights around every tree pillar in the room. It looks magical and being here with Trent means even more to me. I couldn't have imagined coming with anyone else.

We take our seats at the table closest to the stage, sharing a table with a couple of other soccer players and their dates. I see Trent passing a flask back and forth with one of his buddies, which makes me nervous. I don't want him to get drunk tonight. He had promised me beforehand he wouldn't drink, but I don't say anything, not wanting to ruin our prom night.

"Trent, come dance," I beg, grabbing his hand.

"Okay, Maddy," he responds, waving to his friends as we walk away.

Just as we hit the dance floor, the music turns slow and Trent instantly pulls me closer, swaying back and forth.

"I can't tell you how amazing you look tonight, Maddy," Trent whispers.

"You don't look so bad yourself," I respond. Trent does look stunning. The black tuxedo fills out his shoulders, making him look even more muscular and fit. He has let his hair grow out a little since soccer season ended and the waves fall just above his eyes, making him look irresistible when he puts his hand through it. The silver vest he's wearing makes his clear-blue eyes sparkle.

"Thank you, Miss Jennings." Trent brings me closer to him. "I wish we had a room; I would love to see you out of this dress."

"Trent Basso!" I screech. He has never said anything like that before to me. Not that I mind, but it surprises me, making me think he has had a little too much of whatever is in that flask.

"Come on, Maddy. I know I have asked before, but it's killing me. I love you so much and I want to be with you in that way. It will bring us so much closer together," he pleads. I know now that my assumptions are correct; he is tipsy, if not already drunk.

"Well, Mr. Basso. Tonight might be your lucky night, but you better stop drinking from that flask."

"Really?" He pulls back from me, his eyes bulging out of his head in disbelief.

"I wanted to surprise you tonight. I thought we could go up to the barn when we get back to your place, but at this rate, you won't be in any shape."

"Oh, you don't have to worry about that. Let's get Bryan and Kenna and go," he says, pulling my hand.

"Trent, we can wait. We only have one prom." I pull him back to me, holding him in my arms.

"One prom and one first time," Trent says back. I am just about to let him take me, when they announce it is time for the king and queen to be revealed.

"I know it's going to be us, baby. Let's go." Trent pulls me to the front with Mackenna and Bryan.

To my surprise, Gabe walks up to the microphone. "What is your brother doing here?" I ask Trent.

"They always try to get a previous king or queen to announce it and he agreed, since he was in Milwaukee interviewing this week," Trent answers, seemingly annoyed.

"Oh," I say, surprised that he never told me Gabe would be here.

"Okay, settle down everyone. For those of you that don't know me," Gabe starts speaking. The whole school yells 'Gabe'. "Alright, some of you know me," he laughs. "As a previous prom king it is my pleasure to announce this year's king." Gabe opens the envelope. A huge smile spreads across his face and I know instantly whose name is on that envelope. "Trent Basso," he reveals to everyone.

Trent turns to me, kissing me on the cheek, "See you up there, babe." He walks up on stage and Gabe places the crown on his head.

A slim-figured blonde with a friendly smile approaches the microphone after Gabe. "So, now that we have a king, we need a queen. Right, ladies?" She waits for the screams and yells to calm down. "From the looks of your king, I am surprised all you ladies aren't fighting to get up here," she says, laughing at her own joke. Trent's eyes stare into mine as she opens her envelope. "Your prom queen is…Chloe Rodgers."

Trent's eyes close briefly, as do mine. Chloe practically runs in her four-inch heels up to the stage and the blonde puts the crown on her head. Gabe gives Trent the flowers he is to give her and Trent follows his role to a tee, even kissing her on the cheek. She hooks arms with him, smiling like she just won the lottery.

Everyone scurries off the floor as the band starts playing a slow song, signaling the king and queen's customary dance. Trent finds my eyes again when he first descends from the stairs, but Chloe quickly diverts him to the dance floor. I sit close to the dance floor, watching my soul mate dance with an ex-girlfriend, who has always made it clear that she wanted him back.

"It's just a dance, I'm sure he wishes it was you," a deep voice says behind me.

"That's what my mind keeps telling me, but my heart wants to run out there and tear her hideous blonde hair out," I admit.

"I have to say, I am surprised it wasn't you." Gabe sits down next to me, resting his ankle on his knee and stretching his arm across the back of my chair. He's wearing a dark charcoal suit with a black button-down shirt and burgundy tie.

"Not me," I confess. My stomach is churning, watching Trent's hands resting on Chloe's hips. He isn't holding her remotely as close as he held me five minutes ago, but it is still hard seeing him with someone else.

"Why? You guys are obviously the idolized couple around here."

"I'm competition."

"I don't think you are competition. Maybe they are mad because you already won and they never even got up to bat."

"That's the kicker. That little blonde out there got up to bat, hit a double, and will do anything to get up there again."

"Oh Madgirl, you just don't get it," he says, laughing.

"What?" I question him without humor.

"When you're around, no one else exists," he reveals, looking at me in a way that I'm not sure he's talking just about Trent.

The dance opens up to everyone so a few couples make their way out to the floor.

"Come on, let's go make some people jealous." He stands up, holding his hand out for me to take.

I look at Trent, who seems to be chatting it up with Chloe, letting her rest her head on his shoulder. "Sure," I agree, taking his hand and letting him lead me to the dance floor.

Gabe puts one hand on the small of my back and holds my other hand moving me across the floor like he's Fred Astaire. "Where did you learn to dance like this?" I ask in astonishment.

"I needed another elective so I took ballroom dancing. I know, kind of lame," he confesses.

"Not lame…sexy." I smile and he dips me.

"Sexy, huh?" He grins back. "Glad I took that instead of racquetball then."

The song ends and claps roar through the room. My face turns red when I notice people are standing around us in a circle, cheering. I find Trent standing with Chloe next to him. He looks upset, which I don't understand since I am dancing with his brother while he is dancing with an ex.

Gabe and I walk over to Trent, and I instantly go to his side, squeezing myself between him and Chloe. "Thanks for taking care of my girl, bro," Trent says in a tight voice to Gabe.

"No problem," Gabe responds, not noticing that Trent is upset. "I've got to get going anyway so you guys have fun." He goes to leave but then turns around. "Thanks for the dance, Madgirl, it was the highlight of my night," he says, winking at me.

I hear a girl whisper, "What the hell does she have that I don't? One Basso is taken so she grabs another one."

"Thank you, Gabe," I say.

Trent pulls me by my hand, bringing me closer to him and putting his lips on mine. He thrusts his tongue in my mouth, forcing me to open. When my tongue meets his, he eases it slowly over mine until they mingle together, participating in their own dance.

I hear Chloe grunt in frustration before hearing her heels click away.

We slowly push away from each other and he rests his forehead on mine. "Sorry, I don't know why it gets me so jealous when you're with Gabe. When I see him look at you, this rage comes over me," he admits.

"Trent, he's your brother," I state.

"I know, but…"

"No buts, there is no reason to be jealous." I give him a chaste kiss on the lips, smiling up at him.

"I love you."

"I love you, too."

It is midnight when the four of us get into the silver sedan to go home. My feet are killing me so I take off my shoes, resting them on Trent's lap. He rubs them for me while Bryan drives us back to the Basso's. Not wanting us to get a hotel room, all of the parents agreed to let us stay in the Basso's basement together.

Mackenna is sound asleep when we get back so Bryan carries her into the house, placing her on the couch in the basement. I drape a blanket over her. "I guess this is the end of *my* prom night," Bryan jokes, taking the couch opposite Mackenna.

"Guess so," I laugh, hearing Kenna start to lightly snore.

There are two air mattresses blown up on the floor between the couches. I lie down on one of them. Trent looks down at me and then holds his hand out. "Let's go, my queen," he requests and I smile. I guess I shouldn't be surprised that he remembered.

"You guys have about four hours before parents might start looking, make the most of them," Bryan says, turning over to face the back of the couch.

"I intend to, man," Trent replies, pulling me by my hand up the stairs and out the front door. We run to the barn, me barefoot in my dress and him in his tuxedo.

"Stay here for one second," Trent says, stopping me at the doors.

"Okay," I agree. He slides himself through the opening. I stand there, listening to the sounds of animals coming from the nearby woods. I know I am doing the right thing. I have it so much better than other girls; at least Trent loves me and I love him. I can't imagine losing my virginity to anyone else. If I wasn't already one hundred percent sure, I am when Trent opens the barn doors.

He takes my hand in his, encircling his fingers around mine. I see the love in his eyes as he leads me to the ladder. Trent has set up twinkle lights hanging from the ceiling, with lanterns lit at two corners. He also has laid out two pillows and a blanket on top of the hay.

I stand there speechless.

"I know it's still a barn and you deserve so much better…" he says, trailing off.

"Trent, it's wonderful. Thank you," I quietly say. Tears well in my eyes as he gently pulls me down to the blanket.

"We don't have to do anything, Maddy. I know I have pressured you and I'm sorry. I would be content holding you all night," he declares. He moves his hand to the back of my neck, pulling me close.

"No, I want to Trent," I state.

He moves his lips over mine, resting his hands on either side of my face. Our tongues join together and we whimper into one another's mouths. I have never experienced this much passion with Trent before.

"Tell me if you want to stop, okay Mad?"

I nod in agreement, but I don't want him to stop.

His mouth moves down to my jaw, making his way to my neck and then my ear. My eyes close in pleasure when he sucks on my earlobe. He carefully pushes me to my side so he can unzip my dress. He slowly brings the zipper down, taking one strap down my arm and then the other, exposing my bra. His eyes go wide in anticipation.

"You're so beautiful, Maddy." He starts kissing my collarbone, following it to my shoulder before moving down to my breasts. He unclasps my white strapless bra, dropping it next to me. Taking my nipple in his mouth, he flicks his tongue, making it pebble, and he takes his time sucking on each of my breasts. His hands push my dress down past my hips and I lift to help him, leaving me only in my white satin panties.

I put my hands on either side of his face, bringing it back to my mouth, then rolling him over and straddling him. I start unbuttoning his white tuxedo shirt, revealing his muscular chest and hard abs. His hands reach up, massaging my breasts and brushing his thumbs over my nipples. My fingers roam to his pants button and I undo his pants, pulling them down and leaving him only in his black boxer briefs. I place little butterfly kisses across his chest and stomach, making my way up to his mouth. Once my lips meet his again, he crushes into me, now demanding and insistent.

Our hands start to grasp each other harder and I haul his boxers down, adding them to the pile of clothes at our feet. He takes off my white panties slowly while kissing my stomach, and when he comes back up, I feel his hardness at my opening.

Trent feels me tense immediately. "Are you sure?" he asks.

"Absolutely."

"I love you, Maddie," he says as he enters me slowly.

I cringe, grabbing his arms with my hands at the first push.

"Are you okay?"

I nod and he continues to pierce into me until he is fully encased in me. As he finds a slow rhythm, circling his hips while staring into my eyes, a surge flows through me and my body tingles with enjoyment. I know right then that I will remember this for the rest of my life.

"I love you, Trent," I whisper in his ear when he comes down to kiss my neck and shoulder.

"I love you too, Maddy...so much," he whispers back.

After we both climax in a state of complete ecstasy, Trent's body falls on top of mine and I hold him against me, never wanting this feeling to end. He rolls over onto his back, bringing me on top of him. He brings the blanket over us and brushes his hands gently through my hair.

"I wish we could stay like this forever," Trent says, kissing the top of my head.

"Me too. Thank you, Trent."

"For what?" He brings my head up to meet his.

"For being gentle. I couldn't have hoped for a better first time."

"Me either. I couldn't imagine this moment with anyone else."

Chapter 12 – Present Day Great Adventures

"Where were we last night?" Ian wakes me with a grin, bouncing up and down on my bed like a child.

"Out," I say.

"With whom?" He's not giving up.

"You don't want to know. What time is it?" I sit up, resting against my ivory headboard, rubbing my eyes.

"Eight. Gabe will be here at nine and I thought you would want to get all dolled up," he jokes. "So do you want me to guess?"

"Guess what?" I ask. It's way too early in the morning for Ian's games.

"Who you were with?" He throws his legs onto my bed, making himself comfortable.

"Ian, can we please do this another time?' I throw the covers off, moving toward my suitcase.

"Let's see..." He puts his finger up to his lips, contemplating. "Were you with the young strapping soccer star who you have been in love with since birth or his much hotter older brother who has been making your stomach fill with butterflies since we landed?"

"Cut it out, Ian!" I warn and throw a pair of socks at him. I sigh, knowing that he's not going to give up easily. "If you must know, it was the soccer star."

"That's what I thought, seeing as how Gabe stopped by here last night," he tells me. I turn around and see him looking at me with his eyebrows raised.

"What? When?" I question. A sudden feeling of guilt comes over me, though I don't know why it bothers me that Gabe knows I was with Trent.

"Why do you care?" Ian asks tauntingly.

"I don't. I just…wondered." I try to brush it off.

"Keep telling yourself that, Maddy. You better figure out what you want before you lose them both."

"Who's to say I want either of them?"

"Come on, Maddy. I know which one you want, but I am more than happy to sit back and see how this plays out. I just hope the brothers don't kill each other before it's over."

"God Ian, drama much?" I grab my clothes, heading down the hall to the bathroom.

Forty-five minutes later, I walk down the stairs to the newly remodeled kitchen and I am stunned to see my mom sitting down with Ian at the table. She is dressed in a pair of jean capris with a pink button-down blouse that for once isn't two sizes too small. Her hair is nicely brushed in a bob and her make-up is neutral with a small amount of lip gloss. Her recent transformation brings out her natural beauty.

"Good morning, Maddy," my mom says.

"Good morning, Mom. Sorry about last night," I apologize, walking over to the coffee pot.

"Its okay, Ian kept me busy, and then we had some company and we played cards," she snickers over at Ian and they laugh at some inside joke.

"Sorry I missed it, sounds like you guys had a great time."

"We understand you had other things, or shall we say *people* to do," Ian sneers.

"Seriously, Ian, you are driving me crazy and it's only nine in the morning." I turn around, leaning against the counter.

"Honey, I know I can't speak but do you really want to go there again?" My mom stands up, putting her hand on my shoulder.

"Who said I was going there again? It's complicated," I say, hoping this conversation is done.

"It's always complicated with *him*," Ian says, knowingly.

"Do I dare ask who you are talking about?" Gabe inquires, standing in the doorway.

"Please, come in," I sarcastically say, walking over to the sink and chugging my coffee before placing my cup in the sink.

"Good morning, everyone," Gabe announces, leaning against the door frame.

My mom and Ian say good morning in return and we all walk out of the kitchen to the foyer. I shove my feet into my flip-flops and the four of us file out of the house. The heat and humidity are already in full force when we open the door, making me thankful that I wore a tank top and shorts today.

Gabe and my mom walk side by side to the Blue Monster. He must have said something funny because my mom laughs and touches his bicep. A twinge of jealousy hits me, but I quickly shake it off. It's hard to do though when my eyes keep glancing down at Gabe's backside. His shorts fit his ass perfectly, making me wonder what it would be like to grab onto it while he is thrusting into me.

"You might want to wipe the saliva off your chin," Ian whispers in my ear.

I push him and he stumbles into the bushes. "Whoops, careful!" I put my hand in front of my mouth like a southern belle. Gabe and my mom turn around, dumbfounded. "Ian tripped over his own feet," I say, straight-faced.

"Yeah, clumsy me," he lies, waiting until Gabe and my mom turn around before he gives me a small push back.

"Please Barb, I am sure Maddy is fine sitting in the back," I hear Gabe say as he looks over at me.

"Go ahead Mom, sit up front," I tell her, watching while Gabe opens the door for my mom and shutting it behind her. I stand there in disbelief, watching Gabe walk in front of the truck and getting into the driver's side. With no other option, I open my own door and sit next to Ian in the back.

My mom and Gabe chat non-stop on the way to Great Adventures, while Ian checks Facebook on his phone. Kenna keeps texting me messages like "I don't trust him", "Trent's an ass", and "Stay away from him". I don't know how she found out I was with him last night, but I have a good feeling it has to do with Mr. Nosy sitting next to me. I'm still not sure why Mackenna has such a problem with Trent; he is her friend too.

Finally, we arrive at the park and there is a line of cars to pay for parking. Gabe pays the fee for some special pass to get us closer and my mom tries to give him money, but he shoos her hand away.

Once we get into the park and after Gabe insists on paying for all of us, we sit around the water fountain waiting for everyone else to arrive. Those annoying picture people come up to us and we pose for them half-heartedly. Gabe stands next to my mom and Ian next to me. I know Ian put bunny ears over my head, but at this point I don't care. I just want this day over with already.

Everyone else gradually appears and we are all standing in a circle while Jack and Lindsey pass out an itinerary and tell us where to meet for lunch. I take the itinerary out of Lindsey's hands, perusing it. We have specific times and places to meet during the day. I swear they think that everyone else's life should revolve around their wedding.

Caroline is cozying up to Gabe already and a look of disapproval crosses my mom's face. I notice Shawn Edwards walking toward me and I decide that it's time to high-tail it out of this area.

"Come on, Ian." I grab his hand. "See you all at first break," I say, waving my hand while walking away.

"What is wrong with you?" Ian asks, hooking his arm through mine.

"Nothing," I respond curtly.

"Great, *this* is going to be a fun day," Ian mumbles to himself.

"Don't worry, Ian. She just needs a cotton candy and then she will cheer up," my mom says as she walks alongside me. "It has always made her happy." She smiles over to me.

"Cotton candy. I will have to remember that. Blue or Pink?" Gabe chimes in next to Ian and my mom's face beams when she notices him.

"Blue," my mom answers his question. I am surprised she remembers that.

"Shouldn't you be back there with the rest of Belcrest's prom court?" I ask Gabe, looking behind us. I see the sour look on Caroline's face as she watches us walk away.

"I am right where I want to be," Gabe says, winking at my mom and she smiles in return. *Seriously, what the hell is going on between them?*

"Let's go, I am dying to get on Superman. I have never been here," Ian exclaims like a nine year-old boy.

"Never?" Gabe asks, shocked.

"My parents preferred educational vacations. If you ever want to go to Williamsburg, VA, I could be your tour guide," Ian remarks and we all crack up.

"Well, *I* am going to be your tour guide today. After we're done, you will wish you were in Williamsburg," Gabe jokes.

"Sounds good. Now point me to the roller coasters." Ian looks around, waiting for Gabe to tell him which direction to go.

"Superman is this way," Gabe says, pointing to the left.

"You two have fun, I am going to the carousel." I stop in front of the two-story ride, filled with little kids riding their horses and animals as they go up and down. It's a feat for me just to ride on the top floor.

"What?" Ian screams. "We aren't five, let's go." He pulls my hand.

"I don't ride roller coasters," I say sternly, looking him in the eye. I know he is going to push me. Everyone tries, but there's only one person that ever got me to ride a roller coaster and he isn't here.

"Oh, come on," Ian begs.

"No!"

"I will hold your hand the whole time," he says.

"Ian, just go. I will catch up to you guys later."

"We aren't leaving you alone, Maddy," Gabe says. He looks over at my mom and Ian. "I will stay, you two go ahead." A warm feeling spreads across my stomach.

"Nonsense, you two go. I would love some alone time with my daughter," my mom says, putting her arm around me.

Gabe winks at my mom again. If I were counting, that would have been at least the fifth time today already. "Alright then, catch up with us later then?" he asks.

"We will, just have fun," my mom says.

I'm still having trouble believing that my mom wants to spend time with me on purpose. A smile spreads across my lips. I guess it's true when people say that no matter what, you always want to have a relationship with your mother.

My mom and I walk up the stairs to the top floor of the carousel. My mom lets me pick which animal I want to ride first and takes the one next to me. I figure now is as good a time as any to ask her the questions that have been eating me up the past few days.

"So Mom, you look really good. Is there a reason for the change?" I ask, gripping the pole in front of me.

"I don't know. I guess it was just time," she says, smiling and looking down. I can tell she is hiding something from me, but I don't know what it is. I pray it isn't a new man.

"I love it, Mom. You look beautiful," I say and when she looks over, I don't think I have ever seen her so happy.

The ride starts and our carousel horses go up and down with the music. Little kids scream in delight and I can't help but smile. This is the last memory I have of us here, back when my parents were together.

My mom is laughing at the kid in front of us because he keeps trying to get off and his dad keeps putting him back on the horse. "You were like that." She motions her hand in front of her. "I always lacked the patience but your dad would go over and over with you until you felt comfortable."

"I remember," I say. My smile is dim compared to hers and she instantly sees the sorrow in mine.

"I know, honey." She reaches over and pats my knee. "This week is hard."

I nod my head in agreement, afraid that I might start crying right here on the carousel.

When the ride stops, my mom puts her arm around me as we walk to the stairs. "Let's go get that blue cotton candy."

"Thanks, Mom," I say.

"For what?" she asks, taking a chunk off of our newly purchased treat and putting it in her mouth.

"For knowing just what I needed," I say, plopping a blue sticky bite onto my tongue.

"Can we sit for a second?" my mom asks hesitantly, motioning to a park bench.

"Sure," I agree, wondering what she is going to tell me. Will it be about the new man in her life? The reason for her transformation and newly remodeled house? The reason she has been acting concerned about me the last couple of days?

"I wish this could be enough for you but I know it isn't, and I know that there isn't anything I can say that will make it better," she divulges.

"I'm not following, Mom."

"I'm sorry, Maddy...for everything. I should have been a better mother. I should have been there for you, to protect you and watch over you. Instead, I did the opposite and put you in danger," she apologizes. She wipes the tears streaming down her face with the back of her hand. "God, I didn't want to do this here, but you haven't been home much since you got back."

"Its okay, Mom. It was a long time ago and I am fine, see?" I say, reassuring her.

"You're beautiful, smart, and caring. It kills me that I had nothing to do with that. You practically raised yourself," she remarks.

"Oh Mom. I can't say I wasn't bitter toward you, but seeing you like this makes me happy. You look like…" I say, my sentence trailing off.

"A mom?" she asks with a small smile.

"Yeah, a mom," I confirm.

"It took me awhile to get used to it, but I like it too," she says, now with a grin on her face.

"I'm glad." I smile genuinely at her.

"How did I get such a great daughter?" She puts her arm around my shoulder, pulling me into her.

"I don't know. You're just lucky, I guess," I say with a shrug.

"The luckiest mom ever. Thank you, Maddy. I don't deserve your forgiveness."

I let her hug me. I can't remember the last time I felt this close to her.

We get off the bench and start walking toward the rides.

"Maddy, I have to talk to you about something else. I was going to wait until later, but after our heart-to-heart back there, I think now is the time." She doesn't face me, looking straight ahead.

The other shoe just dropped along with my stomach.

"I met someone," she says it so fast, I barely catch it. "Your brother and Lindsey know and they have already given me their blessing."

"Blessing for what?" I ask, taking a couple steps away from her.

"He asked me to marry him. I told him that I couldn't do it without my kids agreeing."

"Who is he?" I ask, closing my eyes and fearing the worst.

"Let's just say that you aren't the only one who finds the Basso men attractive," she reveals, smiling.

"*He* is the reason for this change?" I motion up and down her body.

She nods her head in confirmation, biting her lip.

"What about the house? He remodeled it?" I question.

She nods her head again.

"Why?" My questions are coming faster and she is getting flustered.

"He didn't want you to have to come home to where it happened. Memories of it."

"You told him?" I ask, angry.

She nods her head again.

"You had no right to tell him," I whisper, and I can feel the tears forming. "No wonder he has been so nice to me this week," I mumble, as my voice shakes.

"I'm sorry, Maddy. I wanted to tell him about my past and when that happened to you, it turned the direction of my life another way. He had to know my past in order to accept me." She turns to me now, trying to grab my hands but I back away.

"That's why he was over last night?" I question her again. *He didn't come over to see me, he came for my mom. He didn't care if I was with Trent. How did I read all of this so wrong?*

"Yes. We were going to tell you last night together, but you came home so late." She reaches for me again to re-capture that mother-daughter moment we just had, but I am not ready.

"Mom, just give me some time to absorb this, okay?" I look everywhere but at her.

"Take all the time you need, honey." She steps back away from me.

I walk away, unable to breathe. My heart is racing and, combined with the heat, I feel like I might pass out. I throw what's left of the blue cotton candy in the garbage, as I begin to retrace everything that's happened since I have been here. I start connecting the dots.

Gabe was there when I got off the plane and rented my car for me. He picked me up for every function, always watching me and warning me against Trent like everyone else. Oh my God, he is trying to be my father. I am such an idiot. I thought he wanted me, but he really just wanted my approval to date my mom. No, not date her...*marry* her. Although the thought of them together actually makes me physically ill, the real question that boggles my mind is whether I am upset about my mom dating Gabe or the fact that *I'm* not dating Gabe?

Chapter 13 – College - Freshman Year

I got accepted to State, along with Mackenna and Bryan. Trent had scholarship offers from State and Thrayer University, but Thrayer had a better soccer program so he reluctantly chose there. To say it was devastating to me was an understatement.

When he told me in the barn one night before graduation, I cried so hard I started to hyperventilate. As much as we knew it was the right decision for Trent and his future in soccer, we knew it wasn't going to work for us as a couple. We finally came to the decision that we would spend the summer together and then break up when it was time to leave for school. I say 'we' but it was really more what Trent wanted, though deep down I knew it would never work with us at separate schools.

The summer was amazing. After a huge fight with my mom about one of her boyfriends, I moved in with the Bassos. Since Gabe was still away at school, I stayed in his room but I was rarely in that bed. Each night, Trent and I either went to the barn or snuck into one bed or the other. Mrs. Basso made dinner for us each night and breakfast every morning. Trent and I would play cards with his parents some nights after dinner. I loved being part of a real family.

When summer ended, Trent and his parents drove me up to school to say goodbye. Mackenna and I were rooming together in a co-ed dorm, and Bryan was going to be living on the floor below us. She and Bryan had moved in the day before so they were able to help me get all of my stuff up to the sixteenth-floor dorm room. Mackenna was so excited and I knew I should be too, but all I could think about was saying good-bye to Trent.

A half-hour later, reality hit. For the second time in my life, I wouldn't live ten minutes away from Trent. I wouldn't see him every day or be able to kiss or hug him. Since we agreed on breaking up, he would no longer be mine and I assumed he would be someone else's before the month was over.

I say my goodbyes to Mr. and Mrs. Basso, thanking them for taking such good care of me. Mrs. Basso cries, telling me I am welcome anytime, and Mr. Basso tells me to study hard and concentrate on my classes. They go back to the car to wait for Trent. After brief goodbyes with Bryan and Kenna, Trent walks slowly over to me.

"So, guess this is it," I say. The tears start coming fast and I don't want to cry.

"I guess so. I'm going to miss you, Maddy." Trent leans in, giving me a hug.

"I will miss you, too. Be careful at Thrayer," I whisper.

"I'll be fine. Call me if you need anything and don't believe all those things the college boys tell you." He pulls me back, holding my shoulders.

I nod my head up and down, unable to speak.

"I love you, Maddy. Have fun...we only get to do this once you know?' He smiles, showing his dimple that always makes me melt.

"Trent, maybe we should try the long distance thing?" I blurt out, not ready for him to no longer be mine.

"Maddy, trust me this is killing me, but we made our decision and it's the right one. We have to experience this college thing without dating someone seriously," he says, pulling me in, hugging me longer and harder.

"I know," I lie. I wonder if I should transfer to Thrayer University.

He brings his hands to either side of my face and tilting my head so he can kiss me. I have kissed Trent thousands of times but he must have been saving some skills for right now.

"Man, that is some goodbye kiss," Kenna yells over from where Bryan is holding her tight.

Trent starts pulling me closer, moving his mouth to my jaw and then neck. "Always remember, Maddy. I love you," he softly speaks.

"I love you too, Trent." I give him another chaste kiss.

After one more hug, he is gone.

I am a walking zombie for the first two weeks of school. I go to my classes or the library and then come home. I never go out with Mackenna and Bryan. On Saturdays and Sundays, I stay in bed the whole day, only venturing out for some food, which I bring home to my dorm room. Trent has called me a few times but the calls only last a few minutes and he is more preoccupied with the conversations around him than with me. He seems to be enjoying himself a lot more than I am.

I am sleeping soundly since Mackenna slept over in Bryan's room. His roommate goes home every weekend, so that is usually where she can be found. I hear someone pounding on my door. I decide to ignore it; they probably have the wrong door anyway. The pounding continues and then I hear a familiar male voice telling me to open up the damn door.

I stumble out of bed, cringing when I look down at myself. A tank top and boxers, no bra or underwear. I glance at my closet thinking I should probably change, but he pounds again. I peek at myself in the mirror and the sight is horrifying. I obviously have not been taking care of myself these past two weeks.

"Chill out, I am coming!" I scream toward the door. I decide he won't care how I look so I shouldn't either. I walk over to the door, swinging it open.

"About time, Madgirl." Gabe looks me up and down. "Not sure what look are you are going for...heartbreak girl or I-don't-give-a-shit girl?" he questions, walking into my room and sitting on Mackenna's bed.

"Please, come on in Gabe," I sarcastically say, closing the door behind him and then walking back to my bed.

"So, are you going to throw this whole college thing away because of my dipshit brother?" He is blunt and to the point.

"Why are you here, Gabe?" I ask with equal frankness.

"I had a party last night and Little Ross told me how you have been moping around."

"You still live up here?" I ask surprised.

"Yeah, my brother didn't tell you?" He looks at me dumbfounded. "Of course he didn't," he says, obviously aware of something I am not. "I decided to double major in marketing and economics. I have another year until I graduate."

"Man, you're a go-getter, huh?" Even talking about double majoring sounds exhausting.

"Just making sure I have a future that doesn't involve Belcrest."

"Really?" I question.

"What? You think I want to live the rest of my life in that small town so everyone can know my business?"

"I guess I just thought you were a lifer," I admit, shrugging my shoulders.

"You thought wrong," he deadpans. "Now get your shit together and let's go."

"Go where?" I question, not moving off the bed.

"We are going out to have some fun. You do remember what fun is like, right Madgirl?" He stands up, waiting for me.

"I'm not going anywhere, Gabe." I shake my head back and forth.

"Listen, don't think I won't throw you over my shoulder. So, either you get dressed and come quietly or everyone will be able to see you in your tank top and boxers, which believe me, I am sure they won't mind," he says with a smirk, looking me up and down again.

"You're so annoying. Why do you even care what I do?" I ask, still not moving from the bed.

"You are my brother's girl. If he can't be here, then I will take care of you." He starts looking around on my dresser.

"Now you're the one not in the loop. I'm not your brother's girl anymore," I reveal, trying to keep the tears from streaming down.

"I heard something about that, but you're still Trent's girl. Just look at those eyes." He points to me.

"What?" I ask, blotting my eyes with my fingers.

"You are about two minutes away from crying over him. I'm not asking again, Maddy. I will wait for you outside your door. You have five minutes." He walks out, shutting the door behind him.

I reluctantly throw the comforter off me, getting out of bed. I guess a shower is out of the question so I shrug on my shorts and t-shirt and slip on some flip-flops. We are in the middle of an Indian summer so I want to make sure I am comfortable on whatever excursion Gabe is planning for me today. I brush my hair, putting some mascara on my lashes. I grab my ID, phone, and money and open the door.

Gabe is resting against the wall, playing with his phone while girls stare him down as they walk by. He walks me around campus, serving as my unofficial tour guide. He takes me to his favorite pizza parlor and we lick our ice cream cones from his favorite ice cream shop, laughing over funny stories he tells me about each place we pass.

By the end of the day, my cheeks hurt from smiling and laughing so much. I can't remember a day that I've had so much fun lately, and I can't believe I have Gabe to thank.

In the following weeks, Gabe and I spend a lot of time together. He takes me to the rec center to workout, to the library to study together, and even to a party. Unlike the party I attended with him the year before, I behave myself and he stays by my side the whole time. Trent hasn't contacted me since before Gabe came to my room that day and it strikes me that I haven't even noticed.

We start meeting regularly for dinners on Friday nights and occasionally meet up on Saturday at a bar or a party. He tells me how he wants to be in business for himself and not have a boss. When all of the lay-offs happened at the candy plant by us and he saw everyone around us lose their jobs, he knew then that he didn't want someone else to be responsible for his success.

The way he talks about his family, it is evident how much he loves them. Football is everything to him and it is hard being at school and not playing, but he is still close to a lot of the guys. There are so many things about him that I didn't know.

I find myself telling him things that no one knows about me except Mackenna, Bryan, and Trent. I discuss my parents' divorce, my mom's extracurricular activities, although this comes as no surprise to him. I tell him how I don't ever want to live in Belcrest again, and can't understand how Jack can go back after graduation.

The one topic that we never touch on is Trent, as though it is taboo. I am not sure why Gabe never brings him up, but for me, it is hard enough being around Gabe because he looks so much like Trent. Talking about him is still too hard.

Gabe drives the three of us home for Thanksgiving and I decide to stay at the Basso's. Since Gabe is home this time, I sleep in Doug's bedroom, who can't make it back for the holiday. I call my mom but since I have only heard from her twice while I have been away, I don't think she is very concerned where I am spending the holiday. Jack is going to his new girlfriend Lindsey's house. Trent doesn't come home either due to his soccer schedule.

The Basso's house is filled with extended family for Thanksgiving and they're pretty old school, in the fact that the men watch football all day and the women cook and clean. After dinner, I help Mrs. Basso clean the dishes as some of the guys come back in the kitchen for more food.

"What are you boys doing in here? Didn't you have enough to eat?" Mrs. Basso glares at Gabe and his cousin Reed, who are taking the bread and turkey out and making themselves sandwiches.

"We're growing boys, mom," Gabe responds, winking at me.

"Gabe, you were grown at sixteen." Mrs. Basso hits him with a dishtowel.

"There are some girls that would disagree with you there, Mom," Gabe laughs.

"Gabriel Thomas Basso, I know you didn't just say that, not only in front of your mom but Maddy too," she playfully scolds him.

"Sorry Mom, sorry Madgirl," he apologizes, not looking sorry at all.

They make their sandwiches, taking a seat at the kitchen table.

"Why aren't you in there watching football?" I motion toward the "man cave", otherwise known as the Basso's family room.

"Half time," they both say, their mouths full of food.

I grab a soda, sitting at the table with them. "It must be nice to sit around watching football and eating all day." I start rubbing my feet.

"It's awesome, you should try it one year," Reed jokes. He grins over to me, taking a bite of his sandwich. He is a freshmen in high school. He just started growing taller than the girls, but his face still has acne on it and braces fill his mouth.

"How about we trade spots next year?" I raise my eyebrows while massaging my toes and rotating my ankles.

"Not on your life, Maddy," Reed replies.

We all laugh but I stop abruptly when Gabe grabs my feet, putting them in his lap. He starts kneading my foot with his fist and I can't do anything but tip my head back, closing my eyes. It feels so good. After a few moments, I remember that we're not in a room alone. When I try to pull my feet back to me, he holds them tighter on his lap.

"Thank you, Gabe," I say smiling, but it falters when Mrs. Basso and her sister walk by, giving us curious looks. I don't know if Gabe sees the look on his mom's face, but I see the clear disapproval.

"Anytime, Madgirl." Gabe winks with his sly smile, making my heart beat a bit faster. He only calls me that nickname with other people around, but when it's just us two, it is either Mad or Maddy. I can tell we are getting closer and that the lines are getting blurry. I am not sure how I feel about it.

On Sunday morning, I pack my bags and bring them downstairs to the kitchen. Gabe wants to get back early to study for some test. I place my bag down at the end of the stairwell, walking toward the kitchen when I hear Mrs. Basso talking with Gabe.

"I don't know what is going on with the two of you but you need to stop it, Gabe," she says firmly.

"Mom, we are just friends. May I remind you that you were the one who asked me to check up on her?" Gabe responds back.

"Friends are fine, but nothing more. She is Trent's girlfriend. He would never forgive you and I wouldn't blame him." I hear her slurping her coffee.

"First of all, she isn't Trent's girlfriend. He gave her up when he decided to break her heart so he could get laid in college by God knows how many sluts. Second, if I wanted her, I wouldn't give a shit what Trent said," Gabe says.

"Just remember what I said," she says with finality.

I walk back over to my bag, putting it down loudly so they won't know I overheard them. When I walk into the kitchen, they both smile, acting like the conversation I heard never happened.

After that morning, Gabe seems to distance himself from me a little. He always seems to have study groups or exams. We no longer text or talk every day, and usually when I do hear from him, it's to say why he can't meet me. I don't know how to take it. Is he worried I am getting the wrong idea or does he not want to upset his mother by having a friendship with me?

My dad asks me to stay with him during Christmas break so I go to Michigan instead of Belcrest. Jack is going to be with Lindsey's family and my mom is going on a cruise with her new boyfriend. I will miss Mackenna and Bryan, but with Gabe and I not spending time together, I don't want to be a third wheel.

Trent is only heading home for a few days during Christmas and then going back to campus. His coach is putting on a soccer tournament and supposedly scouts will be in attendance. This is all information I gather from Bryan since I haven't talked with Trent since before Thanksgiving. Both Basso brothers seem to be giving me the cold shoulder recently.

I spend quality time with my dad during Christmas break. It is just the two of us and he is adamant about doing everything together. We have crossed the border over to Canada and drove up to the Upper Peninsula. One weekend, he booked us a room at a resort in Mackinac Island and I am looking forward to a relaxing time at their spa.

"So, you ready to talk about Trent Basso?" my dad asks while driving.

"What's to talk about? We don't really have any relationship lately," I respond coldly. I don't really want to talk about the youngest Basso.

"I know you went to separate colleges, but you guys were friends first. I thought your friendship would prevail."

"You thought wrong. Trent dumped me before college and I have barely spoken to him for five minutes since August," I say, my voice quivering.

"That's a shame. I always assumed you two would marry. Childhood sweethearts," my dad continues talking.

"Guess not," I say curtly.

"Any boys at college?" he asks.

"Not really." I can't decide if I should tell Dad or not.

"That means there is someone." He smiles over to me. My dad is easy to talk to and I know my happiness is his only concern.

"Well, there's a guy I was hanging out with a lot but that has stopped too."

"What happened?" he questions.

"I don't really know. It's complicated," I shrug.

"Did you like him?"

"I think so. I didn't know that I did until after we stopped talking and I noticed how much I missed spending time with him."

"Why don't you say something to him?"

"We can't be together, even if he felt the same way."

"Of course you can, Maddy."

"Dad, it's Gabe Basso," I admit, biting my bottom lip.

"So?" he shrugs his shoulders, looking over at me. "I'm not going to say it doesn't complicate things, Maddy, but if you and Gabe want to see if there's something between you two, you should be able to. Trent has obviously let go of you. I know you don't want any advice from your ancient dad, but can I give you a little?"

"Sure. God knows you are the only parent who cares."

He ignores this comment and continues with his fatherly advice.

"You have one life and if you are lucky, it will be a long one. Love is going to come in and out a couple of times. For some people, they are lucky they meet their love first and never look back, but for others it takes a couple more loves before the right one comes along. Unfortunately, some never find theirs or they weren't selfish enough to take their love when they should have."

"Okay," I say, confused.

"What I am trying to say is that sometimes you have to be selfish. If Trent and his mom aren't happy with you and Gabe, then you have to just say 'go to hell'."

I start laughing.

"In a nice way, of course," he adds, chuckling.

"I don't even know how Gabe feels about me. Maybe I am like a little sister to him."

"Honey, you are so beautiful, he would be crazy not to love you. Not to mention that, from what you are saying, he feels the same but is letting what others say stop him."

I think about what my dad is saying and I can't deny the feelings I have when it comes to Gabe. They are different than Trent. I am surprised how electrifying it feels to be around Gabe. It's a line I can't decide if I want to cross. My dad makes it sound so simple, but in reality, it's not.

"Don't think so hard, Maddy, go with your instincts." He pats my knee and I smile over to him.

"Thanks, Dad," I say.

"Anytime, daughter," he responds with a grin.

My break flies by and soon I am back in our dorm room, readying for the first week back at school.

"So, what did you get for Christmas?" I ask, unpacking from my trip. Mackenna always gets extravagant gifts from her parents.

"A trip to Cancun for spring break," she answers, a smile in her voice.

"That's awesome, Kenna." I am truly happy for her.

"For two," she adds.

"Don't you and Bryan go and get married in Mexico, okay? I want to be at your wedding."

"I'm not taking Bryan, I am taking you," she says, sitting on my bed.

"Are you serious, Kenna?"

She nods her head enthusiastically.

"Oh my God. Thank you, thank you, thank you." I hug her, practically pushing her down with my force.

"You're welcome. We are going to have so much fun, Maddy," she says, clapping her hands vigorously.

"Are you sure Bryan is okay with this?"

"Yeah, he is going on some guy's trip to Miami." She waves her hand in the air. "And before you ask, Trent isn't going."

"I wasn't going to ask."

"Yes you were, Maddy. You don't have to hide all this stuff from me, you know."

"What are you talking about?" I ask, looking anywhere but at her.

"I know it killed you when Trent decided to go to Thrayer. He's an ass for never calling or coming to visit."

"He has soccer; I know it's a priority," I say, making excuses for him.

"Mad, how many girls on our floor come here having relationships with their high school boyfriend and are now single? Long distance is hard but Trent is acting like you never existed. Hell, he hardly talks to Bryan either." She puts her hand on my leg.

"I just don't get it, Kenna. He was my everything and I thought I was his. I didn't really understand why he didn't want to try the long distance thing, but I thought we would at least still talk every day."

"That's why he is an asshole. It's his loss. Now let's talk about Gabe." She smiles at me.

"What about him?" I ask, playing dumb.

"You know as well as I do there is something there between you two."

"Oh Kenna, even if there was something, Gabe distanced himself after Thanksgiving and I can't say I blame him. It's way too complex to ever work." I look at my lap, shaking my head back and forth.

"Maddy, you deserve to be happy and if Gabe makes you happy, you guys should see where it takes you. I see the way he looks at you. Believe me, he wants you. Even Bryan said something on Christmas break."

"What do you mean?"

"Nothing," she says, turning around, obviously trying to hide something.

"Kenna?" I ask, pleading.

"Mad, I don't want to get into more Trent drama with you. It is time you put him aside and move on," she advises me.

"Kenna, you are my best friend. Please tell me what you know. It's not fair for me to be kept in the dark."

"Alright," she releases a sigh. "We saw the Bassos at the tree lighting downtown. Bryan went over to say hello to Trent since the dickhead never called him to say he was in town yet. Just as he got close, he noticed Gabe and Trent arguing about something and he heard your name a few times."

"What did he hear?" I ask, leaning closer to her.

"He just heard Gabe call Trent an asshole and that the way he treated you was wrong and he didn't deserve you."

"What did Trent say?"

"Trent told Gabe that you are his and Gabe needs to stay the hell away from you." She stares at me, her eyes sorrowful. "You aren't his, Maddy. He is out there sleeping with who-knows-how-many girls."

"We aren't a couple anymore, Kenna. He can do what he wants." I don't even feel the first tear fall down my cheek before the rest come flowing out.

"See? This is what I am talking about. You guys weren't just boyfriend and girlfriend. You were best friends. Now he is trying to stop Gabe from having anything to do with you and it's bullshit, Maddy." Anger pours from her body while she embraces me in a hug.

I cry in Mackenna's arms for half an hour before Bryan knocks on the door. I quickly wipe my face, hoping he won't notice my blood-shot eyes.

"Come on in." I release Mackenna.

"How was Michigan, Mad? Did you go to that pawn store? I should have given you something crazy to pawn and you could have ended up on television." His dark hair is pulled back in his hat with his high school soccer shirt and jeans. He throws himself on my bed with us, causing Kenna and I to bounce in the air.

"Sorry, my dad wouldn't let me go. Next time you come with me," I say, laughing.

"That's a date." He winks over to me.

"Stop flirting with my roommate." Mackenna playfully punches his shoulder.

"Can't help it, she's hot as hell. Hey, why don't we have a threesome?" he jokes, pulling both of us in his arms.

"You want a threesome with me and Jennings?" Mackenna asks, cocking her eyebrow up at him.

"Of course. You two would be anyone's dream come true." Bryan smiles up to her, looking as if he thinks maybe it could happen.

"Alright, you, me, and Jennings. Done," Mackenna says, straight-faced.

I stare over at her like she has three heads, but she disregards me.

"Really?" Bryan's eyes look like they are on a bobble head, so wide and big they might fall out.

"Sure. Let me see when *Jack* Jennings is available," she laughs at him.

"I'm game. We'll do it your way first but my way second," Bryan jokes, making Mackenna and I start laughing. He has a knack for making situations lighter and happier and I need his demented sense of humor right now.

Chapter 14 – Present Day

I am trapped in hell. There is no way to get home unless I call a cab and that would cost entirely too much money. My mom is sitting on the bench a few feet away from me. I can see the agony on her face. She has her phone out, texting someone; I assume it's Gabe.

This is all too much information for me to process and come to terms with in a matter of five minutes. Seeing my new-and-improved mom ready to cry, desperately texting the man she loves and probably thinking she made the wrong decision in telling me, makes me go to her.

"Sorry, Mom. I didn't mean to overreact back there. It was just hard for me to process." I sit next to her and the relief in her eyes is evident immediately.

"I understand honey. It's a lot to take in," she says, patting my knee.

"Is that him you are texting?" I ask, nodding my head toward the phone in her hand.

"Yes, we are supposed to be meeting for the lunch now." She glances at the new text that came in.

"I can't say this news isn't hard to take but I will be okay. I just need a little time to adjust. If you want my approval or blessing, you have it. I would never want to deny you happiness," I say reluctantly.

"Thank you, Maddy. You have no idea how happy that makes me." She hugs me hard.

"Let's go see your man, shall we?" I joke.

She looks at me, raising one eyebrow and obviously questioning my sincerity.

"Really Mom, it's fine," I reassure her, wrapping my arm around her shoulders.

I had to tell my mom I was okay with it; what other choice did I have? To see them together is going to be a challenge though, to say the least. It kills me that he knows what happened to me. I wonder if Gabe thinks of me differently because of it. How could he not?

My mom and I walk into the pizza place that is roped off for the Jennings wedding. I swear Jack is taking this to the extreme. More people have shown up. I see the Bassos and Edwards there, along with some other people I don't know. Gabe and Ian are sitting at a table in the back corner so I go over to join them.

"I'll be right there, honey, I want to say hello to a few people," she says, squeezing my forearm and then releasing me.

She walks right up to Mrs. Basso and they embrace each other warmly. How the hell is Mrs. Basso okay with my mom dating her son when she can't stand to be near me? My mom continues making her way through the older crowd until she stops next to a nicely dressed middle-aged man. He is wearing a Hawaiian shirt with khaki shorts. He has a blonde-gray hair with a mustache. His face beams when he sees her and she gives him a kiss on the cheek.

"Hey, scaredy cat. How was the carousel? The horse didn't go too high did it?" Ian teases me.

"That's not what gave me a scare." I look at Gabe and see anguish in his eyes.

"Excuse me," Gabe says, removing himself from the table.

"Oh she told you, huh?" Ian asks.

"She told you before me?" I ask, stunned.

"Well, when he came by last night, she didn't really have a choice," he admits sheepishly.

"I honestly can't believe it, Ian. That was the last person I would have thought it was." I put my head in my arms on the table.

"It's not that bad. Don't you think you are being a little dramatic?" He places his hand on my back.

"No. I honestly don't. What, is he supposed to be my father now?' I turn my head toward him.

"Would that really be that bad, Maddy?"

"You are kidding, right?" I sit up, hearing footsteps approach.

"I thought you could use some beer," Gabe says, bringing over a pitcher of beer.

"Try a couple of shots," I sigh, throwing my head back down on the table.

"Oh come on, Maddy, we'll be related now. You were already practically a Basso, now you really will be one," Gabe smirks over at me.

"There is something seriously demented with you," I say, glaring at him.

"I like to see the positive in situations." He pours me a beer, putting it in front of me.

I take a sip of my beer and look over to my mom, who seems to be overly chummy with that Hawaiian-shirt man. She keeps patting his arm while talking and he can't seem to keep his eyes off of her. The whole table seems to be admiring the two of them. I thought my mom had changed her ways but obviously not. I look back at Gabe, who is smiling while looking at them.

"Doesn't that bother you?" I ask him, pointing toward my mom.

"Why would it bother me?" he asks curiously. Ian looks over at me with confusion. "Hey, if they are happy, that's all that matters."

"So you're into open relationships then?" I ask skeptically.

"What? What they do is their business. It has nothing to do with me."

"Yes, it does. You shouldn't let her get away with that," I say curtly.

"With what? Madgirl, I am completely lost here."

"Listen, if you are going to date my mom, at least make sure she isn't flirting with other people. I wouldn't want her using you." I take another gulp of beer. I really need to get out of here.

"What?" Gabe and Ian start laughing hysterically. Ian is unable to control himself, bending over and slapping me on the back.

"Oh my God, Maddy. I can't believe you thought that she was with Gabe," Ian mocks me.

The whole restaurant is now looking at our table, wondering what is so funny. I feel my face getting redder by the minute. I get up from the table and walk outside. As embarrassed as I am, a sense of relief washes over me.

I barely get out the door before Gabe grabs my elbow, stopping me. "Whoa, Maddy."

"Gabe, just let me go." I pull my elbow back from him.

"Why did you think I was dating your mom?" he asks, leading me over to the park bench out front.

"I don't know. She told me she was dating someone. She made a joke about how she liked the Basso men too. My mind started going back to you and her together...you opening doors for her, having her sit up front. She said the guy was over last night. You kept joking and talking with her today, winking at her every other minute. I guess my mind went right to you when she said it," I ramble, trying to figure out how I got to that conclusion myself.

"Jesus Maddy, you drive me crazy," he says angrily, putting his head in his hands and running them through his hair.

"I'm sorry, Gabe." I play with my hands in my lap, wishing I could start this day over.

"I could give a shit about you thinking I was seeing your mom. I just don't understand why you refuse to acknowledge this." He motions his hand back and forth between us.

"What?" I whisper.

"Please, don't play dumb. I don't know how much more I can take," he says, his anger evident.

"Why are you so mad at me?" I ask defensively.

"That's it, Maddy. I'm done," he yells, standing up from the bench.

"What? Why? Gabe!" I yell after him.

He doesn't acknowledge me, continuing to walk away. I start jogging over to him, but each of his strides is equal to two of mine. I see him duck into the Eagle ride, thinking that there's no way I'll follow, but I don't intend on stopping now.

"Hey lady, no cuts," a boy says to me.

"I'm not riding, I just need to talk to that man right there." I point to Gabe, who is still ignoring me.

"Like I haven't heard that before," the kids sneers, giving me a dirty look.

I ignore him and push past toward Gabe. When I finally reach him, his arms are crossed over his chest and he looks like he is going to beat the shit of out of someone.

"Gabe, please tell me what is going on? Why are you mad at me?" I plead, touching his arm.

"If you don't know, Maddy, it's not worth it. I can't do it anymore." He pulls his arm away from me.

"Do what anymore? Worth what? Gabe, I thought we were friends." I can hear my own desperation in my voice.

"That's exactly the problem," he confesses.

"That we are friends? If you don't want to be my friend, just say so," I whisper, trying to not make more of a scene.

"My God, Maddy, what do I have to do to make you see it?" he asks, throwing his arms in the air.

"Again Gabe, see what?" I scream. With all of the yelling, I suddenly realize that we are at the front of the line so I try to step to the side.

"Ma'am, you need to get behind him if you are riding," the teenage attendant says to me. I look at the kid in disbelief and Gabe starts chuckling quietly.

"Yeah ma'am, are you going to ride with me or not?" Gabe asks me, smirking.

"You know I don't ride roller coasters."

"I've seen you ride them before," he says pointedly. The next coaster rolls to a stop. Gabe gets in, sitting down in his assigned seat. I look at him while the attendant keeps shouting to me to either get in or move out of the way. The blonde behind me looks like she wants to run me over for her chance to sit next to Gabe. The sun is making Gabe's blue eyes sparkle more when he looks at me. For some reason, his face gives me a safe, calming feeling so I hop in the seat next to him, fastening my belt. The metal bar comes down and my throat free falls into my stomach.

Gabe is staring over at me instead of looking at the hill ahead.

"You got me on this ride, so you better answer the question." My heart is beating out of my chest as we reach the middle of the first hill and I am trying to only concentrate on him.

The top of the hill is fast approaching, making my anxiety higher. My heart is beating out of my chest. Gabe grabs my hand, telling me it will be okay. Just as our cart is about to go over the hill, I squeeze his hand and close my eyes.

We begin our rapid descent at the same time Gabe's lips meet mine. His hand rests on my cheek, while his mouth covers mine. His tongue licks my bottom lip, begging for entrance and I instinctively open my mouth. Our tongues mingle together while butterflies fill my stomach. When Gabe pulls away, I stare into his eyes, not noticing that we aren't moving anymore. Then I hear the hollering and clapping around us. I don't remember the ride, only Gabe's mouth and hands. Looking around at the crowd, my face turns a nice shade of pink.

"Come on, let's get out of here." Gabe grabs my hand, leading me away from the ride.

We walk hand-in-hand down the exit ramp. He pulls me over to the train station that is already boarding. We grab an empty row in the back.

He instantly kisses my lips, but this time it is short. "We need to talk," he says.

He grabs both my hands in his, putting them in his lap. "This is so much harder than I thought it would be…let me ask you something?"

"Okay, ask away."

"Do you feel this?" he asks, again motioning between the two of us.

"Gabe, I felt that kiss everywhere, if that's what you are asking."

"Yes...no." He pulls his hands away, brushing them through his hair. "What I am trying to say is...I love you. I know it's complicated as hell for us and I know that not everyone is going to understand it, but I have loved you for so many years. I thought I could get over you when I moved to Florida, but every girl I tried to date never compared to you. There were so many times I wanted to tell you, but one thing after the next has always held me back. I am sick of waiting for the time to be right. I want you to be mine," he divulges, not looking up at me.

"Oh Gabe!" I don't know what to say. I know I love him too, but I can't stop thinking about Trent or his family's opposition to us being together.

"Shit!" he yells and the family a couple rows up turn their heads toward us.

"Sorry," I apologize to them.

"I thought for sure you felt the same way," he whispers, staring at his feet.

"Gabe, look at me." I place my hand on his knee.

He slowly turns his face up to mine, his eyes filled with regret and despair.

"Who said I don't?" I smile over at him. "Gabe, just because I feel the same doesn't mean I think it's a good idea to be together." His smile falters and he shakes his head.

"Maddy, it doesn't matter what anyone thinks. If we love each other, we should be together."

"Your mom hates me, Trent is your brother, and we live in different parts of the country. Nothing about this is right."

"All that matters is this," he says, kissing me again but this time with more urgency. Our lips and tongue can't seem to get enough. His arms are warm around me, fingers gingerly running through my hair. My hands rest on his firm chest. That feeling is there again, as though everything is right in the world when I am with him.

When he pushes back from me, he rests his forehead on mine. "I guess I can't argue with that," I admit.

"I promise you, Maddy, I will protect us. We are worth fighting all this crap for."

"Okay, but can I ask one thing?"

"Anything." His hands rest on my hips, rubbing up and down.

"Can I have more kisses?" I ask, laughing.

"I think I can do better than that." His lips crash down on mine again, cutting off my laughter in the best possible way.

As we depart the train and head back toward the group, the doubts begin to resurface. How are we going to be together? Which one of us will tell Trent? Will I lose him as my friend? What about his mom? The questions just keep running through my mind and I can't escape them. I don't think I can make everyone else upset just to make myself happy. The one thing I know for sure is that there is no way I can face this right now; my brother's wedding has to come first.

"Gabe, hold on a second." I stop him right before we near our family and friends.

"What's up, Mad?" He pins me against the brick wall of a building.

"I don't think we should tell anyone...yet." I see the disappointment on his face so I look down.

"It doesn't matter what they think," he says, kissing my neck.

"I can't ruin my brother's wedding. We don't know how your mom or Trent will take this." I shake my head back and forth.

"Promise me this has nothing to do with Trent?" he questions, pulling away a little bit.

"No, it's not that. After the wedding, we can announce it on the ten o'clock news." I grab his shirt, pulling him back to me. "Please say you understand."

"Alright, but after that reception I am telling everyone that you are mine and I don't care what anyone says." He kisses me so thoroughly my knees almost give out.

"Deal," I say.

After we rejoin everyone, Gabe moves to speak with someone, and my mom approaches me with the mystery man in tow. Although I am happy it isn't Gabe she is bringing over to meet me, I am still nervous.

In the years after my parents' divorce, my mom never really dated anyone, she usually entertained the men at night after I went to bed or wasn't home. By the time I got up in the morning, she would sneak them out the back door like a teenager. I know this is a huge step for my mother and I don't want to make it awkward for her.

"Maddy, where did you and Gabe go? You have been missing the whole afternoon." Looking at the secretive smile on her face, I am suddenly struck that she wants me with Gabe and is ecstatic that we went off by ourselves.

"She rode the Eagle, Barb. You should have seen her." Gabe comes up behind me, laughing. He doesn't place his hand on my back or lace his fingers with mine, but I can feel the heat radiating between us.

"Someone kind of tricked me into it," I smirk, looking at Gabe who winks at me.

"Come on, you barely knew you were riding it," he says, licking his lips and I've never wanted to kiss someone so badly.

My mom looks a bit confused but turns toward the mystery man. "I want to introduce you to someone. Maddy, this is Mitch. Mitch, this is my daughter, Madeline," she says, gesturing back and forth between the two of us.

"Hi Madeline, Mitch Basso." He shakes my hand. His handshake is firm and soft at the same time. I can see the hesitation in his eyes. He is worried I won't like him. Little does he know, it never matters to my mom if I like the men in her life so he has nothing to worry about.

"Hi, Mr. Basso," I say.

"Please, call me Mitch."

"Well then, it's Maddy."

"It's a pleasure to meet you."

"How is it that I have never met you? I mean, I have known the Bassos my whole life and usually attend every holiday…until recently."

"Uncle Mitch lived in Arizona. Never came home much," Gabe chimes in.

"Until last year, that is," Mitch says, smiling down at my mom.

"Am I to assume you are Mr. Basso's brother?" I ask.

"You assume right, younger by two years," he confirms.

"Even though he looks older than me by ten." Mr. Basso comes to Mitch's side, slapping his back in amusement. "Where have you two been all day?" He stares at Gabe and me, but his face is calm and relaxed.

"Just riding some rides," Gabe responds.

"I thought Maddy didn't ride roller coasters. At least, that's what I remember," Mrs. Basso comments, standing alongside her husband.

"Oh Wendy, she rode the Eagle today with Gabe," my mom cheers, not noticing the glare coming from Mrs. Basso.

"How nice that must have been for the two of you. Too bad Trent couldn't be here to join you," she says, the coolness in her voice evident.

"As you know Mom, Trent has stuff to do with the team today," Gabe answers, giving his mom a pointed look.

Fortunately, everyone starts to leave at this point so we all say our goodbyes quickly. We barely reach the Blue Monster before Gabe's lips are once again on mine, forceful and demanding. He opens the back door, leading me in the backseat without his lips leaving mine.

He grabs my hips, pulling me into him and I feel how badly he wants this. His hands grab my ass, pushing me up so my legs straddle around his waist. Ours hands are frantic. He pushes up my shirt, cupping my breasts while I strip him of his. He pulls down my laced bra, freeing my breast and sucking it until my nipple hardens against his tongue. I arch my back, pushing myself against his mouth and moaning in pleasure.

"You are so beautiful, Maddy," he whispers.

My hands reach for his shorts, unbuttoning them, but before I can grab the zipper, Gabe's hand is on top of mine.

"As much as I want this, Maddy, I don't want to take you in the car like we're teenagers." He grabs my hand, bringing it up to his mouth and kisses my palm. "And if I let your hands go where they are going, I won't be able to stop us."

I put my head on his shoulder, knowing he is right.

"It will be worth the wait," he promises, smirking at me.

"I know it will be," I say with a smile.

"Go to dinner with me?" he asks, playing with my fingers.

"I wish I could," I answer, knowing he is not going to like this.

"You can, just say yes."

"I already have plans with Trent," I say, looking down and peeking up through my eyelashes.

"Oh," he says, deflated.

"It's not what you think, Gabe. He asked me yesterday and said he has something to tell me."

"I am sure he does." He rolls his eyes, looking away from me.

"Gabe, it's dinner. Nothing more." I place my hand on his chin, bringing his face back toward me. "I will call you as soon as I get home," I say, kissing him on the lips.

"It better be early," he murmurs against mine before kissing me back.

At that moment, his phone begins to ring. Reaching into his pocket, he thumbs the screen and then puts the phone back in his pocket.

"You can get it," I tell him.

"No, just a work thing." His good mood suddenly dissipates. "We should get going anyway." He nudges me off his lap and starts the car.

He is quiet on the way back to my house and I know it has something to do with the phone call. Gabe has always been so straightforward and honest with me; it feels weird that he is holding something back. I don't want to push too much, but when he pulls in my mom's driveway, I can't keep from asking any longer.

"Is everything okay, Gabe?" I unbuckle my seatbelt, turning toward him.

"Yeah, I just have some unsettled business back in Florida," he answers vaguely.

"Okay..." I say, seeing that is all I'm going to get out of him right now. "So I will text you tonight after I get back?"

"Please," he says softly, not looking up from the steering wheel.

"Okay, Gabe. Talk to you tonight," I say before shutting the door.

I watch Gabe drive away and, despite the fact that it seems as if he's hiding something from me, I'm surprised by how badly I want to be with him in that truck.

Chapter 15 – Spring Break Freshman Year

Cancun's white beaches and clear blue water are just what I need to escape from my hopeless life. As I lay by the pool sipping my orange juice, I can't help but wonder where my life is going. Don't get me wrong, school is going fine...great even. But my personal life is forever in shambles. Since Christmas break, I have only spoken to Gabe twice and only because I ran into him on campus. He never calls or stops by anymore.

It infuriates me that he is listening to his brother and mother, who are both telling him to stay away from me. I miss Gabe's laugh and his smile. I miss the way he grabbed my hand to lead me through a crowded bar or party. I miss the way he walked me to class, even if he was going to be late for his own. I missed the way he knew my favorite food at every restaurant we went to and the way I took my coffee. I miss him calling me 'Madgirl' since no one else calls me that. I just miss Gabe.

Trent is another story. Since Christmas, he has been calling and texting me consistently. I have been ignoring his apology-filled messages. He wrote me off last semester, and I am planning on writing him off for the rest of my life. Mackenna told me that he called Bryan, apologizing to him and of course, Bryan accepted it. They had rekindled their friendship and one weekend, Bryan took the train down to Thrayer to visit him. Mackenna refused to go with him on the grounds that she wanted to support her best friend and I love her for it. I am thankful every day to have her by my side.

I decide to even out my tan, turning over from my back to my front, while picking up my trashy romance novel. I swore I would not be doing any academic reading this trip. Actually, no reading that requires my brain to think at all. So when I saw the shirtless man wrapped around a half-dressed woman on the cover, I grabbed it from the shelf at the airport store. Mackenna laughed, making fun of me, but then picked up the one next to it where the man and woman were even more naked.

The sun heating my skin feels good and I am thankful again for my olive skin tone that I inherited from my dad. Two days in the sun and my skin has turned from clammy yellow to golden brown. Hearing whistling and hollering, I don't have to look up to see who is coming my way.

"What, is it like eighty-five degrees already? I feel bad for those suckers back home where it's probably snowing." Mackenna throws her towel and bag on the lounge chair next to me, oblivious to the few gawking boys up at this hour.

"I see you finally woke up." I put my orange juice back down on the table between us.

"I don't know why you insist on waking up so early. We are on vacation, Maddy." She takes off her cover-up, situating her swimsuit.

"Holy hell, Kenna, what are you wearing?" I question, my eyes bulging out of my head. A quick look around tells me that I'm not the only one to notice her practically non-existent bikini.

"It's new. I know it's a little much but hey, who knows how long I will have this body."

"A little more fabric wouldn't have killed you," I say, rolling my eyes. If I am being honest, I am jealous of her. Not necessarily of her body, even though it is amazing, but of her self-confidence. She doesn't care what anyone thinks of her, and I wish that I had an ounce of the self-assurance that Mackenna has.

"Oh, Maddy. That's a cute suit too," she compliments me. She brings her sunglasses down a bit, scoping me out.

"Thank you. I know it isn't the playboy edition but I like it," I tease, and then we both start laughing.

The one thing about our friendship is that we rarely fight. I can probably count on one hand any fight we've had that lasted longer than an hour. And the ones that we do have are always about Trent.

By mid-afternoon, more college kids are drifting out of their rooms, exploring the pool and beach. Mackenna wants to take a walk so I grab my sunglasses and wrap my sheer cover-up around my waist as we make our way down the beach. Of course, Mackenna doesn't cover up and she looks like she is filming a movie, with her big sunglasses and her dark hair flowing in the breeze. It is intimidating to even walk next to her.

The beach is filled with guys throwing Frisbees, playing beach volleyball, and some are just checking out the girls. With Mackenna by my side, we aren't alone for more than five minutes without guys coming up, asking us to sit down and relax with them. Mackenna ignores them and since I have enough boy problems with the Basso brothers, I am not interested in them either. Some are more persistent than others, but all eventually fall back to other girls around that seem more interested.

It isn't until I notice money blowing by me on the sand that I stop in my tracks. I bend down to pick up the assortment of dollar bills in front of me, wondering where they are coming from. Looking around, I see a guy in a pair of green board shorts a couple steps away, frantically picking up the money, and I contemplate if it is his or he is just reaping the rewards of someone else's misfortune.

Standing there holding the money in my hand, Mackenna sighs impatiently at me as the guy approaches us with his hand out.

"Thank you for picking those up for me," he says, holding his hand toward mine.

"How do I know these are yours?" I hold the bills out of his reach before he can take them out of my hand.

"Excuse me?" he asks in disbelief.

"The money could be someone else's," I respond matter-of-factly.

"Who the hell cares, Maddy, just give him the money," Mackenna says, rolling her eyes.

The tall dark-haired guy looks Mackenna up and down with obvious admiration, but quickly turns back to me since I am the keeper of his money.

"Prove it," I say, ignoring Kenna and focusing on the amber eyes in front of me.

"How exactly do you think I could prove it?" He puts his hands through his brown hair, moving his bangs out of his eyes.

"Um…" I hesitate a second too long and Mackenna grabs the money out of my hand, giving it to jock boy in front of me.

"Here you go." She hooks her arm in mine, steering me forward. "Problem solved."

"Kenna!" I exclaim, trying to stop her from leading me away.

"No, Maddy. I am sure it is his money and if it's not, that's between him and the person who lost it. Let's go."

I glance at jock boy over my shoulder and see him staring at us as we walk away. Most likely he is checking out Mackenna in her playboy centerfold bikini, but he winks when he catches me looking at him and I quickly turn back around.

That night, after an exhausting afternoon of shopping with Mackenna, we are getting ready to go out to a club that we've heard people talking about. I am a little wary after hearing the rumors about Cancun and how dangerous it can be, and since we don't have Bryan or any of the other guys with us, I think this is a terrible idea. As usual, Mackenna won't take no for an answer. She even buys me a new dress to wear, which I think is an even worse idea. The purple dress is entirely too short and shows off way too much of my skin.

"You look smokin', Maddy," Kenna says when I come out of the bathroom wearing her purchase.

"Mackenna," I breathe. If I think my dress is too revealing, then Mackenna's is practically lingerie. It is a stunning red that stops well above her knees and comes off one shoulder, leaving it bare. I pull my dress down a little, feeling self-conscious about my outfit. It is hard to walk around with such a stunning best friend.

"Stop it, Mad," she hisses, grabbing her clutch.

"Stop what?"

"Stop trying to cover yourself up. You look hot. The guys will be drooling," she says, hooking her arm through mine.

"I have had my fill of boys this year; I am good until next year," I confess.

"Oh, some innocent flirting won't hurt you."

We get a cab right away and once we get to the club, one kiss on the cheek of the bouncer and a swing of her hips from Mackenna and we are inside, leaving a line of guys and girls waiting behind us.

The club called "The City" is massive. It has three floors and there are bars in every corner. Girls dressed in little more than Mackenna pass by, selling shots in a variety of colors. Guys and girls are grinding to the disco music, and even though we are in Mexico, almost everyone here is in their early twenties and American.

"Let's go get a drink." Mackenna pulls me over to the bar with a line that is at least four rows deep.

"This is going to take forever. Let's grab a shot from one of those girls and dance," I say, pointing to one of the neon shot trays.

"Awesome idea." She tugs on my arm and I follow her.

We buy two shots a piece, clicking the alcohol-filled test tubes together and toasting our friendship. Under normal circumstances, I am not into dancing in public but the music is so loud and there are so many people on the dance floor, it is the people who aren't dancing that look out of place. For some reason, I push all of my inhibitions to the side tonight. I don't want to think about school, my mom, or the Basso brothers. I don't want to care what I look like or what people are thinking. I just want to feel the music and dance, to be carefree and have fun with my best friend.

I am doing a great job of doing just that, until some guys come up grinding behind us. I never understood why guys think that they can do that to girls. As if us shaking our bodies to the music is an invitation for them to rub their junk across our asses. Isn't that some sort of sexual harassment?

Mackenna quickly shakes her finger back and forth, telling the guy behind her no, and surprising me with how polite she is being. My cling-on grabs my hips, pulling me in closer. Anger starts coursing through my veins and my hands ball into fists beside me. I turn around, putting my hands on his chest, shoving him away from me.

"Get off me," I scream though I doubt he can hear over the loud music.

"What the fuck, bitch?" He comes toward me again.

"Did I ask you to grind your dick against my ass?" I ask him, not backing down.

"If you don't want it, you shouldn't shake it like that," he says, his words obviously slurring.

"Whatever, just go away." I put my hand in his face.

"Bitch," he murmurs before finally walking away from me.

"Way to go, Maddy!" Mackenna comes over, putting her arm around my neck. She is clearly surprised and happy that I stuck up for myself. It is an unusual occurrence. "Let's celebrate with a couple more shots."

I am downing my fourth shot when I hear a deep, somewhat familiar voice beside me. "Maddy, right?"

"Hey, are you trying to pick-pocket people here? I can imagine you would clean up pretty well," I say, smiling at jock boy from the beach this afternoon.

"Yeah, I have my whole team here tonight," he laughs, displaying a dimple in his left cheek. It's adorable.

"I better keep my money close to my chest then." I pat where my money is hidden between my boobs in my bra. I don't know if it's the shots causing me to flirt so blatantly or if it's being in a different country and not knowing anyone. I haven't been myself tonight, but I am loving who I am.

"Careful, that's the first place a thief might look." He stares down at my chest, raising his eyebrows in humor.

"Well, I keep it well guarded," I say with a smirk.

"Let me buy you a drink. I was fortunate to find some money on the beach today." He motions over to a small bar a couple feet away that only sells beer and pre-mixed bottle drinks.

"In that case, you have to buy my friend one too." I point over to Mackenna, who is still chatting the shot girl up about who knows what.

"Of course," he says.

"Mackenna!" I scream over the music, waving her over to me.

"Hey, if it isn't the crook," she laughs.

"He is going to buy us some drinks with his newfound fortune," I tell her and she nods her head in agreement.

"Miles Clybourn." He holds his hand out to me.

"Madeline Jennings and this is Mackenna Ross." He shakes both our hands.

"What do you prefer? Beer or wicked lemonade?" he asks, whispering it in my ear so that I can hear him above all the noise.

"Beer for me and wicked lemonade for her," I whisper back, getting close enough to his ear that when he turns his head, our lips almost touch.

Before I have time to figure out whether or not I want them to touch, Miles has already paid for our drinks. He asks us if we want to join him at his friends' table in the back where it is a little quieter and we agree to follow him.

It ends up being a small roped-off VIP area that Miles takes us to, and I assume that he and his friends paid extra for this. There are three other guys sitting around the table with some girls sitting between them. Miles leads us to a nearby table away from them, and I notice that the girls angrily watch our every step.

"So are you staying at the Hotel Americano?" Miles asks me. Mackenna is staring toward the dance floor and I know she wants to be out there. I figure I can humor Miles a little longer and then we can leave.

"Yes. You?" I ask. It is a little quieter over here, but we still have to lean in close together to hear.

"Yeah. Got in two nights ago. Where do you go to school?" he asks.

"Wisconsin. You?" The questions are the standard for when two college students meet and it is starting to bore me.

"You have to be shittin' me! Me too," he says.

"What year are you?" I am surprisingly shocked as well.

"Grad student, second year," he remarks.

I knew he looked older but not that much older. I am embarrassed to tell him that I am a freshman, so I don't volunteer this information and am surprised he never asks me.

"It's a small world, huh?" he remarks.

"Yeah," I agree. When I look over at his friends' table, one of the guys looks toward me and I can't believe my eyes.

"Little Jennings!" he screams, and Miles looks from him to me, wondering what he missed.

"Grady Smith," I say back. I am astonished that he remembers me as Jack's sister, but since it has been that way my whole life, I don't think much of it.

"How the hell are you? I haven't seen you in forever." He comes around to the back of my chair, hugging me from behind and picking me up until I am standing. "And Ross, looking hot as always," he says, winking down at Kenna.

"Grady," she says, straight-faced.

I saw Grady a couple of times during my first semester when I would hang out with Gabe but not since then.

"Where's your husband?" he asks Kenna.

"Miami," she says.

"You break up?"

"No."

"Dammit," he says. "I was hoping we could get some vacation sex going on," he laughs, but Mackenna doesn't join in. "How do you guys know Miles?"

"Just met him earlier on the beach," I respond.

"You aren't...?" He looks back at Miles, who nods his head in confirmation.

"We aren't what?" I ask, instantly curious.

"You aren't the hot girls that Miles told us all about this afternoon?"

I blush in embarrassment.

"Sorry man, they are off limits." Grady puts his hand on Miles' shoulder, shaking his head.

"Why is that?" Miles asks.

"This little hottie in red has a serious boyfriend, like practically reserve-the-church serious. And this cutie..." he starts, putting his arm around me. "Well, one, she's Jack Jennings' little sister." Miles frowns but doesn't look intimidated. "And two," Grady says, holding up two fingers.

"Madgirl?" My heart jumps in my chest just at the sound of his voice. My mouth goes dry and I can't speak.

"That guy," Grady finishes.

I abruptly look up at Grady, who is staring at Gabe and cracking up. I turn my head toward Miles, who looks disappointed and is now glaring at Gabe. Finally, I look over at Gabe, who has some red-head kissing his neck, her arms wrapped around his waist. I instantly want to throw up.

I grab Mackenna's hand to pull her out of the VIP area.

"Thanks for the drinks, Miles," I say, trying to get away quickly.

"Mad, wait!" Gabe yells.

"What the hell is wrong with you Basso brothers?" Mackenna stands in front of Gabe with her hands on her hips. The red-head finally notices something is going on and stares down Mackenna. Gabe says nothing to Kenna, looking straight at me with pleading eyes.

"Go get yourself another guy, this one's mine," the girl slurs to Kenna, wrapping her arms tighter around his waist. I am not oblivious to the fact that he hasn't pushed her away.

"Oh trust me, you can have him," I yell, grabbing Kenna by her arm and pulling her toward the dance floor.

"You're an asshole, Gabe, just like your brother. Stay the hell away from Maddy, you hear me?" Mackenna is screaming at Gabe as he silently watches us leave.

"Thank you for defending my honor, Kenna, but let's just leave," I say to her once we are absorbed into the crowd and out of Gabe's view.

"I thought he was one of the good ones." She shakes her head back and forth.

"He is, Kenna."

She looks at me in disbelief but follows me outside to catch a cab. Once we get in, I tell the driver to get us to our hotel using the little Spanish I know. A minute later, Kenna's phone rings, startling me.

"Hey baby," she answers, winking to me.

While listening to her tell Bryan how much she loves and misses him, I lean back into the uncomfortable vinyl seat. I can't believe Gabe didn't follow me, but at the same time, I am happy he didn't. I don't know what I would have said to him anyway. How come, just as I am starting to move on with my life, a Basso brother has to come and screw with my emotions?

We get back to the hotel and I can tell that it will be another night of Mackenna and Bryan talking until they fall asleep. I wave Kenna off when she hops on the elevator with the phone still attached to her ear, giving me a look that clearly said she is sorry. She smiles while the doors slide shut and I let out a breath, relieved I am by myself.

I walk out to the pool area. It's been closed for a few hours now but the lights are still illuminated under the water, making it look more appealing now than during the day. Couples linger around the lounge chairs, kissing and whispering with one another. I make my way to the beach where the half-full moon is mirroring down on the low waves lapping against the shore. Unbidden tears fall from my eyes and I decide it's probably best to bring this day to a close.

I turn around after one last sigh at the beautiful view. My eyes widen when I see Gabe sitting in a lounge chair directly in front of where I am standing. I frantically try to wipe away the tears with the backs of my hands, hoping he doesn't notice them.

"I am so sorry, Maddy," Gabe says, as he quickly closes the distance between us. He instantly reaches out, brushing the remaining tears away with his thumbs.

I swallow hard, unable to say anything.

"I never meant to hurt you," he continues.

"Then why did you?" I ask in a whisper.

"Come walk with me?" he pleads.

I nod hesitantly and we take off our shoes, tucking them under the stairs. Gabe rolls his pant legs up so they won't get wet and then he winds his fingers through mine, guiding me toward the water. It amazes me how his presence makes me feel both safe and unsafe at the same time. I know he won't let anyone physically harm me, but the emotional trauma he can inflict will be beyond repairable.

He smiles over to me, looking relieved and scared. "I know I have been an asshole, Maddy, and I can't expect you to forgive me, but I want you to hear me out."

"Alright," I reluctantly consent. My stomach feels like I could throw up at any minute.

"When I came to your dorm room that afternoon to get you out of bed, I was just there as a friend. I knew my brother would want you to enjoy your college life even though he was being a selfish prick. When Little Ross told me about how you were sitting around in your room all the time, I knew I had to do something." He stops, taking a deep breath before continuing.

"Then, after that first week of hanging out with you, something shifted inside of me. I couldn't explain it at first, but I wanted to be around you all the time. I even hung around outside your buildings, hoping to run into you after class. Don't get me wrong; I was always attracted to you. But this was something different, something I never felt before." He stops again. I honestly don't know if I want him to continue.

"As the weeks went on, if I wasn't in class or studying, I was with you. I wanted to introduce you to all of the places that I love around campus, and I enjoyed learning all the things I never knew about you. That's why, when it became natural for us to start touching, I couldn't keep my hands off of you, even if it was just holding your hand or hugging you. It felt so good that, deep down, I knew I wanted more than friendship, but I never wanted to push you." He looks over at me, trying to gauge my thoughts.

"When we went home for Thanksgiving, my mom told me that she saw the way our relationship was changing and I needed to stop it. I knew what I was doing when I grabbed your feet to massage them. I wanted to see how my family would react; if they were willing to let you be mine and not Trent's." His eyes look angry just thinking about it. I already know his mom's reaction from overhearing their conversation, but I decide to keep that to myself.

"I knew I was crossing a line I shouldn't. So I tried to distance myself from you. I didn't mean to hurt you. I figured it was for the best. Then you went to your dad's for Christmas and Trent came home."

"I heard what Trent did," I say and he looks at me, surprised. "Bryan overheard, told Kenna, and she told me."

"Yeah, well..." he runs his hand through his hair. "He told me to stay away from you and I told him he better stop being a jackass and keep his dick in his pants." His eyes now fill with sadness. "I told him if he wanted you, he needed to put you as the number one priority in his life." He stops, but I know that isn't it.

"And?" I ask.

"I told him that I would stay away from you if he did, figuring you'd be better off without the both of us." Gabe stops walking, pulling me to him, and I fumble into his arms. "It's been so hard, Maddy."

"You didn't seem to be upset earlier," I say softly, hurt by what I saw at the club.

"Mad, I met her tonight. I was trying to move on. Grady and the guys brought me down here to get my mind off of you. I don't want her or anyone else, Maddy, but I don't know what to do anymore." He sits down in the sand and puts his head in between his knees.

"I don't know either." I sit down next to him, extending my legs out.

"Can I ask you a question?" He peeks his head over to me and those blue eyes are filled with agony. I nod my head. "How did you feel about us last semester?"

"Um...," I hesitate. How do I tell him that, as confused as I am about him and Trent, he weaseled his way into my heart at some point during those few months?

"Please, Maddy, I have to know." He grabs my hand again, turning toward me.

"Pretty much the same as you. I don't think I truly realized it until after you stopped calling and coming over. It completely destroyed me."

"Really?" he asks, surprised.

"Yeah, really." I bite my lip, looking up at him.

"Doesn't that just make it ten times more complicated? I thought for sure I was alone in this," he says, motioning between the two of us.

"Nope."

"You just made me the happiest and most pissed off guy at the same time."

"Why?"

"I want you, you want me, but I made this promise to my brother." He shakes his head back and forth.

"Don't I have a say in any of this?" I ask, slightly annoyed.

"Trent loves you, Maddy, and I am pretty sure you love him too. I should have never interfered between you guys."

"You didn't interfere. Trent is the one who wanted to break up. Trent is the one who wanted to live out his college days without a girlfriend. So he should be able to fuck a different girl every night of the week and I should wait around until he is ready to commit? I refuse to live my life like that."

"It doesn't change the fact that I am his brother. He should have been able to trust me with his girlfriend."

"OH MY GOD!!!" I scream. "I wasn't then and I will never again be Trent Basso's girlfriend!"

I move to stand up but Gabe grabs my face with both his hands and kisses me. Before I can even think straight, I am lying down on the sand with him half on top of me. He thrusts his tongue in my mouth, and although mine is slow to join in, they finally touch and a surge shoots through my body and I can't get enough. I grab the back of his neck, holding onto him and not wanting to ever let go.

"You have no idea how long I have wanted to kiss you," he murmurs quietly against my lips before claiming my mouth once again.

Gabe and I lie on the beach for two more hours of non-stop kissing, hugging, and touching each other. We don't talk about Trent anymore or why we shouldn't be together. We don't discuss the promise he made. We simply relish our time together, far away from anyone who would judge us.

When we stand up to go back to the hotel, Gabe holds me close to him with his arm around my waist. He walks me to my room and kisses me goodnight. No mention of seeing me tomorrow or what the future might or might not hold for us. I don't know where we stand so I kiss him fully before saying good-bye, just in case that will be the last one.

I am thankful that Mackenna is asleep when I enter the dark room. I drift asleep, thinking only of Gabe's amazing lips.

Chapter 16 – Present Day

"Back to Chicago?" I question Trent, who is leaning back in his black Mercedes.

He nods his head. "How was Great Adventures?"

"Fine," I say hesitantly, hoping he doesn't notice my face turning red. I know I have to tell him, but I can't do it yet.

"So I take it you found out the news?" He looks over at me out of the corner of his eye. If anyone knows how I would take my mom dating someone seriously, it would be him.

"Yeah. So I guess we'll be related now."

"Not in the sense I had always hoped," he jokes. "Kidding aside, my uncle is a good guy. Your mom seems…different since the incident."

"I was really surprised when I got home by all of the improvements. I just hope she's changed for good, you know?"

"I know, Maddy," he says, squeezing my knee in agreement. This is why Trent still knows me better than anyone. He has seen my mom at her worst and knows how it affects me.

"Did your uncle really remodel my mom's house?"

"He had some help, but yeah, he did. I know your mom told him about that night. My uncle asked me about it. Does that upset you?" he asks. I can hear the tension in his voice, since he is well aware that this is a touchy subject for me.

"At first I was upset, but if her being truthful with him keeps her on the right track, then I'm okay with it." I don't mention that I was torn apart when I thought Gabe knew.

"Don't worry, I know my uncle would never tell anyone," he assures me.

"Thanks. I hope not," I say.

We pull up to his condo building a little while later, parking in his reserved spot. Trent opens the door and I see that some of his furniture has been delivered already. It's amazing what money can do. Trent thought I didn't see him slip the salesman extra cash to get the priority service he prefers.

"The couch looks nice," I say, sitting down.

"Yeah, it was delivered this afternoon. Thanks, Mad, I love it." Trent sits next to me, holding a fist full of menus.

"No restaurant?" I ask.

"I thought we could order in. Maybe watch a movie or something. Is that okay?" he questions.

"Of course," I respond, astonished that Trent is choosing to stay in. When we lived together, I think we stayed in a total of two times. He always wanted to eat at every new restaurant, see every show, and dance at every nightclub. Trent Basso staying home on any night of the week was unheard of.

"Here you go. You pick." He hands me the stack of menus and then gets up, walking to the kitchen.

"Do you mind if we get pizza? I haven't had Chicago pizza since the last time I was home. I love New York pizza, but it just doesn't compare to the deep dish here," I request.

"Spinach and onion?" Trent asks, double checking that it's still my favorite.

"Yep, and get half sausage for you," I reply.

"Sounds good."

I hear Trent order the pizza and a salad and then he calls his doorman, letting him know to expect the order. I turn the television on, making myself at home on the couch. I am so comfortable, it almost feels like we haven't been apart. I can see this being our condo and living here with Trent.

"Do you want some wine?" he asks, already getting a glass out and a chilled bottle of Chardonnay from the fridge.

"Sure," I answer.

He comes over, handing me my wine, and I see that look of desire in his eyes that I've seen a million times before. "You're so beautiful, Maddy," he says softly.

"Trent," I sigh.

"Maddy, you've always been the most gorgeous woman I've known," he replies, turning toward the television. He takes a swig of his beer, propping his bare feet on the table.

"Thank you, Trent. You aren't so bad yourself," I compliment him, sipping my wine.

"I'm sorry," he whispers, taking a pull on the bottle again.

"I know, I am too," I say honestly. Lack of love has never been the issue between Trent and me.

We both smile at one another. How do I tell this man that I have loved since I was six years old that his brother snuck in and took his spot in my heart?

Fortunately, we are interrupted by the sound of the buzzer. After paying the delivery guy, Trent places the pizza on the coffee table, along with another beer and the bottle of wine. I have to be careful that we don't drink too much; I cannot spend the night here.

"Oh my God, this is heaven," I moan with a mouthful of cheese and spinach.

Trent laughs, picking a piece of cheese off my chin. "You've always loved your pizza."

"Favorite food," I exclaim, smiling back at him.

"I know. Sometimes I think I know more about you than I do myself," Trent divulges.

"Same here. God, I don't think there is one thing you could stump me on about you."

"Oh, you think so? Are you sure about that?" He smiles over to me. "Okay, let's start easy. Favorite food?" he asks.

"Easy…wings." I answer confidently.

"Alright, favorite drink?"

I glance down at the Amstel Light in his hand and he laughs. "But it's actually orange Gatorade."

"Favorite movie?"

"*Reservoir Dogs* when you're with the boys, but you have always been partial to *Love Actually* around Christmas," I reveal his secret and he nods in agreement.

"Sports team?"

"All Wisconsin except for basketball, and that's Chicago."

"Impressive, Maddy!" he compliments me, finishing the impromptu quiz.

"We could go back and forth all night with one another. I've known you for twenty-five years, Trent."

"That's just it, Maddy. I know I fucked up, but we belong together," he says, taking on a more serious tone.

"We can't turn back time, Trent," I assure him.

"I know, Mad. Believe me…I know," he says with a low and unsteady voice.

"So why aren't you in Europe? I thought you were finishing a season there before coming to Chicago," I ask, changing the subject.

"That's what I wanted to talk to you about."

"What is it?" I place my glass down to face him.

"I'm thinking about retiring."

"Why?" I ask, shocked and surprised. There must be something wrong if Trent wants to retire at such a young age. "What's wrong?"

"You remember when I ruptured my Achilles tendon?" he asks.

"Yes," I answer.

"I haven't been the same since. The surgery fixed it and I have been doing my physical therapy. I was supposed to be in Europe to ease myself back into the States before coming back." He is still not looking at me. I know he knows what I am going to say and he doesn't want to hear it from me.

"I'm not as fast, not as quick. Chicago thought they traded for a number one player, but now they are thinking they got a bench warmer," he admits, shaking his head in disbelief.

"I couldn't even play half the games in Europe, my ankle is still too sore. I don't want to stick around being a has-been, Maddy. If I can't go out on top, I want to retire before I'm known for how many goals I missed in a game, instead of how many I made."

"Trent, you have to give it time. Chicago did get a number one player, a star player," I console him, placing my hand on his shoulder.

"That's why I have been missing some of Jack's wedding events. Chicago's team doctors brought me back to try some things they think would help. I meet with them, and have been doing certain drills and exercises they suggest. Yesterday, I had to meet with the owners and coaches. They told me they will give me one season to prove myself before trading me. I don't want to be one of those players, Maddy. The player that switches from one team to another every year."

"I thought you signed a contract?" I ask.

"I did, but only for a year. I was such an ass. When New York traded me for three of Chicago's players, I told them I would only commit to one season. I was so conceited and full of myself. I practically told them they would be lucky to have me for the year at the cost they were paying me because the next year I would cost double. Now I will be lucky enough to find a team to take me next year." He finally pushes his plate away, but instead of looking at me, he places his head in his hands.

"Stop talking like that. You can do this, Trent. Your body was born to play this sport, and you will recover and be the greatest soccer player again. All the teams will be begging for you," I say, trying to reassure him. I stand up to give him a hug.

"Oh Maddy, thanks but I just don't know." I see a drop of water fall on the couch and I know he is crying. I have seen Trent cry twice in his life before now. It wasn't when he left me at college or when I walked out on him a year ago. Once was when we were eleven and he hugged me good-bye in my driveway before I moved away, and the other time was that night we no longer talk about.

I reach over, stretching my arms around his shoulders from behind. He grabs my hands, leaning his head toward mine, where it is resting on his back.

"I promise you, Trent. We will get you back to where you need to be. I will be here for you."

"Promise, Maddy?" he whispers.

"I promise." I'm not sure what I just agreed to, but Trent being upset always makes me say and do desperate things. He was my best friend and I can't desert him, not when he needs me this much.

Trent turns around and hugs me, wrapping his strong arms around me. We have weaved in and out of a love relationship, but our friendship has remained. Although we grew apart this year, I won't let it happen again and from the look on Trent's face, he won't either.

A little while into the movie, I realize it's getting late and I need to get back home. Gabe is expecting a phone call, I left with Ian with my mom, and I have another packed day tomorrow.

"Trent, I am getting tired. Could you take me home now?" I sit up straighter, pushing the blanket off me.

"Stay the night?" he requests.

"I can't do that, Trent."

"Take my bed, I'll sleep on the couch. We'll go to breakfast in the morning and then talk about us," he says, pleading with me. This is the way Trent works. He will promise me anything, as long as I do what he wants.

"Trent…" I sigh.

"I promise, Mad, I won't try anything." He crosses his fingers on both hands.

"Trent, I cannot stay here. Please take me home."

"Can we at least finish the movie? Here…" He takes my feet into his hands, massaging them.

It feels good, especially after walking around Great Adventures all day in flip-flops. I close my eyes, remembering Gabe's hands rubbing my feet that Thanksgiving in his mom's kitchen. A smile crosses my lips at the thought of Gabe, our time together today, and what the future might hold for us.

A loud noise startles me awake. I notice the stream of light in my eyes before I realize where I am. Shit, I must have fallen asleep. Looking to my left, Trent is standing up, staring at the door.

I turn around to see what all the commotion is about. Gabe is standing in the doorway, pale-faced and obviously assuming the worst. Before I can utter a word, he is out the door.

"Gabe!" I scream after him and start toward the door, but Trent grabs my wrist.

"Let him go, Maddy."

I swing the door open and run down the hall, thankful to find Gabe at the elevators.

"Gabe, please listen to me," I plead, cornering him against the wall.

"No Maddy, I don't want to hear it." I can barely hear his soft whisper and he can't even look me in the eye.

"It was late. I fell asleep and we had both been drinking."

"How convenient. I don't want the details of your drunken fuck, Maddy," he spats, clenching his teeth.

"No, it wasn't like that." I pull on his arms, trying to make him look at me. I can almost feel him slipping away from me.

"I'm such a fool, Maddy. I actually thought you picked me yesterday. I should have known. It's always been Trent, hasn't it?" He starts talking louder, angrier.

"No, I do. I pick you," I answer.

"Answer me one question, Maddy," he says, finally looking me right in the eye. It takes everything in me not to break down; I can see that I have torn this man apart. "Do you still love him?"

I don't answer Gabe. I can't. I do love Trent, but I don't know to what degree or in what capacity.

"That's what I thought. Good-bye, Maddy." He pushes the button for the elevator, which opens immediately.

"Please, Gabe," I beg. I can no longer hold my tears back. He turns around, entering the elevator, and without a look back, is out of my sight and probably out of my life forever. What have I done?

Chapter 17 – College Junior Year

I am relieved finals are over. One more year and I will be a college graduate. I am packing up my dorm room because Mackenna, Bryan, and I will be renting a house. I am thankful I don't have to spend another summer at home with mom and her boyfriend-of-the-week. No more cleaning up her mess or locking my door at night in case a stranger stumbles in. I won't have to wait in my room until I hear her leave for work or act like I am sleeping when she returns in the middle of the night with some guy smelling of booze and cigarettes.

I already lined up a job at the rec center, a requirement from my dad since he is paying my rent and tuition. He's coming out in a couple of weeks to see the house we'll be living in.

My clothes are packed in suitcases and my books in boxes. My closet still consists of a mass of miscellaneous things scattered across the bottom. I find the purple plaid box that I have transported back and forth through the years. I open and then shut it quickly, telling myself that I shouldn't do this now. This is supposed to be a happy day. But of course I open it anyway.

Pictures are scattered in the box, along with little trinkets from the trip, including a bottle of sand with seashells in it. Gabe and I made these together, each bringing one home. A tear runs down my cheek. I should have listened to myself; I shouldn't have opened the box.

After that unbelievable night in Cancun when Gabe kissed me, he showed up at my doorstep the next morning.

"What on earth are you doing here this early? It's vacation." I rubbed my eyes, opening the door wider and crawled back under the covers.

"We have four days, twenty-one hours, thirty-six minutes, and eighteen seconds. Get your lazy ass out of bed," Gabe demanded, pulling the comforter off of me.

"What the fuck is asshole number two doing here?" Mackenna yells, pulling a pillow over her head.

"Let's go, both of you. It's vacation; we have places to be." Gabe stripped us both of our blankets.

"Where?" I asked, reluctantly sitting up.

"Breakfast, pool, beach." He jumped onto my bed, crossing his ankles and resting his arms behind his head. "Now go get ready. I want to spend every waking hour with you before we leave here," he whispered in my ear.

My face turned a nice shade of pink and I automatically stood up, digging for my swimsuit. Gabe and I were waiting by the doorway for Mackenna to join us, but she threw a pillow at us and told us to get the fuck out. Laughing, we left the room and shut the door. Gabe pushed me against the wall, kissing me. "Good morning, Maddy."

"Wow, I could definitely get used to this," I said, smiling up at him.

Gabe and I spent the next four days together. We hung out at the pool, went parasailing, and shopped at the local markets. Gabe showed up every morning and kissed me every night at my door, which is why I was completely blindsided on the morning Kenna and I were leaving when I found the note from Gabe under my door:

Maddy,

I hate that I am writing you this letter instead of telling you. I tried a million times tonight, but I couldn't say it.

Let me start off by saying how amazing these five days have been. When the boys dragged me down here, I never dreamed in a million years that I might run into you, much less that we could be together like we have.

Being able to touch you, grab your hand, or kiss you whenever I want has been something I've wanted for a long time. I meant what I said on the beach that night; my feelings for you run deep. Even though I can't explain them completely, I know you could be the one for me.

Unfortunately, I am not the only one that feels that way. I hope you understand why I have to do this. You could never hate me as much as I hate myself for walking away from a woman so perfect for me, but my brother saw you first. I have to honor my promise to him. I have to let him have his chance with you. Let him prove us both wrong. Let him prove that he does deserve you.

As much as it kills me to not be with you, I hope you find happiness with him. I will love you always, Madgirl.

Gabe

I fold the letter and put it back in the plaid box. Wiping the tears from my eyes, I contemplate how I let him slip out of my life. I have seen Gabe a handful of times since receiving that letter, with nothing more than politely awkward 'hellos' exchanged.

I took Gabe's advice and started talking to Trent a month after we returned from spring break. He was home that summer for a month and I let him take me on a couple dates, but like always, Trent was more concerned about his life than mine. When he received a call to play in Europe for the rest of the summer, he boarded the next plane, swearing we could handle a long-distance relationship.

The phone calls diminished from daily to weekly, and soon two weeks had passed and I hadn't heard from him. When we did talk, it always sounded like a party was going on, with girls and guys hollering in the background. He never returned home before going back to Thrayer University, and he never contacted me until a month after school started.

I wrote Trent off at that point, but he begged for forgiveness, stating that if he wanted a career in soccer, he had to take this seriously and couldn't afford distractions. I reluctantly forgave him and we rekindled our friendship. We lived out the next two years of our college life as friends, e-mailing and texting, accompanied by the occasional phone call.

As I put the box in my duffle bag, Colt walks into the room to grab my boxes. Colt is Bryan's new best friend and will be moving into the apartment as well.

"You okay?" he asks, noticing my tears.

"Yeah." I wipe my face.

"Great. One day and you already have PMS. This should be a fun year," he says with a smirk, grabbing a box and heading out the door.

The four of us progress into an easy routine and I am myself again. I have come to terms with the fact that Trent and Gabe each hold a part of my heart, but I have let them both go. Trent has to pursue his dream of soccer and Gabe needs to find a girl who can give her whole heart to him. I have made peace with this decision and I am content with it.

The four us are having a roommate dinner on Sunday night, a tradition that Bryan made us adhere to. He even made a rotating schedule, two of us cooking the meal each week. Tonight it is Colt and Kenna's turn, and since neither one is even close to a chef, we get a pasta salad and burgers. I wonder what Colt will make during the winter when grilling isn't an option.

Although Bryan tells us all to shut our phones off, I must have forgotten tonight.

"Don't even think about it, Maddy," Bryan warns me with his fork.

"Let me just turn it off," I say to him, having no intention of ignoring the call.

"Make it quick."

"Okay, Dad!" I call out sarcastically. Kenna and Colt burst into laughter.

I dig through my bag, realizing I missed the phone call when I hear the ding indicating a message has been left. I dial it up quickly and am happy to hear Jack's voice.

"Hey, Maddy. I need you to call me back right away, okay?" Jack's voice sounds desperate and urgent.

Before I can dial his number, Kenna's phone starts ringing. I pick it up, instinctively knowing it's Jack calling for me.

"What's going on Jack?" I ask, knowing in my gut that something is very wrong.

"Listen Maddy, I need you to come home," Jack says, sounding as though he has been crying. I automatically think that my mom has finally killed herself by drunk driving or has overdosed.

"Why?" I whisper back to him.

"Just please come home," he begs me.

"I want to know why. What did she do?"

"It's not mom, it's…Dad. He's in the hospital…" his voice trails off.

I drop the phone, putting my head in my hands. Mackenna runs to my side and a second later, Bryan is there, taking me into his arms and assuring me everything will be alright. Colt even puts down his burger, coming over to the couch to see what all the commotion is about.

"We need to get you home, Maddy," she whispers in my ear, while her arms hold me tight.

Kenna packs our bags and the four of us pile into my Jeep. Bryan drives, while Colt sits shotgun. Kenna texts the whole time and I stare out the window. She tries to tell me what is going on, but all I register is that my dad passed out at Jack's and an ambulance was called. Kenna says that my dad hasn't woken up, but the doctors are taking blood and doing some tests to figure what is going on.

Two hours later, we finally pull up to the hospital. Bryan drops Kenna and me off at the entrance, while he and Colt go to park the car. Kenna has taken complete charge of the situation. She rushes to the receptionist to find out where we need to go. She hits the elevator button and then pulls out her phone to text someone.

The elevator door opens to the waiting room and Lindsey is there. She embraces me. "Oh, thank God you made it. Come with me," she says, pulling me away from Mackenna. I look back, seeing Mr. and Mrs. Basso, Doug and his wife, Lindsey's parents, the Edwards and lastly, a set of blue eyes. They stare at me, filled with

so much sorrow that I almost breakdown right then and there. His
eyes are telling me that the news isn't good so that I'm prepared
before I go in. He doesn't walk toward me, giving me the distance he
knows I need right now.

I walk in the room, seeing my dad lying there with tubes and
wires hooked up to his body. A beeping sound comes from the
machines next to him. Jack sits in a chair, holding his hand, with his
head down on the bed. If it wasn't for the beeping of the machines
telling me my dad is alive, I would have thought he is already dead.
Jack picks his head up, relief in his eyes that I am here.

He makes his way to me and I see his dark hair sticking up in
different directions where he has probably run his hands through it a
million times. When his big arms surround me, my tears finally let
loose. I sob into his chest as he smooth's my hair, telling me that we
will survive this. He tells me that our Dad is a fighter and everything
will be okay, but I can't ignore this feeling that it won't.

I take a chair on the other side of my dad, while Lindsey stays by
the windowsill. Jack fills me in on my dad's diagnosis. The doctors
don't know much yet. They are still running tests, but they assume
he had a stroke.

An hour later, a male doctor who doesn't much look older than
Jack, tells us that our dad actually suffered a heart attack and he
needs surgery right away. Right as the young doctor is explaining
what we can expect from the surgery, my mom bursts in the room.

"Oh…nice," she remarks, looking the doctor up and down.
"What happened to him?" She nods her head in my dad's direction. I

can smell the cigarettes and alcohol on her. She is wearing her usual tight black skirt that hangs just past her ass, along with a black halter-top. Her hair is down and curled; her eye make-up is smeared, as is the red lipstick across her teeth. I roll my eyes, already exhausted by her presence.

"I'm sorry, are you related to Mr. Jennings?" the doctor asks, turning to my mom.

"I'm his wife," she remarks and I gasp.

"Ex-wife," I declare, staring at her with what I hope are my most evil eyes.

"Madeline!" She says my name curtly, indicating she wants me to shut up. I do, but mostly to keep her mouth shut as well.

The doctor doesn't skip a beat; he must be familiar with dysfunctional families. He instructs us to go to the waiting room, telling us that the surgery will take approximately four hours and he will come and get us when it's over. We each take our time saying good-bye to dad, conveying our love to him. Jack goes first and then he and Lindsey leave, making me thankful that he will have to deliver the news to our waiting friends. I go second because, for some absurd reason, my mom insists that she should go last.

I walk down the long hallway alone, my heart beating fast. I don't want to face all of those people in the waiting room.

Mrs. Basso is the first to embrace me, whispering in my ear how sorry she is and that they will do whatever I need. I nod my head, tucked in the shoulder of the woman I consider my mother. She holds me tight and relief washes over me, knowing that the people in this room love and support my brother and me.

Bryan and Colt are sitting with Mackenna. She stands up, putting her arm around my shoulders. I think she is going to lead me to the vacant chair next to her, but turns at the last minute, releasing me to Gabe. The feeling of his welcoming arms is far too familiar and comforting, so I collapse into him and he sits down with me on his lap.

He doesn't assure me that everything will be okay or that my dad will pull through. He just assures me that he will be here for me, regardless of what happens. Those words bring comfort to me, and the fact that they came from Gabe means even more.

Gabe and I stay like that for an hour. No one interrupts us. I hear conversations carrying on around us, but we're in our own little world.

"Do you want me to get you something to eat or drink?" he whispers softly to me.

"No, but if you want something, I can get up," I say, slowly getting up from his lap.

"No, I don't need anything." He pulls me back down, intertwining his hands with mine. "I know this isn't the right time, but I am enjoying the hell out of this."

I start laughing and everyone in the room looks over at me, but I can't control myself. I don't know why. It isn't as though what he said was funny. Maybe it is the tension in the room or the fear of something happening to my dad, but it feels so good to laugh.

"You're making me look like a schmuck," he says, biting his lip to keep the smile at bay.

"I'm sorry, I don't know what's wrong with me," I say, placing my head on his shoulder, trying to quiet my laugh.

I must have dozed off because, by the time the doctor comes out, the only ones here are Gabe, Jack, Lindsey, my mom, and Kenna.

"He's out of surgery, but it is still touch and go for a while. We will know more in the morning. He's in ICU, so let him recover tonight and come back in the morning," he instructs.

I don't feel right leaving, but everyone guarantees me it's for the best. I reluctantly leave to spend the night at Jack's. I take the guest room and Gabe goes home for the night. I think my mom thought I would spend the night at her house, but I have no intention of doing that. She probably went back to the bar after she left the hospital anyway.

Jack tells me that Gabe was in town visiting his family when they got the call, but he is leaving to go back to Florida in two days. He says that Gabe and a couple of his buddies bought a house on the beach and are in the process of flipping it, using the extra money to start a real estate company. I know Gabe wants to be his own boss and it doesn't surprise me that he is already attaining that goal.

The next morning, Gabe comes to Jack's to pick me up. Kenna wanted to stay in town, but I told her to go back with Bryan and Colt and I would call them if there were any changes. Although classes haven't started yet, they all have jobs to get back to.

Gabe and I follow Jack and Lindsey to the hospital. The nurses say that not much has changed in my dad's condition, but to be patient because it can take some time.

I tell Gabe to go ahead and leave, but he insists that this is where he wants to be. Returning from a trip to the bathroom, I overhear Gabe on his cell phone. His back is turned to me so I stand silent, waiting for him to be done.

"It's not that big of a deal, only a couple days," he says angrily toward someone. I assume it's one of his buddies in Florida.

"That is nothing. Come on, this is ridiculous." He puts his hands through his hair, leaning against the wall.

"Listen, get your ass up and stop thinking about yourself for once." He turns, looking apologetic and I know instantly who he's talking to. I put my hand out for him to give me the phone and he does.

"Hello, Trent," I say.

"I'm sorry, Maddy. I just got word about your dad. I wish I could be there but they won't let me out of practice," he lies.

"That's okay, Trent," I say nonchalantly. Gabe looks at me in disbelief.

"You know I would if I could, Mad. You understand, right?" he asks.

"Yeah, I understand." Gabe turns around frustrated, throwing his hands up in the air.

"I love you, Maddy. Call me if you need me, okay? I'll keep my phone by me."

"Okay. Bye, Trent," I say.

"Bye, Maddy. Can you give me back to Gabe now?" he requests.

"Sure." I hand the phone over to Gabe. I feel the tears welling up in my eyes, but I am determined not to cry over Trent Basso again.

Gabe takes the phone and walks over to the corner of the room, whispering. Although I can't hear his words, I see the pent-up fury he is unleashing on Trent. He hangs up the phone, throwing it into the chair next to him.

I hurry back to my dad's room before Gabe can see my reaction to Trent not coming. He needs to cool down anyway. When I get back to the room, Jack is smiling up at me with hope in his eyes.

"Was there a change? Did Dad wake up?" I desperately ask.

"He squeezed my hand," he exclaims. "The nurses said that is a good sign."

"Oh my God, really?" I sit down across from Jack, taking my dad's hand, but it's still limp in mine.

Jack and I sit like this, each holding one of my dad's hands, waiting for more movement. We talk about memories of when our parents were together, family trips we took, and holidays spent together. I know the divorce was my dad's fault as much as my mom's, but that doesn't change the fact that she has never been a mother to me. I suddenly realize that she never came to visit him today, making me hate her even more.

Lindsey and Gabe come in about an hour later.

Jack excitedly tells them the news about my dad squeezing his hand. Lindsey kisses his head, hugging him in happiness.

"You guys go get something to eat, Maddy and I will stick around here," Gabe tells them.

They look at each other, assessing one another's thoughts. "Thanks, Gabe." Jack gets up, taking Lindsey's hand. "Call me if anything happens."

"We will, just go relax," I instruct them.

"Get up." Gabe taps me on the shoulder.

"Why?" I question, still sitting down.

"Because." He takes my hand, lifting me onto his lap.

"Oh, I see," I say, resting my head on his shoulder.

We talk about my school and where I want to live after I finish. Gabe tells me about his friends and the house they bought.

An hour later, my dad's machines start going off. Alarms are blaring and my dad's body begins thrashing around. Gabe runs out of the room to get the nurses, but a medical team is already running toward him to get in the room. They tell him to take me out in the hallway so he grabs my hand, pulling me out the door.

I huddle next to Gabe, waiting for them to come out and tell me he is alright. Ten agonizing minutes later, a doctor leads us to a private room down the hall, telling me what I have feared since the first call came from Jack. My dad is dead. He suffered another stroke and this one took his life.

Jack returns after Gabe texts him, and he breaks down crying while Lindsey holds him close, whispering in his ear. I am surprised to find that, for once, I have no tears to shed. We are each allowed to go into the room to say goodbye. Jack takes ten minutes to my two. I can't stand to see him lying there, limp and pale. This shell of a body isn't my father.

Two days later, we bury my dad. Gabe stands by my side the whole time. Kenna, Bryan, and Colt come down from school to attend the wake and funeral. Kenna helps Lindsey plan the post-funeral luncheon. Doug, Jack, Mr. Basso, Mr. Edwards, Bryan, and Gabe are the pallbearers. Trent never comes home.

My mom shows up drunk, wearing a short and insanely tight black dress and spike heels. The man she brought with her wears jeans and a black button-down shirt with tattoos up and down his arms. His greasy hair is slicked back and they both reek of cigarettes and alcohol. My tears finally appear when she walks in. Unfortunately, they aren't tears of sorrow, but tears of rage. How could she disrespect my dad like this?

I grab her arm, pulling her into the private family room. "What the hell are you doing?" I seethe through my teeth.

"Madeline, don't make a scene," she says, swaying to the side.

"Me make a scene? You show up hammered to my dad's funeral."

"I'm not drunk, Madeline. Excuse me if I needed to have a few drinks before coming. Have some sympathy, this is hard for me."

"Are you serious? Sympathy for you? Jack and I are burying our father today. You should be here for *us*, to console *us*," I say with a rising voice. Jack and Gabe have found their way in the room, while her "date" hovers by the doorway.

"Madeline, you're being so dramatic," she says, waving her hand in the air before stumbling into the wall.

"Dramatic? You brought a date and you are dressed like a slut. You make me sick!" I yell. Gabe tries to pull me out of the room, but I yank my arm out of his hands. "What kind of mother are you?"

"Maddy, just stop," Jack states, standing between the two of us and putting his hands in front of me.

"Yes, Madeline, this isn't the time," she says, her voice cool as a cucumber.

"Jack, how can you let her get away with this?" I complain.

"Listen, we are here to bury dad, so let's give him peace. The people out there loved him and they deserve to grieve like we do. We can discuss these things later," he calmly says. Jack is forever the mediator between us.

"I could give a shit about talking later. This is unforgivable. I am done with you," I scream, walking out of the room with Gabe in tow, leaving Jack to deal with my mother.

I push past her boyfriend and walk outside. I can't believe that the one parent who gave a shit is no longer on this earth.

I stay at the Basso's for the next week until Gabe goes back to Florida. Saying good-bye to him is harder than I expected. He never kissed me or touched me inappropriately, but I felt closer to him once again. When we get to the airport and I walk him to the terminal, I feel the tears starting to fall down my cheeks.

"Don't cry, I will call you when I land," he says, bringing me into an embrace.

"I'll miss you. I can't thank you enough, Gabe," I say.

"I am only a phone call away."

"I would have never gotten through this without you."

"You are stronger than you think, but I was happy to be here for you."

"Good luck with the house thing. Tell Grady and Ryan I said 'hi'." I pull away.

"I will. Have a great senior year and think about coming down after you graduate." I see the anguish in his eyes and know he doesn't want to push me, but I so desperately want him to. Part of me wishes he would beg me to move down there to be with him. I know how he feels though; he still doesn't want to betray his brother.

"We'll see," I say with a shrug. "Bye Gabe." I give him one last hug.

"Bye, Madgirl," he says softly, placing a hand on each side of my face. He brings his lips to my forehead and kisses me good-bye, his lips lingering. Abruptly turning around, he walks to the security area, but turns around one last time and winks to me before disappearing in the crowd of people.

Chapter 18 – Present Day

I open the condo door to Trent standing in the kitchen. Glass bottles and alcohol are spewed across the floor.

"So, what happened, other than Gabe dropping all of the alcohol for the bachelor party on my floor?" he asks, his voice cocky.

"What do you think? He left," I say, not bothering to turn around.

"Figured as much. Maddy, you have to stop fighting this. We are meant to be together, always have been."

"Trent, not now," I stutter. Tears are still streaming down my face.

"Let him go."

"I can't," I whisper. I grab my purse off the kitchen counter, searching for my phone. I need to get out of here, and the sooner the better.

"Stop it, Mad. I will take you home," Trent says.

"You don't have to. I can call someone or catch a train that will get me closer to Belcrest." I start walking out but he grabs my arm, pulling me back.

"Just let me take you home." Trent grabs his keys off the counter and leads me out of his condo, leaving the mess at the front door.

The forty-five minute drive is quiet, neither one of us saying much. Once we get off the freeway, Trent finally starts the conversation I have been avoiding.

"Jesus, Maddy, what do I have to do?" he asks angrily.

"Trent, we have tried…numerous times." I close my eyes, unable to look at the love pouring from his.

"No, *you* tried. I kept messing it up. I swear, Maddy, I've changed," he admits.

"Trent, I wish I could give us another shot, but I can't do it. We have always been better at being…friends."

"Maddy, I can't be your friend. I miss you. That night you walked out on me is the night that I realized that you are the one I need in my life."

"Trent, you just don't get it. You have been everything to me for half my life. But the other half of my life…" I can't stop the tears that start again, so I let them fall.

"What Maddy?" he asks, so softly that I barely hear him.

"You destroyed me. I don't want to pick myself up from that again. One of these times, I won't survive."

"I'm sorry. I know I have been a jackass to you, but I swear if you give me a second, third, or whatever chance this is, I will prove it to you." He grabs my hand.

"Trent, that's not the only reason," I say quietly.

"Gabe?" he confirms, pulling his hand away from mine.

"When you were destroying me, he was picking me up. You both hold a place in my heart and I don't want to lead either one of you on, but..."

"What do you want from me, Mad? Anything, just name it," he says, pulling into my driveway.

"Nothing. Trent...you are who you are. I either have to accept it or not." I put my hand on his face. The sweet face that gave me my first kiss, my first experience with sex, and most of all, my first love.

"Please don't choose him," he begs, shaking his head back and forth.

"Trent," I sigh.

"Give it time. Think about it, Maddy. You have always been the one for me. You take care of me, believe in me and love me, no matter who I am. Do you know how great it is to know that you don't love me because of my money or because I play professional soccer?"

"There are girls that don't care about that, you just don't hang out with them," I point out.

"No girl compares to you. I will spend the rest of my life making this up to you."

"Trent, I'm sorry," I whisper.

"No, Maddy…don't," Trent says, stuttering his words.

"I love him, Trent," I admit.

"Take as much time as you want, don't decide now," he says desperately, ignoring what I just said.

"I don't need more time," I respond.

"Don't do this, Maddy. It's me…your Ricky…your Romeo," he begs. "Please, Maddy."

"I'm sorry, Trent," I whisper, getting out of the car. Before I can get away, he grabs my wrist.

"I'm not done, Maddy. I will prove myself to you. Just because you pick him, it doesn't mean I will stop trying to get you back," he says, releasing my arm. I exit the car without looking back at him.

"Finally, girl. I have been calling you all night." Ian runs toward me, pulling me into an embrace when I enter the house.

"What's all that?" I ask, looking over his shoulder to the scattered pictures across my living room floor.

"Your mom and I are trying to find a picture of your dad." He walks back over to the coffee table.

"Why?" I ask, placing my purse on the new bench in the foyer and following him.

"Jack and Lindsey want to display a picture with a lit candle at the church and reception in honor of him," my mom answers, carrying two glasses of iced tea. She is wearing another nice new outfit and her hair is perfectly styled in a bob.

"That's nice." I pick up some of the pictures, thumbing through them.

"Your mom said she is having a hard time finding the right one," Ian says. "I must say though, your dad was a gorgeous man."

"Like Jack," my mom and I say at the same time. We look at each other and she smiles at me, but I don't smile in return. I am not ready for the mother-daughter relationship she wants.

Everyone who knew my dad when he was younger was able to see the close resemblance to Jack. The dark hair and striking green eyes are the first thing people notice, but if you looked closer, it was their high cheekbones and narrow nose that made them look so much alike.

"Yeah, I see it. Both complete hotties…such as shame. Which brings me to my next question," Ian says, a devious smile on his face.

"Do I even want to know?" I ask, certain that I don't.

"Are there any men in this town that play for my team?" he asks. "Kenna has been taking me around town since you have been *busy* but I haven't seen anyone. And trust me, I know when I see them."

I roll my eyes in his direction. "I guess I never noticed. Around here, they are probably still hidden in the closet," I say with a shrug.

"I can tell you where to go, Ian. There is this bar about twenty minutes outside of Belcrest. In my high time, I went in there and couldn't figure out why no one was hitting on me until the bartender told me to look around," my mom embarrassingly admits.

"Let's go tonight, Maddy," he excitedly says, hopping up on his knees and clapping his hands in anticipation.

"I'm exhausted and I have to take care of some stuff," I say and both are absolutely true.

"Maddy, you need a night away from those boys," he pleads. "Clear your head. You know you love the gay bars because no one bothers you there."

"We have the Bar-B-Que," I object. I'm not sure why I don't want to go. Ian and I have so much fun going out in New York and he is right, I always favor the gay bars because no one comes up behind me, trying to hump me when I dance.

"After," he begs.

"Um…"

"You should go, Maddy. These boys have been running you wild the whole week. Once Friday comes, it will be crazy. Go enjoy yourself," my mom pushes.

"Okay. After the Bar-B-Que. Let's invite Kenna too," I say.

"We can invite everyone. Barb, did you want to come?" he asks her.

She looks from Ian to me and shakes her head, but her eyes looks distraught and upset.

"I'm surprised you kept all these pictures," I say, changing the subject.

"Why?" my mom asks.

"I don't know. I just figured after you and dad divorced, you wouldn't want reminders around," I respond, shrugging my shoulders.

"Ian, would you excuse us a minute?" my mom asks him. Poor Ian, he keeps getting shut out due to family issues. I owe him tonight.

"Of course, Barb." He winks at me while getting up and going upstairs.

"Maddy, I know I wasn't the best mother, especially after your dad and I divorced." She swallows hard, hesitantly grabbing my hand with hers. "But I did love your father and our family together. When he asked me for the divorce, I knew it was coming and I also knew it was my fault."

"Dad asked you for one?" I ask, flabbergasted. I had thought for sure it was the other way around.

"Yes, but he had every reason to. I was gallivanting around behind his back for years. I don't know if it was because we married so young, or I was just being self-centered. I felt like I missed out on something by marrying my high school sweetheart. Then he had to start going out of town and I was responsible for you and Jack all the time. I assumed he was cheating on me so I decided to start living my life." She squeezes my hand.

"After he asked for the divorce and I knew it wasn't because of another woman coming between us, I lost it. I started going out more and drinking more. Somewhere in all of that, I forgot I was a mother and I abandoned you and your brother. Jack was older so he probably embraced the freedom it allowed him to have, but you were so young. I'm sorry, Maddy." She takes a deep breath before continuing. "I wish I could say your dad's funeral was my low point, but we both know it wasn't."

I nod my head in agreement. I can't talk about that fateful night, especially in this room. It might be redecorated, but I can still visualize the night with perfect clarity.

"The way I came to the funeral, bringing that guy and being drunk when you and Jack needed me there for you…I'll never forgive myself for that. I guess a small part of me always thought that your dad and I would get back together." She takes a sip of her tea and I see that her hand is shaking.

"You were so right to yell at me that day. I wish then that I had realized what I was doing to you. I know you can't forgive me and I understand, but I do want to tell you something."

"Okay," I whisper.

"After that night, I checked into a rehab facility. I have been clean for two years now."

"That's good," I say, but wonder if she thinks that knowing this will make it all better. "Why didn't you tell me?"

"I wanted to prove it to you. I'm sorry I wasn't there for you…I'm sorry for everything."-She pats her hand on my knee, standing up and walking away.

This trip just gets better and better every minute. I am happy for my mom, that she is finally getting her life back on track. But I still resent her for what she did and what she didn't do for me, and what I lost because of her.

It makes me realize it is time for me to go there; I have been ignoring the pull since I arrived. The problem is, I can't ask Gabe to take me and I can't ask my mom because I don't want her asking any questions.

I dig through my drawers in my room, finding my running shorts and shirt. Luckily, I have a pair of old running shoes in the closet as well. The shorts and shirt are a little tight, considering my body has changed over the years but they will do. It's only a mile away and this way, I can escape without anyone knowing where I am going.

When I get to the cemetery entrance, I'm not prepared to see Trent's car there. I see him up on the hill, kneeling on the ground. I don't want to interrupt him so I stay by his car until he is finished. I wonder if he comes here often.

I am mesmerized watching him, as he sits to the right of the headstone. His lips are moving as if he's talking, and he wipes his eyes a few times. He didn't forget; this whole time I thought he had. I cannot stop the tears, not this time.

I am staring at the ground when I hear him walk up to me.

"Hey," he says, his voice shaky.

"Hey," I say in return.

"Do you come here a lot?" he asks.

"My first time since that night," I shamefully admit. "You?"

"Every time I come back to town."

I look up, surprised at his response.

"I know you think I don't care, Maddy, but I do," he says with bitterness.

"No, that's not it." I shake my head back and forth.

"It's okay, I have been a selfish prick most of our lives. I deserve you thinking that I don't care." He puts his hand on my arm. "But this," he says, motioning up the hill. "This is something I will *never* forget."

I gulp hard, trying to get my emotions under control.

"Well, I will leave you alone." He kisses my cheek and walks over to the driver's side of the car. "By the way, nice running clothes. I think I remember tearing those off of you a time or two," he says with a smirk, trying to lighten the uncomfortable situation.

I smile up at him but say nothing more.

I wait until Trent drives away before heading up the hill. I slowly walk up it, looking at the numerous headstones with last names I recognize of schoolmates or neighbors. Everyone in town is, or will one day be buried in this cemetery.

Finally, I reach my destination. The headstone reads "Jennings". It is my dad's family's headstone. My grandparents and one uncle are also laid to rest here. I sit down, ready to face him. The angel statue next to his name reminds me I should have come sooner.

"I wish you were here," I say, concentrating on my dad for the moment. "You always gave me the best advice." I run my hand across his name. "I don't know what to do about Gabe and Trent, let alone Mom. What has happened to my life?"

I sit in silence, listening to the birds chirping and leaves rustling in the wind. The cemetery is off the main road, so there is no noise of cars or people. I don't know what I expected when I came here. I pick at the weeds around the family plot, contemplating leaving and thinking maybe this was a mistake.

"I miss you…every day," I softly say. "I know I haven't been here, but there isn't a day that goes by that I don't think about you." I touch the angel, caressing the outline of it with my thumb.

"I hope you will forgive me. Isn't it absurd that I am asking for your forgiveness, when I can't forgive Mom or Trent?" I ask, wishing he could answer.

"I know you would tell me to forgive them. You were never one to hold grudges. God, why did you have to die on me?" I put my head in my hands, crying. "My life is a disaster, Dad. Gabe found me at Trent's apartment today and he thinks I slept with him, but I didn't. Trent wants me to desert Gabe and move right back in with him, but I love Gabe. Now Mom tells me she has been clean for two years and expects me to forgive her like nothing has happened. I have been living my life for three years with no one to look out for me or guide me. I am so mad at you for leaving me," I say, my voice getting louder as I pound my fists onto the ground.

As I look at the angel again, my body starts shaking and I unable to breathe. Jack once asked me if I knew where it had come from, but I told him I had no idea. Hopefully, someday I can tell him the truth. After a couple of minutes, I take deep breaths and exhale them slowly, finally able to calm down.

Fifteen minutes later, I am able to stand up and say goodbye. I kiss my fingers, placing them on the headstone and the angel. I am filled with peace as I leave the black iron gates. I know what I need to do; I just need to figure out how to do it.

I walk back through downtown on my way home, where I run into the one person that probably hates me more than I hate myself over this mess.

"Madeline."

"Hello, Mrs. Basso," I respond. Could my day get any worse?

Chapter 19 – Spring Break Senior Year

Once school starts back, time seems to slow to a crawl. Mackenna, Bryan, and Colt always make sure I'm not alone. If Gabe isn't calling, he's emailing me, and has even Skyped a couple of times to see how I am holding up. As much as I love my friends' concern, I desperately want to be alone.

Against my better judgment, I reluctantly agreed to go on a trip up north with my friends for Spring Break. I figured I could go on long walks or read a book while I was there.

I came home from class early one day to hear Mackenna and Bryan yelling at each other, which is unusual for them. They usually only argue about one thing, or should I say, one person. My heart sinks into my stomach.

"He is not going with us," Kenna spats at Bryan.

"What was I supposed to say? He is one of my best friends." Bryan sits at the table, placing his head in his hands.

"*Was* Bryan. He *was* one of your best friends. He *was* one of mine too, but what he did to her is unforgivable. You saw how much it killed her when he didn't come." Mackenna is talking about me, but where is Trent going with us? Wait…oh shit!

"She didn't seem so upset in Gabe's lap," Bryan scoffs.

"Bryan Jacob Edwards. She had to find comfort somewhere and he was the one there, not your jackass friend," she shouts back at him.

"Come on, Kenna. You know she has feelings for Gabe."

"Maybe…but that doesn't excuse Trent's actions," she says, sitting next to him.

"I know that, but it's hard for him too. You have to see his side of all this."

"No. He has no side. He made his choices. I don't give a shit if he is trying to backtrack now. He cannot come with us."

"Kenna, we need another person to share the cost. The cabin is costing a fortune, and we need as many people as it can sleep," Bryan points out. I am fortunate to have my dad's life insurance money and Kenna never has to worry, but Colt, Bryan, and the others are using money they should be saving. He's right that it is cost effective to have as many people as possible.

"Why does he want to come? All of a sudden he wants to hang out with us? Why, Bryan?" Kenna is still fuming.

"I don't know. He called, asked if we had plans. I told him and he wanted to know if he could tag along with us."

"You're telling her," Kenna says, pointing at Bryan.

"No point, I heard it all," I say, opening the screen door.

"Maddy," Kenna sighs.

"It's okay, Kenna. Bryan is right; we need as many people as possible. It's a big enough group, I will just keep my distance," I say, walking to the stairwell.

"Are you sure, Maddy?" Bryan asks, his eyes warm with concern.

"Yeah, it's fine," I reply, walking upstairs to the comfort of my bedroom. I am willing to deal with this, but I have to tell Gabe and I am not so sure he will be.

Gabe and I aren't dating, but I'm not going to leave out the fact that Trent is coming and have him find out later. When I went home for Christmas, I stayed at Jack's, never seeing Trent. Gabe came over a couple of nights, but I never asked if Trent was home and he never divulged the information. Since I don't know how fast word will travel, I decide to call Gabe right away.

"Hey, it's me," I say.

"Hey you. How are you doing? Getting excited about your trip?" he asks. I hear him shuffling papers behind him.

"I guess, are you busy?"

"Never for you, Madgirl. You sound…not like yourself. Something wrong?" he questions, his voice etched with concern.

"Um… I don't know how you are going to take this," I say, hesitating.

"Hit me with it," Gabe's voice relaxes.

"Okay, I'm just going to spit it out," I admit.

"Maddy…" Gabe's stern voice tries to reassure me it will be okay, but I know it won't.

"Trent is coming with us to the cabin." I say it so fast I don't think he will hear it, but the silence on the other end confirms he did. "He called Bryan and asked. The other guys need all the people they can get to keep the cost down. I didn't want them to say no just because of me..."

"Maddy, stop talking," Gabe's gravelly voice interrupts me. "So this is Edwards doing?" Anger fills his tone.

"He is the one who agreed that he could come, but it's fine. It's a big group so I can keep my distance from him," I say, knowing I sound desperate.

"You might be able to, but Trent can't. Maddy, I think this is a very bad idea. I am half tempted to call Edwards myself to talk about this." Gabe's tone turns fatherly and I don't like it.

"Listen Gabe, I know the situation isn't ideal, but it's fine. I will be fine."

"I'm sure you will be," he mocks.

"What does that mean?" I bite back at him.

"When it comes to Trent, you are always okay with him being there. It just sucks that he doesn't feel the same."

"Gabe...why are you saying this?" I softly ask.

"God Maddy, seriously? You honestly don't see this as a bad idea?"

"No." I shake my head, although he can't see it through the phone.

"You know what? Whatever. Go ahead and go. Have a *great* time."

"Gabe, don't be like this," I beg softly.

"Maddy, we aren't a couple. I have no say whether you go or not." He's angry again.

"I want you to be okay with this."

"Sorry Maddy, I'm not," he says curtly.

"Please, Gabe," I plead one more time.

"Listen, I have to go see a house. I am going to be late. Have fun at the cabin. Give my brother my best." The phone goes dead as he hangs up on me.

I reluctantly give him his space, waiting for him to cool off, but a week later, he still hasn't called, e-mailed, or texted.

A week later, we are all in my Jeep on the way to the cabin. There is a caravan of five cars, including Trent's truck. He has brought a few friends, which helps tremendously with the cost.

"So Maddy, funny thing happened the other day," Bryan says, putting his head between Kenna and me in the front.

"Yeah?" I turn down the music a little.

"Gabe called me," he says, not sounding happy about it in the least.

"Really?" I ask, trying to sound nonchalant.

"He chewed me out for letting Trent come to the cabin. He must have screamed at me for ten minutes," he says. "Do you have any idea why he would call *me*?"

"I told him it was you that said Trent could come," I admit, smiling at Kenna.

"That's what I thought. I wish you three could get your shit together," he says, leaning back down in his seat next to Colt. I turn the radio knob up again.

I keep my distance the first night, even though Trent is following me around, asking to talk. I have refused him enough times that my hand starts automatically going up when he comes around. Colt tries to run interference, but he is trying to get with a girl named Kristi, so I tell him I can handle Trent Basso.

"I know you can, Maddy, but I hate what that asshole did to you. If I had my way, he wouldn't be up here with us," Colt says, putting his arm around me.

"You will be happy when you have money left for the semester," I say. "Thanks for caring though."

He shrugs, going over to sit next to Kristi. Trent is occupying his space within seconds.

"Do you need any help?" he asks.

"No, I don't. Just go and have fun." I shoo him away with my hand.

"I want to talk to you," he begs.

"I don't."

"Come on, Maddy," he says, placing his hand on my arm.

"Listen, Trent. I didn't want you here. You are here to keep the cost down. If your plan is to keep hounding me all week, I will leave." I tear my arm away from him.

"You keep telling yourself that, but I am pretty sure things will change by the end of the week," he whispers in my ear, making goose bumps crawl up my body.

No, No, No. Don't fall for his tricks, Maddy.

By day three, I can't take it anymore. Every time I walk out of the room, he follows to get me alone. I am trying so hard, but I feel myself losing my willpower. Gabe was right; he won't keep his distance. I should have listened to him. Maybe I should leave.

Kenna decides tonight's a girl's night in and the boys go into town to some bar. We play drinking games and I am reminded how much fun this trip was supposed to be.

By the time the boys get back to the cabin, it is late and I am plastered, along with the rest of the girls. So when Trent comes and sits next to me, putting his arm around my shoulders, I don't protest. Kenna is staring holes through me and Colt looks sympathetic to what is happening. They probably see it before I do. I relax into Trent's body, snuggling next to him. It feels natural and I can't stop myself from resting my hand on his leg.

"How much alcohol did it take for you to stop fighting this?" he whispers in my ear.

"Fuck you, Trent!" I stand up fast, yelling at him and the room gets quiet.

"Let's go somewhere, Maddy." He tries to grab my hand but I pull it back.

"If you want to talk, let's talk right here," I furiously say, pointing to the ground. I don't know if I am mad at what he said or because he is right. I can't fight this between us.

"No, let's go somewhere more private." He rubs his thumb up and down my arm, insinuating that talking isn't what is on his mind.

"Jesus, Trent, you are such an asshole. How can you come up here and act like you didn't screw me every which way? You should have been there. My fucking father died, Trent. If anyone knows about my family, it's you. How much my dad meant to me," I scream at him, but it doesn't seem to faze him.

"You go, girl," Kenna says behind me.

"Kenna!" Bryan yells, telling her to stay out of it.

"From what I hear, you were well taken care of...by *my brother*." Trent stands up, glaring down at me.

"He was there and you weren't. Surprise, surprise. Trent wasn't there when I needed him. But who is always there for you? Me," I say, pointing at myself.

"You keep playing fucking games, Maddy. Who is it this week, me or Gabe?"

"Give me a break. You broke up with me, Trent. Leave Gabe out of this."

"Why should I leave Gabe out of it? You have probably fucked us both. So Maddy, which brother fucks better?" The room gasps in shock. I smack him across the face, running out of the room.

"Maddy," Mackenna calls after me.

"I got this, Kenna," Trent says.

"You better make this right, before I kick your ass, Basso," I hear Mackenna yell.

I sit next to the lake with a fuzzy head and a stinging hand, wondering how the hell I got into this situation.

"I'm sorry, Maddy, I shouldn't have said that." Trent comes up behind me. "You just got me so angry."

"Why do I make you angry, Trent?" I don't turn around.

"The whole thing with Gabe, it pissed me off," he admits.

"I never slept with Gabe," I say, hearing him come a little closer.

"I know, but…you're mine, Maddy. I figured we would always be together."

"You seem to only want me when it's convenient for you." I still can't look at him, so I focus on the moon gleaming down on the lake.

"I'm a shit. I should have come home for you when your dad died, but it pissed me off that Gabe was the one that called me. You didn't call me and he was there, so I figured you made your choice."

"I didn't call anyone. It was a coincidence he was there. Yes, he comforted me. He got me back up on my feet."

"Yeah, I heard," he scoffs, throwing rocks into the water.

"From who?" I ask.

"My mom. She told me you stayed the week and Gabe stayed to be with you. She chewed me out for not coming home, too." He makes a rock skip three times.

"Good, because it was a shitty thing for you to do, Trent." My eyes finally meet his and the moon is making his blue eyes sparkle more than normal. "You have to let me go."

"I can't, Maddy," he says, placing his hand on my face, wiping a tear from my eye.

He's inching closer to me; I knew I shouldn't have drunk so much. I am losing my willpower and I don't know if it's the alcohol or Trent. "You have to, Trent. I can't live like this anymore."

"You are mine...always." His lips crush into mine and the warmth spreads through my body. His hand moves from my cheek to my neck, pulling me closer and keeping me firmly pressed against his lips. He licks my bottom lip, asking me for permission to open and, knowing that the words he just spoke are true, I oblige. His tongue meets mine and they dance together like they always have.

He pushes me to the ground, resting on top of me. His hands roam my body and finding my breasts, he squeezes them through my shirt and I can't stop the moan that escapes.

"God, I've missed you," he whispers. His mouth quickly moves from my lips to my neck and then over to my ear. "Please, Maddy, I need you."

"Yes," comes out of my mouth before I realize what I'm saying. I need to feel him too.

"Let's go." He gets up, grabbing my hand and pulling me toward the boat house.

We walk upstairs and there isn't a bed, but Trent finds a blanket, sprawling it on the floor. He leads me down to it, joining me. His mouth covers mine again, urgent and demanding. I feel his hands go up my shirt, pulling down my bra to release my breasts.

"Please, Trent. I need you inside of me," I plead with him.

"You will have me soon, but I need to explore your body more. I've missed it." He pushes up my shirt, lifting it over my head. Then he releases my bra with one hand, pulling the straps down my arms and freeing my breasts for his viewing. "So fucking perfect, Maddy." He bends down, taking my breast in his mouth, licking my nipple, and making it peak while massaging the other one with his thumb.

"God, Trent," I moan, arching my back.

His hand runs down my side, placing his finger along the waistline of my jeans. "You make it hard to go slow."

He undoes my pants, pulling my zipper down, and I gasp from the pleasure that is building within me. I need a release and he is making me beg for it.

"Trent," I groan.

"I know, baby. Soon." He puts his finger on the outside of my underwear. "So wet." Pushing my silk panties to the side, he rubs his finger up and down, making me wetter.

I can't take it anymore. I roll him over on his back, pulling off his shirt, unbuttoning his pants, and pulling them down along with his boxer briefs. Trent finds my mouth once again as he grabs my breasts, kneading them together with both his hands, and I shed my jeans and panties.

Straddling him, I slowly let him enter me, trying to control myself. His hands come down to rest on my hips. He moves me closer and then pushes me back from him. It feels so good, I don't want him to stop, but he puts his thumb on my clit, rubbing it gently in a circular motion and it undoes me.

"Trent, harder. I need you harder," I say. He suddenly flips me over, spreading my legs wide and he slams into me over and over again. I hear the wetness between us and I can't hold back anymore. "OHHHHHHH TRENT." I come, feeling him pump into me two times before he releases my legs and falls on top of me.

I hug his naked body to me and he props up on his elbows. "You're so beautiful." He kisses me again, this time slow and easy. Resting his head on my chest, my fingers comb through his hair while his run softly along my ribs. Soothing...comfortable...home.

"Oh shit," I whisper to myself when I wake up the next morning. I know I am naked before I even get up. "Shit, shit, shit," I repeat, looking over at Trent lying naked under the blanket I just escaped from. Feeling around for my clothes, I scramble to get them on so I can get out of this boathouse. When I stand up, I have to immediately sit back down. The room starts spinning and I think I am going to be sick.

"Ahh...come on, I'm not that bad," Trent's voice startles me and I jump.

"Trent, we shouldn't..." He puts his finger to my lips.

"Don't even say it, Maddy. What happened last night was a long time coming." He moves his finger, kissing me and I think I might actually throw up in his throat.

"I don't think so. It was a mistake, Trent." I push him back onto the blanket.

"You can't deny this, Maddy. We have been meant to be together since we were little. You are my soul mate," Trent says, moving closer again.

"Oh Trent, I think I am just an easy lay for you." I get up and walk unsteadily down the steps away from Trent.

Running has been my release since my dad died. The more that's on my mind, the longer I run. I might hit my record today.

Once I hit the porch, the cool Wisconsin morning breeze hits my face. I look out, noticing that the sun is starting to burn the dew off the grass.

I decide on the Whitetail Trail, which means I have to follow the blue triangle signs. The clear air up here feels good going in and out of my lungs. It makes the running that much more enjoyable.

The fact that I can never face Gabe again is the first thing that goes through my mind. God, he was right to tell me he didn't think it was a good idea. Whatever has been going on between us will be over now.

Trent is another story. He seems genuine, but he always does until he breaks me in two again. Do I give him another chance? No, I will not do it to myself again. Whatever happened last night is over and done with, and there's nothing I can do about it now. Trent Basso has to get out of my life if I am ever going to survive.

With a mile left of my run, I slow down to absorb the scenery. The tall trees are just starting to get their leaves after a long hard Wisconsin winter. I am just about to exit the trails and head back to the main road when I hear footsteps behind me. I don't have to turn around to know who it is. Rolling my eyes, I say, "Trent, for the love of God, can you leave me alone?"

"I don't know who Trent is, but seeing you in those shorts, I know why he won't leave you alone," a deep voice that I don't recognize says. I can tell he is a couple steps behind me and I don't want to waste time turning around. I don't know if I can outrun him, but I have to give it a shot. I run as fast I can toward the cabin and when I get to the front of the house, I run right into Trent.

"Whoa baby, what is it?" he asks, holding me tight.

"There was…" I can't breathe between the running and crying. "A man." I take a deep breath. "He was following me."

"Stay here." He sits me on the porch and walks a little way down the road. A couple of minutes later, he returns, shaking his head.

"What did he look like? I didn't see anyone." He motions me inside.

"I never turned around, I just ran," I say, staying put on the rocking chair on the porch. I can hear laughing in the kitchen, but I am not up for being around everyone.

"I wish you could describe him, but you did the right thing by running away." He puts his arm around my shoulders and pulls me close to him. "It's okay, I have you now. No one is going to hurt you, but." He holds me close, trying to stop me from shaking. "Please don't go out running by yourself anymore."

"You don't have to worry about that," I confirm.

After that incident, Trent and I stay close all week. I still have no desire to get back together and we don't sleep together again, but I do laugh at his jokes and sit next to him on the couch. I even let him kiss me goodnight a few times. It all makes me more confused. Is Trent really ready to have a relationship? I am just not ready to answer that question yet.

Sunday afternoon, everyone is packing up and I know I have to say goodbye to Trent. Kenna has gotten used to him being around me again. Although she gives him dirty looks, she never verbally attacks him again.

Trent walks over to my Jeep, wrapping his arms around me from behind. "I'm going to miss you," he whispers in my ear while nipping at my neck with his mouth.

I turn around, pulling myself out of his arms. "Trent, I can't get back together with you yet. Let's see how you do when we aren't around each other," I say.

"I thought we were well on our way," he says, confused.

"You have always been good when we were around each other, it's the distance thing you need help with. Let's see where this takes us, okay? We can decide if we want to do this at graduation."

"Are you kidding me, Maddy?"

"No, these are my rules. If you want me, Trent, you are going to have to prove yourself before I get involved again," I say, leaning against my truck.

"Alright." He shakes his head, smiling. "I'll prove it, but Maddy..." He leans in close to me. "You better be ready to be swept off those beautiful feet." He kisses my neck and disappears back to his truck.

"Ready, Maddy?" Colt comes up, throwing his bag in the back.

"Yeah..." I touch my neck. "Yeah, let's get out of here."

We have two months until graduation, long enough for Trent to prove if he really wants to be a part of my life. I am keeping to my word this time. The problem, of course, is Gabe. I don't know what to tell him, but I know I have to say something before he finds out from someone else. He hasn't talked to me since he hung up on me that day, so I am not sure it is even his business anymore.

When I get back to our house, I go up to my room to call Gabe. My fingers hover over his name, but I can't make myself press the call button. Then my phone starts vibrating in my hand and I see Gabe's picture, my heart plummeting. I can't believe I'm going to do this to him.

"Hello," I say as though I don't know it's him.

"Please tell me what I just heard is not true," he says, his voice dripping with anger.

"Gabe, let me explain," I say, not sure what I am going to say.

"No need, Maddy. If you want to chance yourself with him again, I am not going to talk you out of it."

"Gabe…"

"But do not come to me when he breaks your heart. Not *if* Maddy, *when,* because you know he will. You also know where I stand with you and I refuse to do this anymore," he snaps.

"Let's remember, Gabe, you are the one who walked away from me. You are the one who couldn't break your promise to Trent," I say, angry.

"I thought what we had meant more to you, but I guess I was wrong. I actually believed you would pick me over him. How ridiculous was I? Have a great time with my brother for however long it lasts." He hangs up on me, again. Ugh.

I lie down on my bed and the tears start once again. I think I have cried more in the last year than I have in my whole life. It kills me the way Gabe talked to me, but it hurts more knowing that he just thinks I'm some stupid girl following a guy who will break her heart. A knock on my door pulls me out of my misery.

"Come in," I say, quickly wiping away my tears.

"It has been a total of four hours. Tell me he hasn't already broken your heart?" Kenna comes in the room and sits on my bed.

"It's not Trent, its Gabe. He found out about me and Trent, and I just got off the phone with him."

"Did you honestly think he would be cool with this?" she asks, the condescension clear in her voice.

"No, I just wasn't prepared for how I would feel, knowing he hates me."

"Oh, Maddy. Gabe could never truly hate you. But I don't know what to tell you." She wraps her arms around me, giving me a hug.

We both know there is nothing she can say that will make the situation better, so I let her hold and comfort me.

The two months leading to graduation go by fast. Trent has stuck to his word, calling me every day and even coming up on two different weekends. I still am not committed to making our relationship work yet, but he's making great strides. Gabe never called me again and I don't have the nerve to call him. I miss talking to him, but I know I can't have both of them in my life.

Graduation is here and we are all getting ready when Trent walks into our house; his graduation was last weekend. We are going back to Belcrest for two weeks, and then I am moving to New York with Ian. Trent is going there to play for Soccer National League after being signed at the end of this past season.

Mackenna and Bryan are staying in Belcrest. Bryan has gotten a job across the border in Illinois, but it will be close enough for them to stay in our hometown. Why they want to stay there, I have no idea. What Kenna doesn't know is that Bryan is asking her to marry him tonight after our party.

"Let's get going, graduates. Party time is over." Trent looks delectable in his tailored blue suit.

"Party time is tonight," Colt yells over to him, fixing his cap in the mirror.

Trent walks over to me, grabbing my gown from my hands. "Let me." He holds it open while I put my arms in it, covering up my navy and white dress. "You look beautiful...as always." He kisses my cheek.

Graduation goes off without a hitch, and afterward, we have a party to celebrate. Trent spends the night...in my bed. Nothing happens, but it feels good waking up in his arms.

I don't know if it is the alcohol or nerves about what the future might hold, but I suddenly feel sick and have to rush to the bathroom. I throw up and my body feels cold and clammy. This is the worst hangover I have ever experienced, and I didn't even drink that much.

Two days later at the Basso's, I still don't feel any better. I can't eat anything and I am throwing up every morning. I lie in bed most of the day, moving only between the bed and the couch.

I think we both are refusing to admit what the problem might be. Ignorance is bliss for us, but after day three, I know we have to do it. I tell Trent to go and buy a test and he nods in agreement.

Luckily, his parents are out of the house running errands in town, so we sneak up to the bathroom and I pee on the stick. We sit on the edge of his bed, setting the timer on my phone. He holds my hand while we wait in silence.

My alarm rings and I slowly walk over to the stick on his nightstand. Before I get there, he grabs the stick and says, "No, we aren't doing it here." Holding my other hand, he pulls me out of the house. He heads to the old barn where it all began, and we climb the ladder up to the second floor.

"Alright, are you comfortable, Maddy?" he asks.

"Yes. Are you ready?" I ask him back.

He pulls the stick out where we can both see it, and I close my eyes for a second before looking down.

"Two lines means?" Trent asks.

"I'm pregnant," I sigh.

Chapter 20 – Present Day

I have had enough heart-to-hearts today. The last thing I need is a lecture from Mrs. Basso.

"Are you out for a run?" Her eyes examine me up and down.

"I was...yes," I say, trying to pull down my shirt and shorts as she appraises me.

"Walk with me, will you?" She motions the way I just came from.

"Um..." I stutter, trying to think of an excuse.

"Please, Madeline. We need to talk," she says, her voice sounding a little softer.

"Okay." I turn around, joining her. She cut off her long blond hair, but the shortened style fits her, bringing out the blue eyes she shares with her boys. Wearing a pair of workout pants and t-shirt, I assume she just came from the gym. She has always been concerned with staying fit.

"How is New York?" she asks. Seriously? She is going to try and have a casual conversation with me?

"It's okay," I shrug.

"Have you found a decorating job yet?" She looks over at me, taking a drink of her water bottle.

"Not a permanent one yet, no," I admit, keeping my eyes forward.

"That's a shame," she says, sounding genuinely sympathetic. I still have no idea what this is all about.

"Well, it's a hard business to get into. I knew it when I decided on it as a major." I shrug my shoulders.

"You're talented, you will find something. Maybe you should consider something outside of New York." I can't help but glance over at her in surprise. "Don't look so surprised, Maddy. I have always believed in you."

"I guess we will see what the future holds," I respond.

"Speaking of the future, what exactly are your plans?" she questions, her voice sounding cold and indifferent once again.

"Not sure what you mean?" I want to hear her say it.

"Regarding my two sons, I want to know how you think you will rectify this situation," she says, confirming my suspicions as to what this conversation is really about.

"I don't really know," I softly say.

"Which one do you love?" she asks, as though it is as simple as that.

"I love them both," I admit.

"No, you don't. I am actually starting to believe you don't love either one since you are stringing them both along." She stops at a park bench in the middle of our town square, patting the seat next to her for me to join her.

"No, it's not that. It's because I love them both that I don't want to hurt either of them."

"Huh." She looks over at a family with a young girl. The mom is relaxed on the park bench while the dad closely follows the little girl with brown curls, who walks a couple of steps and then falls down. They both laugh, smiling at one another each time she falls.

"I thought that would be you and Trent," she says sadly. I can't have this conversation.

"Sorry." I bite my lip in nervousness. I feel bad that I took that away from her but she will have other chances.

"You think I blame you." It is a statement not a question, but I answer anyway.

"Don't you?"

"God no, Maddy. I don't blame you, it just makes me sad." Her eyes continue to focus on the young family in front of us.

"Do you think Trent is capable of that?" she asks, pointing to them again.

"I thought at one time he was, but I'm not so sure now," I state honestly.

"He has always been about himself. On one hand, I am so proud of his drive and success, but the way he got there leaves something to be desired. I'm not blind to my son's faults, Maddy." Her eyes finally drift from the family back to me.

"He's a good man, Mrs. Basso," I assure her.

"Yes, he is. So is Gabe, even though they are so different."

I nod in agreement.

"Don't get me wrong. I see why you have fallen for them both, even though I'm obviously biased," she says, laughing nervously.

I have no idea what she wants me to say so I just sit beside her quietly

"Listen, Maddy, I am going to cut to the chase, okay?" She turns her body directly toward me, crossing her legs.

"Okay." I gulp hard and angle my body toward her. This is where she tells me to leave her family alone.

"I love you, Maddy. You are the daughter I never had. Ben and I would be happy to have you join our family, but this has gone on too long. Seeing my boys fighting and destroying their relationship is tearing me apart. Do you know Trent is driving back and forth from Chicago because Gabe's at the house? They haven't talked to each other for over two years. If one comes home for a holiday, the other doesn't. I know I have been cold to you, but I see you as the reason my family is in distress." Slow tears start to flow down her cheeks, but she catches them automatically.

"I'm sorry. I know I have caused problems between them over the years. I assumed after I left Trent that they would rekindle their relationship." My stomach hurts, realizing how much I have torn the Basso family apart.

"Are you kidding? It's made it worse." She smirks as though she knows something I don't.

"After hearing what you just said, I am not surprised you hate me. I ripped your family apart."

"I never hated you. I was upset, yes. But someone recently told me that I should talk to you and help you understand where I am coming from."

"Really? Do you mind me asking who?" I know this isn't the time to ask who is trying to get Mrs. Basso to become my ally again, but I am eager to find out.

"Your mother." She smiles up at me. "She has really turned over a new leaf, Maddy. You should be proud of her."

"She's like a new woman," I say, rolling my eyes.

"I know it's hard but give her a chance. Although she has hurt you, she does love you so don't shut her out." She pats me on my knee.

"We'll see," I say, recalling exactly why I left this town in the first place. Everyone likes to get into everyone else's business.

"In regards to my sons, please do me a favor and choose. I thought you had walked away from both of them, but I see my boys fighting over your attention more than ever. I honestly can't take it any longer. I want my family back. I know it's a hard decision, but whatever you decide, they need to know it's final. Once you ultimately choose, the other will have no option but to accept it, and I pray over time their relationship will heal."

"I understand, Mrs. Basso."

"Soon, Maddy, please do it soon. My family is on a tightrope and I am afraid it is going to snap soon, never to be repaired." Her blue eyes are dull with pain as she divulges her worst fears.

"I know. I promise I will." I nod again slightly.

"Thank you. See you tonight," she says, patting my knee once again and leaving me to my thoughts.

I sit on that park bench for another fifteen minutes after Mrs. Basso walks away. I stare at the family across the way. The man bends over, handing their little girl over to the mom and kissing her on the lips. I can't help but smile at them.

Would that have been Trent and I if things were different? If I am being honest with myself, the answer is 'no'. I'm not sure Trent would be able to appreciate a simple life after getting a taste of being a celebrity. He loves the spotlight, the clubs, the fancy restaurants, and everything that comes with being a soccer star.

Looking at the family, I can't help but see Gabe and myself. I know without a doubt that Gabe would put his family first. He would appreciate having a wife and children and would love them unconditionally. A twinge of pain hits me, thinking that might never happen after this morning.

All I know is that Mrs. Basso is right. I am going to have to break one heart or the other, and I'm going to have to do it very soon. I get up and leave the family, who continue to enjoy one another's company, oblivious to the many conflicting thoughts running around in my head.

I come downstairs from showering and getting ready to find the Bar-B-Que already in full swing. All of the bridesmaids are fawning over Lindsey in the living room while drinking their fruity margaritas. I smile as I walk by them, reminded that that's the way it should be. Lindsey should be the center of attention.

Guys are spread out across the backyard, drinking and playing corn hole, while Mitch and Mr. Basso man the grill. Trent is over by Bryan and Ian, tapping the keg. Mackenna is at a table talking with some other girlfriends who are rubbing her belly. I don't see Gabe anywhere. I should have called him or texted him at some point today, but I haven't had the nerve and thought he might need a chance to cool down.

I turn around to go back into the house, thinking I must have missed him, when he walks out onto the porch. I am surprised to see he isn't alone. Caroline's arm is entwined in his, and they're laughing about something, their heads leaned in close. When he finally notices I am standing there, he looks me up and down.

"Oh, hey Maddy," he says, continuing to walk by me. My eyes automatically follow them, but the rest of me is frozen in place. He sits down at a table and she takes the seat next to him, scooting her chair as close as it can get. He looks back up to me, making sure I noticed, and then turns toward Caroline again, putting his arm around her chair.

That ass is trying to make me jealous and damn if it's not working. I can't take seeing him with someone else so I quickly go inside.

The older women are mingled around the kitchen table, laughing and smiling at each other. It is nice to see my mom has friends and I'm beginning to think that Mrs. Basso is right. Maybe she has changed and it is time I give her a chance.

"How are you, sweetheart?" My mom comes up to me, putting her arm around my waist.

"I'm okay, Mom." I lean into her, letting her comfort me.

"You sure? You don't look okay," she remarks.

"Really... I'm fine. Go enjoy yourself." I nudge her toward her friends again.

She follows my instructions and I suddenly realize that, even with all of the alcohol around the house tonight, she and the other ladies aren't drinking any of it. My heart swells a little with hope.

I need to hide out for the rest of the evening so I escape to the family room, where there are no Basso brothers present. All of the older men and Jack's friends have started a euchre tournament. I decide to join in, knowing that it will keep me away from the drama for the night.

Three hours later, it is down to Mitch and me, partnered against Doug and Mr. Basso. Surprisingly, Mitch and I make a good pair, and based on the way he plays euchre, I know that I can trust him with my mother. My dad always said you could tell a lot about someone's character from the way they play cards. Mitch plays honestly but can give and take a little trash talk, telling me he is a good guy with a great sense of humor.

During the last two rounds, the older women come down to watch their loved ones play cards. My mom's eyes light up when she sees that Mitch and I are partners. Trent, Bryan, and Kenna come in too, complaining about the mosquitos. I don't see Gabe and I work hard to keep my mind focused on the cards, rather than what he and Caroline are doing.

Mr. Basso and Doug end up winning the tournament, but Mitch gives me a huge hug, complimenting my playing after the game is over. He doesn't seem upset that we didn't win, and even laughs when Doug puts an 'L' on his forehead, implying that he is a loser. A man that can handle defeat with grace is another good sign.

The party dwindles down after the tournament and Ian is anxious to cash in on my promise to go out. As I change into dance club appropriate clothes, Ian says, "Please don't kill me, Maddy."

"What did you do, Ian?" I ask, already annoyed.

"I might have invited a couple people outside to go with us." He winces, biting his lip and trying to act innocent.

"What people, Ian?" I grab my short pink skirt.

"A couple of Jack's friends, a couple of bridesmaids, and maybe Trent."

"In other words, Gabe, Caroline, *and* Trent?" I ask, hoping he's going to tell me that I'm wrong.

"Maybe." His high-pitched voice confirms that I am right.

"Ian…I have managed to avoid drama all night. And now I'm supposed to hang out with all three of them? Well, at least Kenna can help me run interference."

"Um…Bryan and Mackenna left. She wasn't feeling good," Ian says, obviously sorry for having to relay the news.

"You owe me so big. You better find some gay guy to take Trent off my hands," I joke.

"I would be happy to oblige," he laughs.

On top of everything, Gabe is going to drive us since he has the most room. I am surprised Trent seems alright with this, since Mrs. Basso said they aren't on speaking terms. I guess he figures Gabe is with Caroline so it won't make much of a difference. Now there's a depressing thought.

The club is packed with a line out the door. For once, Gabe is the one who gets us in rather than Trent. Apparently, he knows the doorman from college, and he even scores us VIP passes to the upstairs bar and lounge. Of course, Ian isn't having any of that. He is here to meet some guys and dance, and therefore deserts us five minutes after we enter.

The remainder of us sit in a round booth, holding two different conversations. Caroline seems to want Gabe all to herself, placing her back to Trent and I. Trent is trying to hold a conversation with me, but I just stare at the dance floor, occasionally glancing at Gabe from the corner of my eye. The waitress comes over and I

immediately order tequila shots. Gabe declines, but Trent and
Caroline join in.

Two rounds later and I am ready to dance. I grab Trent, leading
him to the dance floor. We snake our way to the center of the crowd,
and I notice that Gabe and Caroline have come up right behind us.

Trent wraps his arms around me tight, placing his hands on my
hips and guiding them to the rhythm. I place my hands on his
shoulders, moving my body up against his. Looking over Trent's
shoulder, I can see that Caroline has her ass in Gabe's crotch,
circling it while bending down and touching the ground. Gabe is
holding her hips firm to his body, but his eyes are holding mine.

We continue to dance like this until I am not able to watch
anymore. I pull Trent over to the bar for another round of shots and
take two to his one. I can sense the alcohol running through my
body, and love how it makes me feel loose and carefree.

We hit the dance floor again and Caroline is still grinding on
Gabe's crotch. Does she not have any other moves? The dance
competition that Caroline and Trent are not privy to continues, with
both Gabe and I trying to make each other more jealous by the
minute.

The competition ends when Caroline moves her body up Gabe's,
kissing his neck and sucking his earlobe. He leans into her and looks
as if he is going to kiss her. I can't handle it any longer.

"I have to go to the bathroom," I whisper in Trent's ear.

"I'll be at the bar," he whispers back.

I walk through the crowd until he can't see me and I sneak out the front door. I need some fresh air and I don't want to deal with him right now.

I am leaning against the side of the building with tears streaming down my cheeks. I need to go home. Although I can't blame Gabe for moving on, I can't stay here and watch them anymore either. I have strung him along for six years, consistently picking his brother over him. I have to let him go, maybe even both of them.

"What the hell are you doing out here, Maddy?" Trent walks out of the club, finding me.

"Sorry, I just needed some air." I quickly wipe the tears from my face, hoping my mascara hasn't run.

"Do you want to talk about that?" he asks, pointing to the inside of the club.

"No," I say, sitting down on the cement sidewalk.

"Do it anyway," he demands.

"What do you want me to say?" I ask.

"Oh good, you found her." Gabe is standing a couple feet away. "I'll see you inside."

"Gabe," I plea and he stops. I see his back rise and fall from his breath.

"What, Maddy?" he responds, not turning around.

"I need to talk to you," I say and Trent gives me a sideways glance. "I'm sorry, Trent. I need a minute with Gabe." I put my hand on his knee, begging him to give us some time alone.

"No," Trent says, staying firm in his spot.

"What?" I ask, astonished.

"I said no," he deadpans.

"Trent, don't be an asshole. Just give us a minute." Gabe turns around, walking toward me.

"Watch it, Gabe," Trent warns him.

"What are you going to do?" Gabe counters, meeting him chest to chest.

Gabe is sober and Trent is a little drunk so I know how this will end, and since I am drunk too, I think I should get in the middle.

"Come on, guys. Let's forget this and talk about it tomorrow. We can go inside to dance some more." I place a hand on each of their chests.

"Stay out of it, Maddy," Gabe warns.

"Don't talk to her like that," Trent says back. They are each pushing harder against my hands and I am slowly losing control.

"She isn't yours, Trent."

"She has and will always be mine," Trent confesses. "So stay the fuck away from my girl, Gabe." I freeze.

"Your girl? How many times have you left *your* girl when she needed you? How many times have I had to step in, Trent?" Gabe spat. "If you treated her like she deserved, or hell, thought of her before yourself, we wouldn't be having this argument, would we?" Gabe yells, and Trent punches him in the mouth.

"You son of a bitch," Trent says, shaking his hand and flexing his fingers.

"You're calling your own mother a bitch, asshole." Gabe punches him back in the stomach but when Trent tries to hit him again, Gabe ducks out of the way.

The boys move away from me. Before I can stop him, Gabe hits Trent in the face again, knocking him to the ground.

"Trent!" I scream, but he doesn't get back up. I rush to his side and look back at Gabe. He is staring down at us with sadness in his eyes.

I stare back at him, begging with my eyes to stop this. To come down and help his brother, but he shakes his head.

"Keep picking up his pieces, Maddy. Pretty soon he will swallow you whole," he says and walks back into the bar.

Chapter 21 – 22 years old

I put my hand on my stomach. I still can't believe that I am carrying Trent Basso's baby. Trent and I told his parents last night, and to say that they weren't thrilled would be an understatement. They were livid. Trent's dad retreated to the living room, turning on some sports channel while silently fuming. Mrs. Basso sat us at the kitchen table, lecturing us on safe sex and how careless we had been. I wanted to tell her that was a moot point, but I sat there quietly, nodding my head in agreement.

A half hour later, Trent and I stood up from the table and Mrs. Basso astonished me by embracing both of us. She murmured how we would get through this and that she loved us both. I hope to be half as great a mother as her.

The next morning, Mrs. Basso comes into my room. I am sleeping in Doug's room, since the Basso's still don't want Trent and I to share a bed. Another moot point, but I don't mention that to them either.

Sitting at the edge of my bed, she puts her hand on my leg. "Maddy, I think I came up with the perfect plan," she says and I sleepily wonder why she isn't saying this in front of Trent.

"Okay," I quietly respond, scooting up against the headboard, and adjusting my tank top to cover my stomach.

"You and Trent go to New York," she says. So far I like her plan.

"Then when you get close to delivery, you come back here to have the baby." Not anymore.

"Why?" I ask.

"Well honey, New York is no place for a baby. Trent will be traveling a lot and you don't want to be left alone." She stands up, straightening out my clothes and putting the freshly laundered ones in the drawers.

"There are a million babies that live in New York," I counter.

"You and Trent are young. If I could come out there and help you I would, but you know I have to work. It's best if you come back. Once Trent's season is over, he can come back here to join you." She is now moving Doug's trophies around, wiping the invisible dust with her hand before placing them back on the dresser.

"Or I could go back to New York when the season's over," I say, raising my eyebrows.

"Maddy...I think you should come here. It's easier that way," she declares.

"Easier for who?" I whisper to myself.

"Just think about it, Maddy. Trent will be busy with the team…you don't know anyone there." Her voice goes soft and it dawns on me what this is really all about.

She doesn't think Trent can be the father, or partner, he should be. She thinks he will leave me there alone in a strange city with a baby, and without anyone to help. If his mom thinks he will desert me, how am I supposed to trust him?

Patting my leg one more time, she looks at me with those pitiful eyes and exits the room with a handful of dirty laundry. Anger absorbs me. How can she not believe in her own son? Does she really think he is that selfish? He will surely prove her wrong. Yes, Trent has been selfish, but I know he will be there for his child. There is no question about it. I believe in him.

Running into Trent's room, I find him still asleep so I crawl in next to him. Hopefully his mom doesn't decide to have a little chat with him right now too.

He wiggles when I wrap my arms around his waist, kissing his back. "Now that's the way I like to wake up," he says groggily, turning around to wrap his arm around me and pulling me closer. "You better hope mom doesn't find you in my bed," he jokes.

"She's already doing laundry," I laugh. There is never a piece of dirty clothes at any given time in this house. I don't know if it's because she has three boys, but she practically lives in that room.

"What do you want to do today?" he asks.

I shrug, happy to stay where I am right now.

"Sounds good to me," he smirks, knowing what I am thinking. "I can't wait until we get to New York, to our very own place. We can stay in bed all day if we want." He plays with my hand that is draped over his stomach.

"Not if your mom gets her wish," I say bitterly. I was going to tell him in a different way, but I am still angry that she doesn't believe in him.

"What are you talking about?" He sits up a little, still holding me close.

"You're mom thinks I should come back here when I am close to having the baby," I divulge.

"Really?" He doesn't seem surprised or upset.

"Trent, she wants me to come back to Belcrest during soccer season." I am trying to get the point across, but he doesn't seem to understand what I am saying.

"I know, maybe she has a point. I don't really want you in New York by yourself with the baby when I'm not there." He grabs my hands and I know where this is going. He only grabs both of my hands when he has something horrible to tell me.

"I'm fully capable of handling myself. Plus Ian is out there, he will help me," I remind him.

"Maddy, that's not the same thing. When the season's over, I can come back and get you and the baby. We can go back to New York, together." I pull away from him, but he continues to hold my hands tight in his.

"Absolutely not. I'm not going to be stuck in Belcrest while you go around doing whatever you want. I'm the one who never wanted to live back here, remember?" I tug hard, releasing my hands from his. I stand up and slam the door behind me.

"Maddy!" I hear him shout from behind the door.

I run down the stairs out the front door and head to the safest place I know.

A few minutes later, I hear footsteps coming up the ladder. Trent sits down next to me, propping his elbows on his knees and leaning against the hay barrel.

"I'm sorry, Maddy. I never meant for you to think I was leaving you," he says, sounding regretful.

"I just feel like your life will remain the same and everything I worked for will come to nothing. I will never be a designer. You and your mom want me to stay in the one place I hate to raise our baby. Trent, this is not MY baby, this is OUR baby." I sit cross-legged, playing with a piece of straw.

"You don't think I know that, Maddy. I want nothing more than to raise this baby with you. I'm sorry for being a jerk in there. I honestly was just thinking of you and the baby, I swear." He puts his finger on my chin, raising it up, and lightly brushing his lips with mine. "We will figure this out...together."

"Okay," I say, still unsure how this will all work out, but happy that we are on the same side now.

Two weeks later, Trent and I are getting ready to leave for New York. Mrs. Basso had me go to the doctor to get on pre-natal vitamins and make sure everything was okay. They said that everything looked good, but to make sure I see a doctor when I get there to have the necessary check-ups. They did an ultrasound, which showed that I was ten weeks along.

Trent and I decided we would go to New York and have the baby there. After I deliver, we will decide together what is best for us as a family. He had already rented a one-bedroom apartment in the city before he found out that I was expecting, so we will have to look for something bigger in the coming months. I don't really care where we live, as long as I am with him.

Mackenna is picking me up for some girl time before I leave. Her dad is going to buy a shop for her so that she can open her own photography studio in town. She is so talented, not only with candid shots, but posed pictures as well. Even her landscapes are amazing. I am going to miss her so much. She is the only reason I have contemplated coming home after the baby.

Since I am with Mackenna, Trent is going out with Bryan. It is nice to see their friendship rekindled again. Trent is lucky that Bryan is so forgiving. After Mackenna and I go out to eat at my favorite restaurant and get ice cream at the Dairy Mart, she drops me off at my mom's house to pick up some things I had left there. I figure my mom will be out so I can sneak in, grab my stuff, and then Trent can come to get me after he and Bryan are done.

It isn't surprising to find my mom's house dark and quiet. It is Friday night, the start of my mom's weekend binges. I don't turn on any lights, since I can't bear to see the old ratty furniture and worn-out shag carpeting. There are empty wine bottles on the counter in the kitchen and the fridge is empty, unless you count wine and beer.

Rolling my eyes, I go upstairs. The third stair still squeaks and the railing is missing from when we painted five years prior. I walk past her room, seeing clothes strewn across the floor and bed, along with more wine glasses and beer bottles littering the nightstands. All courtesy of her guests, I assume.

Shaking my head, I take a deep breath and walk the short distance to my room. I can instantly tell that she hasn't stepped foot in here since I last left. Dust coats all of my pictures, my dresser, and even my bedspread and pillows. Opening my closet where clothes are hung from high school, I grab my bag in the back. Trent should be here soon and I want to get out of here as soon as I can.

I take my purple flower photo box, putting it in the bag, along with some other mementos from high school. I am scrambling in my desk drawer, looking for a letter from my dad, when I see a car's headlights in the driveway. Thinking it must be Trent, I run downstairs to open the door for him.

Right before I get to the bottom of the stairs, I hear a key in the lock. Shit, it isn't Trent. I slowly back up the stairs as they enter the house, figuring they will head straight to her room and I can sneak back out, but that damn third stair. My right foot hits it, just as she wobbles past me on her way to the kitchen. She looks over and continues walking so I assume she is too drunk to see me. I continue my retreat upstairs.

"Madeline," she says as she walks back my way. I freeze on the fifth step, praying she passes out. Her drunken partner walks up behind her, glancing my way.

"Hey, I'm Bill." He puts out his hand for me to shake. Is he kidding? I roll my eyes, standing firm on the stairs. He is wearing a silk button-down shirt. All the buttons are unbuttoned, except for the bottom two. His chest is filled with large amounts of black hair. His hair is gelled back and he sports a soul patch right under his bottom lip. The cheap cologne fills my nostrils, making me nauseous. "Alright then." He pulls his hand back, running it through his hair.

His hand grabs my mom's ass, pulls her closer and turns her to face him, immediately thrusting his tongue in her mouth, never once taking his eyes off me.

At this point, bile starts rising up my throat and I know I have to flee this scene before I get sick.

"I will let you two," I say, motioning with my finger "do your…thing." I continue up the stairs quickly, listening to my mother's moans. I imagine he will take her right there in the foyer.

"Are you sure? I would love a mother and daughter threesome…Madeline," he shouts out to me.

I get up to my room and the lock the door.

Automatically, I grab my phone and text Trent to hurry up and get here. I fumble through the rest of my drawers, quickly grabbing what I came here for. I will never return here again.

Once I think I have everything, Trent texts me back. He is on his way, but he and Bryan were at a bar one town over so it might be fifteen minutes or so before he gets here. I decide I will wait outside for him, glad that it's a nice summer night.

I throw my duffle bag over my shoulder and slowly open my door, looking down the hall at my mom's door. It is shut so I quietly slip out of my room, turning off the light as I tiptoe down the hall. When I get to my mom's room, I am relieved to hear silence. Good, they must have passed out. Just as I turn to make my way down the stairs, my mom's door opens up and a gust of musky cologne hits me right in the face.

He is standing in the doorway. My mom is sprawled over her bed with her skirt up to her waist and no underwear on. She is still wearing her red hooker boots, but she is out cold. Fear hits me and I know that I have to get away. I am pretty sure that he can take me, but I figure if I can get down to the kitchen, I can probably find a knife to defend myself.

"I was just coming to get you. Your mom passed out on me," he leers with a sleazy smile across his lips.

"My boyfriend will be here any minute," I warn, and casually start walking down the steps. I don't want to alert him to my plan of defense.

"Don't worry, it will only take a minute. Your mom has already prepped me so I just need you to finish." He follows me down the stairs and I swallow hard. Tears are pricking at my eyes and I am praying that Trent gets here fast. I begin to second-guess my decision to leave my locked room.

When I get to the bottom of the stairs, I debate going left to the kitchen or right to the door. Something tells me to go left so I follow my gut.

"Sorry to disappoint you, but I'm not my mother. The apple didn't fall from *that* tree," I say, turning on the light in the kitchen. My eyes start searching desperately around the countertops.

"No, you're definitely not your mother." He looks me up and down again. "I'm sure you are much tighter." He stays in the doorway, trapping me in.

"Listen…I am not going to sleep with you. My very large boyfriend will be here any minute, so I suggest you get your shit and leave or go upstairs and after my mom sleeps it off, I am sure she will be happy to fuck you." Opening a drawer, I find a knife. Not a big one, but enough to wound him and give me time to get away.

"That's where you are wrong, sweet one," he slurs. He walks over to the fridge and I start making my way to the doorway he came from, the knife behind my back. "You are going to fuck me right here in this kitchen." He cracks open a beer, taking a fast pull from the bottle and slamming it down on the counter.

I turn to run toward the door, but he grabs me around my stomach from behind, throwing me to the ground. The duffle bag slams to the floor and I hear glass breaking. Before I can get the knife out, he is on top of me, unbuttoning my pants. I bring the knife up and he puts his fingers around my wrist bending it back until I release it.

"Did you really think you could hurt me?" His hand reaches down my pants and underwear and I feel his fingers inside of me. I release the tears that are building, letting them spill down my cheeks. I scream for help but I know my mom will never hear me.

Luckily, he has to release my wrist in order to undo his own pants and pull mine down. I pick up the knife again and slash his shoulder with it, attempting to squirm my way out from under him. Crawling backwards, my back hits the wall and I slowly stand up, letting the wall support me.

"You bitch," he spats at me, helplessly lying on the ground holding his shoulder.

"Get the fuck out," I tell him, the bloody knife still in my hands.

"Not on your life, sweet one." He starts toward me and I am prepared to stab him.

"Don't come any closer," I threaten, but he doesn't listen and instead rushes me, pushing my body against the wall.

He grabs my hair, pulling my head down while holding my wrist with the knife down at my side. He licks my neck and says, "You smell so much better than your mother. Like fucking heaven and I can't wait to be inside you." He takes his hand out of my hair to push my pants down, but realizing he needs both hands, he takes the knife and throws it across the room.

Knowing I have no other means of defense, I start begging him. "Please, don't do this." He tosses me toward the stairs and pain flares up to my shoulders as my back hits the second stair hard. He jumps on top of me, managing to pull my pants off completely. "I'm pregnant," I plead, but he doesn't stop.

"Nice try. I bet you are still a virgin which will make this so worth it." He grabs my breast with one hand and moves my underwear to the side with the other. Right before he is about to enter me, I hear my mom's front door open.

"Maddy?" Trent calls. I have never been so thankful and embarrassed at the same time.

"Trent!" I scream and Bill covers my mouth, hoping he won't find us.

Trent comes up, grabbing Bill and throwing him down the stairs. He glances up to me and I see the fury in his eyes. Grabbing Bill by his silk shirt, Trent punches him right across the face, knocking him out. Once Trent knows Bill isn't getting up, he comes over to the stairs, carrying my jeans.

"Maddy, are you okay, baby?" He holds me close to him while I cry into his chest. "Did he…" he hesitantly asks.

I shake my head back and forth. "No, you got here just in time."

"Oh, thank God." He yanks his phone out, calling 911.

"Trent…" I look down at the stair.

"Oh shit, Maddy." He pulls me closer, telling the operator that we need an ambulance right away.

I hear her demanding voice before she reaches my room. "Where is she? Madeline Jennings?"

"Ma'am, are you family?" The young nurse makes her first mistake.

"Yes, why else would I be here?" she exclaims.

"May I ask the relation?" Second mistake for the nurse. One more and she will get the wrath of this woman.

"I am her mother," she surprisingly announces. She's telling the truth. She has always has been more of a mother to me than my own.

"By all means, Mrs. Jennings, go ahead. Room 208," the nurse says apologetically.

The clicking of her heels is loud in the quiet hospital. I knew Trent would call her. I didn't want him to. I already feel so guilty and ashamed, but he didn't know what to do when I shut down.

"Oh, Trent." She embraces him and I can feel both their eyes shift to me.

"Maddy, sweetheart." Her hand touches my back and tears instantly fall from my face. I am facing the window, trying to shut out everything that happened.

"Talk to me," she begs. I can't turn around; I can't face her.

She sits behind me, rubbing my back in small circles while telling me it will be okay. Trent did the same thing, but it's different coming from her. My rapid breathing and gasping to catch my breath through my tears is starting to slow down a little.

"Trent dear, go get something to drink and give us a minute. Your father is in the waiting room down the hall."

He leaves the room and she scoots up so her body rests against the headboard, putting my head in her lap and brushing my hair with her manicured nails.

"Honey, you can talk to me," she softly says.

"I lost it," I whisper into her stomach, tears staining her dress.

"I know, baby. I know." She listens, not saying anything more.

"I shouldn't have gone there. Only shitty things happen to me there. I should have known something like this would happen. It's all my fault," I admit.

"No, Maddy. You didn't deserve what happened to you. Don't you ever think that," she says, stopping her hand for a second.

"Trent must hate me. I killed his child." I start crying harder.

"No, he doesn't." She keeps running her fingers through my hair while I continue to cry.

Eventually, sleeps overtakes me and when I wake up, it's still dark outside and his mom is no longer holding me. Trent is slouched down in the chair next to me, his hand lazily hanging on the side of the bed.

He is so handsome. I imagine what our baby would have looked like. If it was a boy, would it have been the spitting image of Trent? Would he have had those crystal blue eyes? Would he have been athletic like his father or more artistic like me? We will never know because I did something stupid and took that away from us.

"Trent," I whisper. He stirs but doesn't wake up, so I nudge his hand with mine. "Come here." I scoot over on the bed, holding the covers out for him.

A small smile spreads across his face and he climbs in with me. "Always, Maddy." He holds my head in his hands, kissing the top of it. "I will always be here to hold you."

Chapter 22 - Present Day

I help Trent up to his feet when I see some guys and girls taking pictures of us. Here we go again. We will be front page on all of the gossip sites before midnight. I flag down a cab, practically pushing Trent in. Luckily, the few cab companies that operate in this small town hang around, just in case. Once I am in the car, I text Ian to let him know that I will see him back at home.

Trent rests his head against the window with his eyes closed as I think about what Gabe just said. He's wrong when he says that Trent has never been there for me when I needed him. Gabe doesn't know how he picked up the broken pieces when all I wanted to do was curl up and die. Gabe doesn't know that because I never told him.

Sure, he knows about Bill Monroe; the whole town found out about him. He was arrested for sexual assault, pled guilty, and is still serving his twenty-year sentence. But he, along with the rest of the town, doesn't know that I miscarried Trent's baby that night.

I didn't want him or anyone else to look at me differently, so I begged everyone that knew to keep it to themselves. I guess it doesn't matter now since he doesn't want anything to do with me. He walked away from me tonight, and I can't blame him. He deserves better than me.

The cab drops us off at my mom's house and we enter the dark living room. A sense of fear still hits me when I first walk in, but the changes my mom has made help. Also, my therapist has done wonders with me.

"Here you go," I say, handing Trent a bag of frozen vegetables. I am still baffled by the fact that my mom has food in her freezer.

"Thanks," he mumbles.

"Why don't you spend the night here?" I ask.

He smiles brightly and moves to stand up.

"On the couch," I add.

"Yeah...right." His smile falters and he sits back down.

"I'll go get you a pillow and a blanket," I say, leaving the room.

By the time I get back, Trent is already asleep and I hope that he doesn't have a concussion. I decide to curl up on the recliner next to him in case he needs me during the night.

I am jolted awake by a very drunk Ian. "I can't believe you left me there. What the hell, Maddy?"

"They got into a fight, people started taking pictures, and I had to get him out of there," I explain, rubbing my eyes.

"I heard. Some guys I was hanging out with were talking about Trent Basso getting his ass kicked by someone outside. I figured out who the other guy was all on my own."

"Oh great, I don't even want to go online now." I roll my eyes in disgust.

"Um…there is someone at the door who wants to talk to you," Ian says, sheepishly looking at me.

"No..." I can't see him now.

Ian nods his head, raising his shoulders in apology. "I'll stay here and look after Trent."

"I'm sure you will," I joke, getting up.

When I walk around the corner, Gabe is standing by the door, looking at the ground. I see so much sorrow on his face that I almost break down. What have I done to these two brothers?

"Can we go for a walk?" He motions toward the door and I nod my head in response.

"Trent here?" he asks. I nod again.

"Is he okay?" I hear the remorse in his voice.

"Yeah, he'll be fine," I reassure him.

"May I?" He places his hand out, asking permission to hold mine.

"Of course," I respond, letting him entwine our fingers together.

"I'm sorry for what I said, Maddy. I was just so angry after seeing you on the dance floor with him. And I'm sorry for what I was doing with Caroline." He walks us down my driveway toward the main road.

"It's okay, you are probably right. I have always put Trent's life in front of my own." I want to tell him not always, but I don't know if I can.

"Oh Maddy, I didn't mean it like that. I was just pissed that you picked him over me again," he admits.

"But I didn't." I stop walking, looking at the moonlight streaming across his face. God, he's gorgeous. "If you would have stayed yesterday, you would have known that I didn't pick him. I was only comforting him; he is going through a hard time right now."

"You mean his ankle and the fact that he might not play again? Jesus, Maddy, don't you see?" He shakes his head. "You are his crutch, his savior. You are there for him when he feels down or unsure of himself, but as soon as he's better, he drops you. Doesn't it ever bother you that he is never there when you need him?"

It is time he knows the truth, even if I am sure he won't want me anymore. I can't let him to continue thinking that Trent has never stood by my side.

"You don't know this because I kept it from you, but he saw me through a time I didn't think I would survive," I disclose.

"What are you talking about, Maddy?" he asks, sounding confused. From what he knows, he has always been the one there for me. I take a deep breath.

"Remember Bill Monroe and what happened?" I ask, knowing he remembers. You don't forget when someone you love is almost raped.

"Of course," he responds, looking at me with apprehension.

"I was pregnant when it happened." My eyes start to water.

"Don't, Maddy, it's okay. You don't have to tell me this."

"Yes, I do, Gabe. You deserve to know." I wipe away the tears, taking another deep breath so I can speak.

"It was Trent's baby. Well...you probably already figured that out," I say, my voice shaking. "I was hurt badly when I tried to get away that night and I miscarried."

"I'm sorry," he says, his voice a whisper.

"Anyway, Trent and I had plans to move to New York and raise the baby there together. After I miscarried, I shut him out. I couldn't handle it. Your mom came in the hospital room and took over until I cried enough to fill ten buckets."

"My mom knew?" he asks, disbelief evident in his voice that the people he loves had deceived him.

"Yeah, that's my fault. I swore her to secrecy. Anyway, after I got out of the hospital, I couldn't even get out of bed and Trent had to get back to New York to start practice with the team. I told him I wasn't going to go, and that he probably didn't want me anyway since I killed his baby. He stayed back with me, telling the team a personal matter came up and he couldn't make it. The general manager threatened to take away his signing bonus if he didn't get there the next day, but Trent stayed with me for two more weeks. He would come into my room at night and hold me when I cried, but gave me the space I needed during the day." I shudder, remembering the darkest time in my life.

Gabe squeezes my hands in encouragement. I begin walking again, following the same path that I ran earlier.

"One night, Trent came in my room and I assumed he was going to climb into bed with me, but he was fully dressed with his backpack on. He told me to get my ass out of bed and get dressed. I fought him but he dragged me out of the bed, throwing my clothes at me. When I still wouldn't go, he picked me up and put me in his truck. I refused to speak to him so I had no idea where he was taking me, nor did I care really. Then he turned in here," I say, motioning to the cemetery in front of where Gabe and I now stand.

"Oh, Maddy." Gabe seems reluctant to follow me but he does.

"We walked up to my father's headstone. I had been back many times since his funeral, but I knew Trent never came. Him taking me there made me more furious, because it brought back the time in my life that he disappointed me the most. Now he wanted to come here? I started screaming at him, telling him how I felt he had thrown me aside all those years. I told him I hated him and never wanted to see him again, that he should go to New York without me and live the happy bachelor life he's always wanted. Instead of taking me up on my offer, he wrapped his arms around me tightly so I couldn't run from him. He must have held me for fifteen minutes before I was finally too exhausted to continue fighting."

Gabe and I walk through the iron gate and I wipe the tears from my face. He remains silent, giving me time to collect myself and continue.

"I knelt down in front of my dad's headstone, apologizing for what happened, and I was surprised at how much better it made me feel. Trent sat next to me the whole time with his hand on my back.

Then he opened his backpack and pulled out that angel." I point to the small angel statue on the right of my dad's headstone.

"He said that we needed to properly mourn our child and that this statue would represent the baby we lost. That night, Trent and I said good-bye to our baby and I finally started to slowly heal."

I don't tell Gabe about how we stayed there until sunrise and how hard it was for me to walk away, but that Trent gave me the strength to make it down that hill. That was Trent's moment and mine.

My fingers brush along the angel and slow tears run down my cheeks. It was the worst time of my life but I survived it.

"I know it's not enough, but I'm so sorry," Gabe says, pulling me from my thoughts. "I wish you would have told me so I could have helped, but I understand why you didn't." He puts his arm around my shoulders, pulling me to him. "That was you and Trent's time. He needed to see you through that and I am glad he stepped up to the plate."

"I'm sorry I never told you, and I understand that you will look at me differently now." I get up quickly and start to walk back down the hill.

"Mad, wait up," he says, jogging up behind me. He pulls my arm, turning me around to face him.

"You want to know what I see?" he asks but I don't answer him.

"I see the most beautiful girl I have ever met. It's not your looks, it's you. You are strong and independent and what you just told me proves it to me all over again. What you had to go through shows just how much you can persevere when the odds are against you. I love you so much and I want to be with you in every way possible. I want to be there for you when you need me, to reassure you of your strength when bad things happen. I want to be the reason for your smiles and laughter. I want to make you happy and feel loved. So the only difference in how I feel is that I now love you even more than I did before," he says and then takes a deep breath.

"But I can't do it anymore, Maddy. I can't keep putting myself out there for you to continue to pick him. I am starting to look like a pathetic jackass, and I want someone who wants me just as much as I want them. I want someone by my side that loves me as much I love them. As hard as it is for me, I have to walk away from you." He grabs my hands and squeezes them.

"No, Gabe. I picked you. Please…" I plead.

"Shh…" he puts his fingers to my lips. "Can I have one last kiss?" He leans his head toward me, our lips are barely touching. "Maddy?" He wants permission so I nod my head, tears still streaming down my face.

Once his lips hit mine, I open automatically. If this is my last time kissing Gabe Basso, I don't want to waste any time. His tongue explores my lips and mouth until it finally meets mine. He moans in my mouth and I moan in his. He licks my bottom lip right before he sucks it into his mouth, but comes back to my mouth deeper and harder. I wrap my arms around his neck and it is taking everything in me not to wrap my legs around his waist. Then he pulls away from me.

"It's late. Let's get you home." He starts walking back toward my house. Putting my head down, I follow, trying to think of something to say to change his mind. I love him so much. But I am reminded of the phrase, *If you love them, let them go*. I love Gabe enough to let him find the love he deserves, and he definitely deserves someone better than me.

Chapter 23 – New York

Trent and I left for New York two days after our intimately private funeral. Luckily, the general manager of his soccer team was understanding after Mrs. Basso called him and explained the situation. Unfortunately, Trent was not as understanding that his mom called his new boss. In her defense, she was able to get his signing bonus back. She's a persuasive woman.

We moved into the one bedroom apartment he had rented in the city. It was minimally furnished with a sofa you could spring a quarter off of, end tables that were nicked and scratched, and a bed that sagged a little in the middle. But it was ours and it was in a nicer part of town than most kids directly out of college should have been able to afford. Trent is a great soccer player and they pay him well, considering he hasn't yet proved himself in the league.

He is supposed to practice for a month and then start up with the team. Until then, he doesn't have to travel, which is great for us. We explore the city, finding small local restaurants and places to eat and hang out. Trent goes to practice during the day and the nights are ours. We spend time together enjoying each other's company.

A week after we arrive, I am lying on the couch and flipping through channels when Trent walks into the room, holding out his hand.

"Where are we going?" I ask, taking his hand.

"Surprise," he says, leading me into the bathroom.

"Oh, Trent," I sigh. The bathtub is filled with rose petals. There are red, yellow, pink, and white petals floating on top of the water. Lit candles illuminate the small space. "It's beautiful."

"It's for you." He kisses the back of my neck slowly, pulling up on the hem of my shirt and bringing it over my head.

I feel my body tremble. Trent and I haven't been intimate since the incident and I don't know if I can do it.

"We will take this slow and if you want to stop, just say so. I don't want to rush you. Right now, let's just take a bath." He reaches around my waist, unbuttoning my shorts and they fall to the floor.

He moves in front of me and I notice that he has already removed his shirt and is working on his pants. Kissing my collarbone and neck, I feel his hands move to my back and seconds later, my bra joins my shorts and shirt on the floor.

"You're so beautiful," he whispers in my ear, as his fingers hook the sides of my panties, pulling them down. His body follows his hands and he trails soft kisses across my stomach.

"I love you, Maddy," he says, coming back up to my lips once I step out of my panties.

I am standing there with my hands at my side, unsure of what to do.

"Come on. Let's get in while it's still hot." He holds my hand as I step into the water.

My eyes close when the warmth of the water surrounds me, making me feel like I'm wrapped in a cozy cocoon. I sit with my knees propped up, holding my legs close to my body. Before I realize it, Trent is across from me and his wet chest has rose petals stuck to it.

"Relax," he says, slowly bringing my legs to him and massaging my feet. "Lean back, baby." I follow his instructions, resting against the warm tub and stretching my legs on top of his. He moves his muscular legs to the outside of my hips, and brings out a jar of salt scrub. Taking one of my feet out of the water, he rubs the salts into my foot, deeply massaging the bottom with his thumb. I moan in delight. He follows suit with my other foot and then begins to move his hands up my legs. Instinctively, I pull away.

"It's okay baby, it's just me." I settle down again at the sound of his voice. "Every inch of you is gorgeous. How did I get so lucky?" He is giving my leg small kisses as he comes closer to me.

I swallow a hard gulp, reminding myself that this is Trent.

His hands move across my body like silk and a rush of arousal hits me. His fingers brush between my legs and I pull them together, but he uses his other hand to gently open me up again.

"You okay, baby?" he asks and I nod, though I'm still unsure. "You feel so good," he says, inserting a finger, "and so wet." He kisses my shoulder.

"Trent," I moan.

"Yeah, baby?" he asks.

"Don't stop, it feels so good," I admit.

"Never."

We stay in the bath, touching and feeling each other until the water goes cold. Trent wraps me in a towel, carrying me into our bedroom. More rose petals are sprawled across our bed and candles are lit on the dresser. He lays me on the bed and brings out a bottle of lotion. He spreads it across my legs, my stomach, my arms, and finally my breasts, as he sucks on each of my nipples.

He crawls on top of me and I can feel the tip of his erection at my entrance. I immediately tense, but he lifts my chin with his finger, saying, "Look in my eyes, baby." When I look in his beautiful blue eyes, I only see him.

He enters me slow and steady, and starts moving in slow circles as the pressure starts to build inside of me. I place my hands on his shoulder blades, pulling him closer to me. I want his body against mine. I need to feel the familiarity of us together, making love.

Trent rests his arms on either side of my head, kissing me slowly while gently thrusting into me. I moan into his mouth, the pleasure surging through me. Not being able to hold off any longer, we both groan as we release together. He stays inside of me for a while after, continuing to kiss me and say sweet things. Then Trent cleans me up and comes back to bed, cradling me in his arms. We talk until we fall asleep and he never lets me go.

After that night, sex consumed our lives daily. We christened every inch of every room in our small apartment. Fortunately, Mrs. Basso had talked me into going on the pill when we were at the hospital, so we didn't have to worry about condoms.

A month later, Trent started playing soccer with the team, which took him away from New York a lot. Ian frequently slept on our couch, keeping me company. I landed a job as an assistant to an interior designer, which pretty much meant I answered phones and checked on orders. I didn't mind though because at least it was something to get my foot in the door. Not to mention, I wanted to be available when Trent was home so it really was perfect.

The first two months were great. Trent would rush home after practice or an away game and we would spend every moment together. It wasn't until a game against DC United where Trent was put in as a starter that things changed.

He made headlines by scoring three goals and suddenly he had a following. He continued to be a top scorer, which only brought more media attention to him. Unbelievably, he led his team to the Soccer National League cup and they won, resulting in a new lucrative contract and making him the top earner in the history of the league.

Trent started changing before my eyes. He moved us from our tiny one bedroom to a high rise, two-bedroom condo with a doorman, saying he wanted to keep me safe. After practices, he began to stay late, stating he needed extra workouts to increase his muscle mass in order to remain a top performer. I had to admit that his body was amazing before, but it was downright incredible now. I just hoped I was the only one getting to enjoy it.

Our quiet evenings at home have now been replaced by shows, clubs, and appearances around the city. Our cheap diner dinners consisting of milkshakes and cheeseburgers seem to be history, and instead we are eating high-priced meals in candle-lit restaurants with a bottle of wine.

In the beginning, it was exciting but I have grown tired of it and prefer staying home now while he goes out. Slowly, I've stopped hearing from him when he's out of town, and he no longer rushes back to me. He returns long after I go to bed and I sneak off to work, trying not to wake him.

We don't make love anymore, just fast sex that leaves me unfulfilled. Trent's arms no longer wrap around me securely at night and instead, our backs face each other in the king-size bed we share.

One day after a long day at work, I turn the doorknob and Trent is in a tuxedo, smiling and holding a bouquet of roses.

"What are you doing?" I ask.

"Come with me." He pulls me by my hand to the bedroom.

On the bed, a black gown is laid out with a pair of strappy high heels. "It's stunning," I say.

"No, you will be stunning in it," he whispers in my ear, standing behind me.

"Where are we going?" I ask.

"Surprise," he says. "You have half an hour to get ready."

I hurriedly take a shower, curl my hair, and put my make-up on. I can't keep the smile off my face. I am thrilled to have my Trent back. Questions fill my mind, namely whether or not is he going to propose and whether or not I'm ready for that.

He helps me into my dress, kissing my neck and shoulders like he used to, while telling me how beautiful I am and how much he loves me.

"Tell me where we are going," I beg him.

"No way," he says, slipping something around my neck. "Pull that gorgeous hair up." He clasps it shut and I feel it with my hands.

"Trent, you shouldn't have." I can feel the cold element on my chest.

"You deserve it, baby." He kisses my shoulder, leading me over to the mirror.

He stands behind me as I admire the exquisite ruby necklace that hangs from my neck. "I love it," I say, staring at him through the mirror.

"I love you," he says back at me through the mirror. "Now let's go and celebrate."

"What are we celebrating?" I ask, walking down the hall and throwing my cell phone in the new clutch Trent bought me.

"I'm not saying anything until we get to the restaurant," he says, grabbing his wallet and keys.

"Can you at least tell me the name of the restaurant?"

"Sure. Sparrow's, your favorite." He smiles back at me and I don't bother telling him that it's his favorite restaurant, not mine.

"Sounds great," I say instead, smiling in return.

We make our way downstairs and I can't help but notice that there is a limo waiting for us. Trent has gone all out tonight. I look at him and he motions for me to step in first. The limo driver opens the door for us and we climb in. When the limo pulls away from the curb, Trent opens a bottle of champagne.

"I can't hold it in any longer." He is giddy with excitement. "Maddy, we're going to Chicago. I've been traded." He hugs me in a tight embrace.

"What?" I ask quietly.

"Did you not hear me? New York traded me. I'm going to Chicago. You think we had it good here, you should see how much they are going to pay me." The gleam in his blue eyes is shining bright. Trent is happier than I have ever seen him, and I don't want to disappoint him by telling him that I don't want to leave New York.

"That's great, Trent. I'm so proud of you," I say, hugging him back.

We pull up to Sparrow's and there are loads of photographers outside. Ever since Trent led the team to the Soccer National League cup, there always seem to be paparazzi around, following us to shows and restaurants and trying to snap pictures of us. Gossip columnists have started calling him 'the sexiest guy in soccer'.

Trent gets out of the limo first, holding his hand out for me to join him. I can hear the clicks of numerous cameras and I hope that I look good enough to be seen on his arm. The last thing I want is to be publicly humiliated.

We enter the restaurant and are led toward a table with about fifteen other people.

"I thought it was just us celebrating," I say, pulling on his arm before we get to the table.

"It will be. Later, baby." He brings us to the table and everyone starts clapping for him. "Thank you, everyone." He pulls my chair out for me and I smile widely, trying to hide the disappointment of having to share Trent as best as I can.

He takes the seat between some red-headed girl and me. I don't recognize anyone and can only assume that these must be the people he hangs out with when I don't go out. "Everyone, this is Maddy." He puts his arm around me, kissing my temple and three women give me dirty looks.

I wave my hand 'hello' to everyone.

That is about the last attention I get from Trent for the rest of the night. He is Mr. Comedian, entertaining the table like he is being paid. The girls are fawning over him and the guys are high-fiving him. No wonder he loves this crowd; they kiss his ass.

They laugh at every joke he tells, even when it's about them. I can't help but notice that no one else makes fun of him though. They compliment him every chance they get, telling him how awesome he is and what a great game he played and how Chicago is so lucky to have him and how New York is stupid for trading him.

The scary part is that Trent enjoys every bit of it. His laugh isn't even genuine. It's some transformed mixture of sounds I have never heard from him. This is the new Trent and I can't stand this obnoxious self-centered man.

I am thankful when the check comes, and I'm not sure why, but I'm somewhat surprised when it is handed to Trent. No one at the table offers up any money. Wasn't this a congratulatory dinner for him? These people are mooches; they don't care about Trent.

Walking out to the foyer of the restaurant, the red-headed girl, whose name apparently is Cammi, comes up to Trent and winds her arm through his. "Tre, let's go clubbing…to celebrate."

Trent looks over at me and I shake my head no.

"Sorry Cam, not tonight," he says. *Cam? What the hell?*

"Oh come on, Tre, you never pass up clubbing," she whines and a brunette comes up on the other side, pushing between Trent and me. *Oh, hell no.*

"I am sure that Madeline," the brunette looks at me questioningly, as if she's confirming my name, "can make it home by herself. You can even give her the limo and we can take cabs."

I swear if Trent goes along with this, I will strangle him right here in front of all his 'friends'.

Trent looks at me like he is trying to figure out if I will be okay with it, but then says, "No, no. Maddy and I are going home. Have a great evening, ladies. Gentlemen." He starts to walk away but both ladies kiss him on the cheek and everyone whines to him when we leave. *Sorry mooches, I guess you'll have to buy your own drinks tonight.*

The limo is already waiting for us when we exit the restaurant. I don't wait for Trent to finish shaking hands before I hop in. You would swear he is a rock star the way he acts. By the time Trent joins me I am fuming, but I don't want to start a fight in front of the driver so I wait until we get home.

I am quiet the whole way home and surprisingly, Trent is too. Both of us stare out separate windows. He opens the limo door before the driver can even get there. I walk by, thanking the driver and greeting our doorman with a smile.

"Good evening, Ms. Jennings. Mr. Basso," he says as we walk quietly to the elevators.

"Benny." Trent nods at him.

We are silent the whole way up the elevator, down the hallway, and through the front door. Once the door shuts, I retreat into our bedroom, slamming the door behind me.

"What the hell, Maddy? Are you going to tell me why you are so pissed off?" Trent opens the door, standing in the doorway.

"What do you think? Are you sleeping with just Cammi or both of them?" I ask.

"Are you crazy? No, I'm not sleeping with them." He starts loosening his tie while walking into the closet.

"Whatever. You didn't seem to mind her hand on your thigh," I spat, taking off my shoes.

"Gimme a break, what was I supposed to do?"

"Tell her to stop or simply remove it and place it back in her lap. Take your pick, *Tre*," I say with a sneer.

"Why don't we talk about what this is really about?"

"What do you *think* this is about?" I stand with my back to him and he unzips my dress.

"You don't want to leave New York," he states knowingly.

"You're right, I don't. But that isn't why I'm mad. Are those the people you go out with when I don't go?"

"Yeah, some of them." He shrugs his shoulders.

"They're moochers, Trent. They are using you for your money and connections." I strip out of the dress, placing it on the bed and grabbing my pajamas from the drawer. "You are different with them and I don't like it."

"What do you expect? You never want to go out, all you want to do is lie around this apartment or hang out with Ian. I needed to find friends and I like my group. I have fun with them. Remember what fun is like, Maddy?" I turn to look at him and see that he is now wearing black slacks with a button-down shirt.

"Are you going back out?" I ask, pulling my long hair in a ponytail.

"Yep," he says.

"Trent, we need to talk about this. You are just going to leave?" I ask.

"Yes, I am. I don't want to fight. I have worked my ass off to get where I am and tonight I want to enjoy this. I deserve it."

"Don't you want to work this out, Trent?" I ask, knowing the answer already. This is the way Trent says goodbye. He ignores whatever it is until it goes away. He has done it to me my whole life.

"Jesus Maddy, what do you want from me? I pay for this apartment, I buy the food, and I get you nice things. All I get in return is grief from you. It's always something else I should be doing," he says, starting to walk down the hallway.

"Trent!" I call out but all I hear is the door slam shut. "Good-bye," I whisper to myself. A few tears fall from my face, but there are no sobs or screams that come out. I can still breathe fine as I walk down the hallway to pack my suitcase.

A half hour later I have two suitcases packed. I leave the black dress hanging on my side of the closet with the shoes under it. The necklace now lays on his nightstand. I don't leave a note. He knows why I am leaving and I am quite certain he won't come looking for me. The pictures of us remain on the dresser and walls, and he can keep all the items I decorated our apartment with. I want nothing from this place or Trent.

Ian is at the door to help me out. He is taking me in until I can find my own place. I don't cry as I lock the door and slide the key under for Trent to find when he comes home tonight. I give Benny a hug good-bye at the elevator and he doesn't ask me why I'm leaving. Ian hails a cab and I take one last look at my place with Trent. Not one tear falls from my eyes as I climb into the cab.

Ian cradles me in his arms but there are still no tears. I am sad for what we have become, but I should have left a long time before now.

A month later I am walking past a newspaper stand on my way to work. My boss has actually given me more responsibility lately and I am still living with Ian. It turns out his roommate wanted out, but didn't want to leave him in a lurch. A newspaper reads, *Soccer dream gone to Chicago.* There is a picture of Trent with Cammi by his side, kissing his cheek and crying. I never heard from him after I left.

His mom tried to call me a few times but I never answered. Kenna calls me every day. She never tells me what everyone is saying, even though I know what they think. I don't care though, I know the truth. The online gossip had a field day with our breakup, showing Cammi instantly taking my place and saying that Trent's small-town girlfriend just couldn't compare to the city girls Trent was bedding. I choose not to believe it. I know firsthand how they lie and convolute stories to boost sales.

I see my therapist twice a month and my life is continuing without Trent Basso. I am making it on my own and I love it.

Chapter 24 – Present Day

After a horrible night's sleep, I make my way downstairs where I smell bacon and eggs. My mom and Mitch are in the kitchen, laughing with each other. I see Mitch playfully smack my mom's butt and she turns around, pretending to be irritated. He wraps his arms around her, kissing her, and the genuine happiness on my mom's face is evident. I am so happy for her. She obviously has worked hard these last two years to stay sober and get her life straightened out.

Trent and Ian are still asleep in the family room so I go over and make sure Trent isn't unconscious. The bruise across his cheek is pretty bad and I cringe, thinking of how upset Lindsey might be with the pictures. We will definitely have to use some heavy make-up.

When I walk in the room, I hear Trent snoring. Breathing a sigh of relief, I decide to go in the kitchen and help my mom and Mitch. They are sitting down at the table eating. Mitch is reading the paper, telling my mom about a storyline and my mom is fiddling on her phone. They look like a couple that has been together for years.

"Hey guys," I announce, making my way to the coffee maker.

"Good morning, Maddy," Mitch's deep cheerful voice says to me.

"Good morning, sweetheart," my mom adds, placing her phone down on the table. "How was last night?"

"It was alright," I answer, wondering what she has already heard.

"Not from what I heard..." she says, raising her eyebrows at me.

"From who?" Ian must have woken up and then went back to sleep.

"It's online, Mad." She holds up her phone smiling and Mitch starts laughing.

"What is?" I walk over to my mom, grabbing her phone. I read the article from one of the gossip columns and laugh. I am bent over, cracking up with Mitch and my mom, when Ian and Trent make their way into the room.

They are both rubbing their eyes and yawning, stopping at the door and looking at the three of us inquiringly.

"What is so funny?" Ian asks, narrowing his eyes at us.

I glance at both of them but I can't control myself long enough to fill them in, so I hand my mom's phone to Ian. Soon he is joining in with us before passing the phone to Trent.

"What the fu--" Trent starts, before Mitch cuts him off.

"Trent," Mitch says sternly. "Ladies." He motions his hand toward my mom and me.

"They have made up stories before but this...this is ridiculous." He starts reading the story again.

"I absolutely love it, even if I am the scorned lover." I put my hand over my heart, sighing like Scarlet O'Hara.

"It's alright, Trent, you can admit it. Lots of athletes have come out of the closet recently," Ian jokes, placing his hand on Trent's shoulder and everyone is laughing, except Trent.

"You're telling me they can't see the resemblance between Gabe and me?" Trent shakes his head back and forth, still reading the headline trending the Top Ten. *Trent Basso's high school sweetheart finds out he's gay.* There is a picture of me, leaning against the wall crying, while Gabe and Trent look down at me

"He's your lov-er," I say, resulting in a nasty look from Trent, who obviously does not appreciate my humor at this moment. "Oh Trent, no one believes these things."

"Yes they do, Maddy. After you left me, people honestly thought I was with that Cammi girl. You should have seen how many people yelled things at me on the street. Women would come up to me, calling me a man-whore. Older ladies stopped to tell me girls like her only want me for me for my fame and money, that I should be concentrating on trying to get you to forgive me for cheating. It was unbelievable. The first few times I would argue back, but they never believed me." He finally hands my mom her phone, walking over to the coffee pot.

"Now they will think you cheated on Maddy with Cameron, not Cammi," Ian spouts and the other three of us try to hide our giggles.

"Just let it out guys." Trent gives us permission to laugh and we all oblige.

"The truth will come out. I am surprised there's no picture of the fight," I admit.

"Fight?" Mitch and my mom ask in unison. Ian and Trent both give me a look and I bite my lip in regret.

"Um..." I stumble. Not like they can't see Trent's eye, but they must not have noticed it yet. So I grab Trent's shoulders, turning him around and they both gasp.

"Gabe?" Mitch asks. We both nod our heads, confirming his suspicions.

"Maddy, I need to speak to you." My mom doesn't wait for me to respond before she grabs my hand, pulling me out of the room. Ian raises his eyebrows as I pass him, wiggling his finger back and forth, informing me I am in trouble. I stick out my tongue in response.

Once we get to the living room, my mom sits me down on the new couch. "Maddy, I know you don't want to hear this from me, but you have to put an end to this."

"Don't worry, Mom. I plan on ending everything today," I confirm to her.

"Alright, because if they are physically fighting now, it will only get worse. Now who did you choose?" she asks, smiling at me.

"No one," I confess and a sad expression crosses her face.

"Why?" she questions. "I thought at Great Adventures..." she starts but I interrupt her.

"Gabe told me last night he doesn't want to be with me and I can't blame him." I have to keep telling myself it's for the best, that he deserves better.

"And Trent?"

"I love Trent and I always will, but I just think...I can't." I shake my head and my mom embraces me.

Her show of affection warms me all over. I have missed this my whole life and nothing can compare to be comforted by your mom. I need her to tell me everything will be alright.

Right on cue, she says, "Everything will work out Maddy, just wait and see."

"Maddy, Maddy!" Ian screeches, stopping in his tracks when he sees my mom and me. "Oh sorry," he says, and starts to back out of the room.

"It's fine, Ian. What is it?" I ask, curious what caused him to tear in here like the house was on fire.

"They have the fight on there now." He bites his bottom lip, Ian's tell-tale sign that there is more to the story. "The good news is that you are no longer the scorned lover." He walks back into the kitchen, leaving me to wonder what the bad news is.

I walk into the kitchen, grabbing the phone out of Ian's hands. Scrolling down the article, I see a picture of me standing between Gabe and Trent, my hands on both of their chests. The title reads, *Trent Basso's ex-girlfriend tries to stop boyfriend from hitting him.*

"It will be fine, Maddy. No one believes it anyway," Trent says, repeating my words back to me. He's smiling with his head on my shoulder, looking way too pleased with himself.

I shove his head with my palm off my shoulder. "They're making Gabe into the bad guy," I sulk.

"He is," Trent whispers.

"Trent…please, just be quiet," I say, glaring at him.

"Let's just have some breakfast. Mitch and I made you guys a feast." My mom brings over plates of food to the table.

"What a great idea, Barb," Mitch chimes in.

"You should call him, Trent," I instruct him.

"No way. Why would I?" he asks, looking at me in disbelief.

"To give him a heads up. He knew the doorman at that club. I'm sure his name will be released soon." I bite into a piece of bacon.

"Too late. Update," Ian announces. "*Brothers fight over same girl,*" Ian discloses the headline. "*Trent Basso and older brother Gabe are in love with the same woman, the soccer star's ex-girlfriend, Madeline Jennings.*"

I stand up to go upstairs and get my phone. If Trent isn't going to tell Gabe, I will.

"Let it go, Maddy," Trent yells up to me.

I sit on my bed, grabbing my phone from my purse. I have five texts, two from Ian last night and three from Kenna this morning, insisting I call her immediately. I am grateful that my phone is listed under Ian's name so the press won't find me. After my breakup with

Trent last year, I cancelled my number after being bombarded by so many calls.

Me: Have you been online?

Gabe: No, but already heard.

Me: I'm sorry.

Gabe: It's not your fault

Me: Still...

Gabe: I can handle it

Me: Ok, well...let me know if you need anything

Gabe: Sure

"*A source close to Gabe Basso informs us that the love triangle has been going on for years. Apparently, Ms. Jennings has forced a wedge between the two brothers, who now hate each other,*" Ian reads as I enter the kitchen,

"Just put it away, Ian," I snap. My mom is nervously chewing on her nails while Mitch seems to be comforting her. Trent continues to eat his breakfast like nothing is happening, which only pisses me off further.

"Shouldn't you be calling your agent or PR person to make a statement?" I rudely ask Trent.

"Um...no. They aren't going to do anything. It will die down." He puts another piece of toast in his mouth.

"Trent. For once can you think of someone beside yourself?"

"Ohh...this site says you left Trent for Gabe last year," Ian continues.

"Seriously Ian, enough!" I screech.

"I'm just trying to give you all the juicy details," he says, grinning.

Ignoring him, I glare at Trent as he continues to sip his coffee and eat his breakfast as if he doesn't have a care in the world.

"Maddy...Gabe's a big boy, he can handle himself." He stares at his plate, while my eyes bore into his head.

"You could at least make a statement," I tell him.

"Fine. Can I at least finish my breakfast?" he asks, annoyed.

"I guess so," I sigh, rolling my eyes.

"Ohhh...ouch," Ian says quietly to himself, but I can't help but want to know what drew that reaction.

"Do I even want to know?" I ask.

"Nothing big. They don't have a lot of information. Just Trent being injured, you coming to his rescue, Gabe being upset, and so on and so forth."

I sit in the chair, biting my lip and staring down at the table while everyone else finishes their meal. I jerk my head up when a phone starts ringing and Trent stands up, digging in his pocket to retrieve his phone.

"What?" he demands with obvious irritation.

"Yeah, I know." He nods his head in agreement.

"Is he there?" he asks whoever is on the other end.

"Mom..." he draws out. Oh, shit.

"Fine, give me a half hour," he says.

He ends the call, shoving his phone back in his pocket.

"Ms. Jennings, Uncle Mitch. Thank you for the breakfast." He places his plate in the sink, walking to the door.

"Maddy, can I have a word?" he asks, nodding his head toward the front door. "See you, Ian." He clasps his hand on Ian's shoulder while walking out of the room.

I stand up, pushing my chair in and follow Trent out of the room.

"What's up?" I ask.

"I'm sorry about in there," he says, motioning to the kitchen with his hand. "It's just that you are so worried about him. What about me? I am the person who will have to deal with this for weeks. They will follow me around, hounding me for pictures, asking questions...."

"He's your brother, Trent," I interrupt, not wanting to hear about his celebrity-life problems. "He didn't sign up for this. Imagine what it could do to his business."

"He's not my brother, Maddy. No brother would do what he has done," Trent says, glaring at me.

"I really want you guys to mend this," I request, placing my hand in his.

"Sorry Maddy, I can't do it. Not to mention, he doesn't want to anyway."

"How do you know?" I ask.

"When you left me, I thought maybe we could put all of this aside and be brothers again but he refused. He told me it was unforgivable what I did to you. So I'm sorry Maddy, but it's not me."

He pulls his hand away from mine. "Anyway, I just wanted to apologize for being an ass, but what else is new right?" He opens my door, looking at me one more time before shutting it behind him.

I place my hand on the doorknob, ready to run after Trent and make him feel better. Instead, I turn toward the stairs because, regardless of his sulking, I have had enough of worrying about Trent's feelings. He certainly has cast mine aside enough over the years.

Taking a shower, I let the warm water flow over my body which relaxes my muscles but won't quiet my mind. One thing that everyone seems to agree on is that Trent and Gabe need to mend their relationship. Trent just confessed that he tried but Gabe refused him. Since I am the one that came between them, I should be the one to bring them back together. And if I can't have Gabe, they should at least have each other.

After I finish getting ready, I look through my old purple floral box, finding the MASH prediction that Mackenna made for me when I was eleven. I sigh heavily and fold it up, putting it back in the box. As much as I wish this MASH was my current life, it can't be.

I hide the box back on the shelf in my closet, suddenly remembering another purple box and a rush of excitement hits me. That box contains exactly what I need to show Gabe why he needs to patch up his relationship with his brother. I rub my temples, trying to remember where I had it last. I shake my head, knowing I never took it to New York. Is it at the Bassos? God, I hope not. Then it finally dawns on me. Grabbing my phone and purse, I race down the stairs, almost slipping on the bottom two.

"Mom, can I borrow your car?" I frantically ask her.

"What's up, buttercup?" Ian peeks around the corner, curious.

"Mom?" I ask again, ignoring Ian.

She looks at Mitch and then back at me. "Of course. Where are you going?" she questions.

"Jack's place. I have to end this, Mom." She rifles through her purse and hands the keys to me.

"Thanks," I say and start out the door. Before I can get it open, Ian grabs my arm.

"Oh no you don't. I smell drama and where drama is, I am." Ian hooks arms with me and we head out together to my mom's car.

Chapter 25 – Present Day

Jack has been storing my boxes in his attic and Ian reluctantly agrees to go up there after some heavy persuading on my part. A half hour later, Ian comes down the stairs with my purple plaid box.

"You have a bunch of other shit up there." Ian motions with his thumb up the ladder he just came down.

"Thank you, Ian," I say, ignoring his comment and concentrating on the box. When I lift the lid, the smell of the beach practically floats to my senses. Closing my eyes, I can almost feel the sun on me as I remember playing volleyball with Gabe and our midnight walks along the beach. I recall his hands on me as he held me close and those luscious lips kissing me goodnight.

"Jack, could you call Doug? I have a plan," I yell toward him, walking down the stairs.

"Maddy, Linds and I are extremely busy, can't this wait?" Jack walks into the room, holding some kind of tulle and ribbon that he is using to try to make a bow.

"Just please go call Doug. It's time his brothers grow up." I lead the way into the kitchen, sitting down with Lindsey and helping her tie boxes of candy into little tulle packages clasped with ribbon. Ian sits down too and soon we have an assembly line going.

Two hundred tulle presents later, a scheming plan has been put into place. We've recruited not only Jack and Doug, but Mr. and Mrs. Basso as well. They convinced Trent that the bachelor party should be here at the Basso's instead of a club in Chicago, where photographers would be waiting for him to show up. Since Jack is only concerned with who is there and not where his bachelor party is being held, it made my plan that much more possible.

Trent is still at his parents' house so I text him to meet me at the barn in a half hour. After jotting a down a quick note, I hand the letter to Ian.

"Make sure he reads it," I instruct Ian, holding it firmly in his hand.

"I will, Maddy." He practically has to rip it from my hands. Although I will always cherish the goodbye love letter that Gabe wrote to me after our time together in Cancun, it's time I let it go.

"Ian, let's go." Jack puts his hand on his shoulder, motioning him toward the hallway.

Ian reaches over, giving me a huge hug. "Good luck, honey. I will be waiting for you afterwards." Then he retreats down the hall.

"Are you sure?" Jack asks me, not following Ian. "I thought this was going to end…differently," he says, faltering over the words.

"It's for the best," I say.

"For who?" Jack questions but I don't answer. I just wrap my arms around him, trying to assure us both that this is the right decision.

I pull out of my brother's driveway and follow the boys toward the Basso's house, parking along the side of the road closest to the barn. Déjà vu hits me, reminding of all the times I parked my red Jeep in this very same spot. I think about all the nights we made love or had wild sex there. The nights he held me until I fell asleep or comforted me when I cried over my mom.

The tall grass scratches my legs as I follow the path up to the barn. I push the wooden door open and see that Mr. and Mrs. Basso have already been hard at work, preparing it for the bachelor party. There are poker tables and chairs strewn around, as well as long tables along the walls for food and beverages. The barrel in the corner indicates that there is a keg coming soon. Jack is going to love this.

I climb the ladder up to my hideaway spot with Trent. I am surprised to see him waiting for me, resting against the hay bale. When his eyes meet mine, it makes me want to run back down that ladder, out of the barn, and back into my mom's car. I reluctantly walk over to him, thinking about the fact that I will never be here again. I take a seat next to him and he grabs my hand, smiling over to me.

"Trent," I sigh heavily, releasing the breath I've been holding for the last two minutes.

"Maddy, I am truly sorry for this morning. I have already called Eric and made a statement. I told them that the fight outside the bar was just us brothers messing around and that you were trying to get us to stop before someone got hurt. I didn't explain the pictures of you crying though, since I didn't know how."

"Thank you." I bite my lower lip, unsure of how to begin.

"What did you want to talk about?" he asks.

"Um...well..." I stutter, "we need to talk about us," I finally say.

"What about us?"

"We need to say good-bye to each other as a couple," I say bluntly.

"So you are choosing him?" he asks coldly.

"I'm not choosing anyone," I respond, shaking my head back and forth. "I want you two to get past this fight and be the brothers I know you can be."

"Maddy, I told you this morning that I tried. He doesn't want to. Not to mention, I'm not willing to sacrifice you for him." He stares down at our hands clasped together.

"Trent, can I ask you a question?"

He nods his head up and down.

"Would you marry me?" I ask, hoping he knows that the question I've posed is hypothetical and not a sincere request.

"In a couple years, yeah," he says with a shrug.

"No, I mean right now. Fly to Vegas and be married by the end of the night."

"Maddy..." he sighs.

"Trent, I love you and I know you love me, but you can't deny we have changed through the years. There was a time when you would have jumped at those words and had me in your car, driving to the airport before I could blink. We aren't those kids anymore. Our paths have separated and unfortunately--"

"Someone took my spot," he interrupts.

"That's not the reason, well…it's not the only reason. We gave it everything, Trent, but we don't want the same things in life anymore. You love the clubs and parties, whereas I like staying home for quiet nights together. Our time in New York showed us both this," I say, looking at him pointedly.

"You mean the world to me and what we have shared over the years will never be forgotten. I will continue to support you and be your friend, but I cannot be with you in any other way. Not anymore." I look down at the flower blanket beneath us where I lost my virginity and a tear slips down my face.

"I told you, Maddy. I've changed," he pleads.

"Please Trent, don't fight me on this. You know this is the best thing for both of us." I say, knowing it's the truth. I just hope Trent can see it.

His blue eyes study me for what seems like an eternity. My eyes don't waver and I can't tell what he is thinking which scares me.

"Do you love him?" he softly asks.

"Trent, this has nothing to do with him," I say.

"Maddy, just answer the question."

"Yes," I whisper.

"More than me?"

"Trent…" I breathe in exhaustion.

"Actually, don't answer that. I don't think I could handle the answer anyway." He throws a piece of hay to the ground.

"I never meant for it to happen and I know he didn't either, Trent. You have to believe me."

"It's my fault. If I wouldn't have been such a douche all those times….." he says sadly, shaking his head.

"It might not have mattered, Trent. We tried to stay away from each other."

"Not very hard," he deadpans.

"Trent, we did," I beg him, but then he turns his head and I see a small smirk on his lips.

"Shh…" he says, putting his finger against my lips. "I'm going to miss you."

"I told you Trent, I am here for you whenever you need me."

"Promise me, Maddy. Promise me we will always be friends. I can't lose you." He drops his gaze back down from me.

"I promise," I answer truthfully. I will always be there for Trent.

I wrap my arms around his shoulders, pushing myself closer to him. He returns my affection with arms around my waist.

"I love you, Maddy," he whispers in my ear.

"I love you, too," I whisper back.

Another five minutes pass and I know I need to get out of here before Gabe arrives. I don't want him to see me here.

"Have fun tonight," I say to Trent as I give him one last hug.

"I have a feeling I won't remember any of it after this," he says, gesturing between the two of us, "I plan on getting completely wasted."

"Be careful, Trent," I say, my voice serious.

"Always," he says, grinning at me.

I am retracing my steps back to my mom's car when I see Gabe making his way down from the house.

"Maddy?" he questions, clearly surprised to see me here.

"Hey Gabe," I say, trying to keep my voice casual.

"What are you doing here?" His eyes don't have their usual sparkle and I wonder if it's because of me, or because of what's going on with the press.

"I was talking with Trent," I admit.

"Oh." He puts his hands in his pocket and I sense that it's to keep them from touching me. His hands have always found ways to touch or caress me, no matter what we are doing.

"You got the letter?" I ask, changing the subject.

"Yes, thank you. Your friend Ian is very convincing. Here." He digs the letter out of his pocket, handing it back to me. "It reminded me of how important my brother is to me."

"Good, I'm glad. I hope you both can make amends and have a friendship again," I say sincerely, stuffing the letter in my back pocket.

"Well…thanks again, Maddy."

"You're welcome, Gabe." I turn around, sensing his eyes on me until I am swallowed up by the trees.

When I am safely in my mom's car, I finally let the tears flow. I weep for the boy I have loved for so long and the man that will never be mine. I cry, knowing that Gabe's arms will never securely wrap around me, and his soft lips will never kiss mine again. I lean my head forward against the steering wheel, unable to drive away from the man who holds my entire heart.

Chapter 26 – Present Day

The next morning I am drinking coffee at the kitchen table, trying to get rid of my bachelorette party hangover, when Ian walks through the front door.

I look up at him questioningly, and he holds up my mom's extra key that she hides in the faux rock on the front porch. He makes his way to me in the kitchen, still wearing the clothes he wore last night.

"Where were *you* last night?" I ask, snickering.

"Well…" Ian says, his voice insinuating that he might have hooked up with someone. "If you must know, I spent the entire night taking care of your drunk-ass ex." Now he sounds annoyed. Oops.

"Oh, I was wondering why you never came back last night." I get up, grabbing him a cup of coffee.

"You don't have to, Maddy. I can get it." He moves over to the cabinet to get his own mug.

"No, I insist. It's the least I can do, and I'm really sorry this trip hasn't been that fun for you." I tilt my head, displaying my best apologetic expression.

"It's fine. You know I love your family and your friends, Maddy. Just wish I could have spent more time with you." I fix him a coffee just the way he likes it and he smiles at me, though I notice a speck of sadness in them.

"Ian, I'm going home with you," I joke.

He remains silent, taking a gulp of his coffee and resting his head in his hands from exhaustion. I rub my hands through his hair, massaging his scalp and he moans in pleasure.

"You know I couldn't have done this without you, right? And that I'm indebted to you for the rest of my life?" I ask him.

"Now you're talking," he says, and I can tell he's got a smile on his face.

"So, how bad was Trent?" I ask.

"Remember when he won the Cup?" I nod, remembering. "About twice as bad. Mr. Soccer Stud wouldn't leave the barn, pulling out some old ass blanket and even slept alone on the upper level." He shakes his head in disbelief. "I couldn't even get him go to the main house this morning. Finally, Gabe threw a bucket of cold water on him and that got him up." He starts laughing. "Oh, you should have seen Trent, it was hilarious."

"Glad to hear the infamous Basso brothers' pranks are back on," I say with a smile.

"After last night, they are in full swing. What Trent did to Gabe after his stunt…" he continues.

"I don't want to hear about it, Ian. I'm glad you had fun with them. They are a great group of guys. I just can't bear to talk about them right now." I grab the pot, refilling my cup.

"Them or *him*?" he asks, grabbing the pot out of my hand. "Never mind, I already know the answer."

Before I have a chance to contradict him, my mom walks into the kitchen, looking completely put together and void of any hangover. "Maddy, we need to get to the beauty salon."

"I know, I just need this last cup of coffee." I start to sit back down, but my mom takes my coffee and pulls me by my free hand out of the kitchen.

"No, we should have already left. This is Lindsey's day and she doesn't need the stress of us being late," she says. As we make our way up the stairs, she calls out to Ian and Mitch, telling them that we'll see them at the church.

"I can't believe my son is getting married today," she says wistfully and I'm happy for the reminder. This is Jack's day and I'm happy that the three of us will be sharing a joyful occasion for the first time in quite a while.

A half hour later, my mom and I walk through the salon doors. It is the only beauty shop in town, and therefore Lindsey and her bridal party are the only clients this morning. Caroline and three other bridesmaids are already getting their hair styled into different hairdos. Lindsey's blond hair is in a mess of large curlers as she sits in front of the make-up stand.

"I swear, Maddy…late again. You are lucky it's my wedding day and I'm too busy floating on cloud nine to be mad at anybody," Lindsey says happily, while the lady puts foundation across her face.

"Sorry, Linds," I apologize, going over to give her a quick hug.

"It's okay. Like I said, nothing will get me down today. I will be Mrs. Jack Jennings in a few hours," she says with a huge smile on her face.

"And my sister," I chime in.

"And my daughter," my mom adds.

"I can't wait." Lindsey says.

An hour later, I am trying to sit still while Diana, the owner of the beauty salon, puts my hair up in a tight ponytail. She curls small pieces of my brown hair, tucking them under. When it's all done, I have about thirty bobby pins and an entire can of hairspray in my hair, but it looks absolutely gorgeous.

When I get to the make-up station, I look around and realize that I'm the last girl to finish. I should have known Caroline would pick a time to confront me when no one is around and I can't get away from her.

"So, you told me he was available." She brings a chair up next to me, and Bridgett, the girl applying my make-up, peeks through the corner of her eyes at her.

"He is," I respond, looking at her through the mirror. To be honest, she looks stunning. Her red hair is pinned into a bunch of tight twists and turns and then it flows into large curls, hanging down in a cascade of waves. Her plum eyeliner and mascara make her green eyes stand out. I can't remember which color dress she is wearing, but I imagine none of the guys will be able to take their eyes off of her.

"Listen, I know what you are doing, Madeline. You can't have them both," she says, sneering at me.

"Not that it is any of your business, but I don't have either one of them. They are both single and available," I snap back, causing Bridgett to stop applying my eyeliner.

"That's not what Gabe says. He told me he is seeing someone and I'm not blind. I see the way he is always looking at you..." She starts to go on but I've had enough. This is Lindsey's day. It's not about me, Gabe, or Trent, and it sure isn't about Caroline.

"Look, if Gabe is seeing someone, then I didn't know about it. I swear. And bottom line, I'm not with either Trent or Gabe, nor will I be."

"Keep telling yourself that, Maddy. I honestly don't know what is so damn special about you. Those boys might be single, but they definitely aren't available." She turns on her heels, stomping away from me.

"What was that all about?" Bridgett whispers to me after she leaves.

"She wants Gabe Basso," I say shortly.

"Ohh...well, I can't blame her there. Before he moved away, he was one of Belcrest's most eligible bachelors. The other being Trent, of course." Bridgett gives me a knowing smile that tells me she is well aware of my history with the Basso brothers.

I grin at her through the mirror and then close my eyes, allowing her access to my eyelids. One more day and I will back in New York, I remind myself.

After arriving at the church in the limo, we file in through a back door while Doug makes sure that Jack is nowhere in sight. I find my emerald green dress hanging among the rainbow of others, then grab it and make my way to the changing room. My mom and I have to be ready for pictures in just a few minutes so I change quickly. The shoes I'm wearing are already killing my feet and I have a feeling by the end of the day, my feet are going to need a massage. *Gabe gave the best foot massages.*

I hear the boys laughing and joking as my heels click down the steps. I stop at the end of the stairway, my hand supporting me on the railing. Closing my eyes, I take a deep breath, thinking once again about Jack and Lindsey. Like taking a plunge into a cold pool, my feet hit the floor and I turn the corner. Those blue eyes find me immediately.

Gabe is the most handsome man in casual clothes, but in a tuxedo, he is downright breathtaking. I see that the vest he is wearing is yellow, which means he won't be standing with me at the ceremony. I cringe at the thought of him dancing with someone else.

"Hey, Maddy." Trent comes alongside me, breaking my gaze from Gabe.

"Hey, Trent. How are you feeling?" I ask and can't help a small smile.

"Better after about a gallon of water," he says, smiling back at me.

"That's good. I guess I better get going to the pictures." I step away, seeing my mom posing with Jack.

"Yeah...you don't want to delay the ceremony." His hands are in his pockets as he rolls back on his heels.

"See you later," I say, noting that his vest is orange. I should have known that Jack and Lindsey would know not to stand me next to either Gabe or Trent. Good decision on their part.

"Maddy," Trent calls out to me.

"Yeah?" I ask.

"You look beautiful. Save me a dance, okay?" He raises his eyebrows in question.

"Of course," I answer.

Twenty minutes later, we are done with our side of the family photos. The groomsmen are sitting around the pews, waiting for their turn. A smile forms on my face as I watch the three Basso brothers joking around like they used to when we were young. It reconfirms to me that I made the right choice. I find Gabe's eyes on me every so often, but he never approaches me and always looks away quickly when our gazes connect.

My stomach seems to constantly ache, and I feel like I could throw up at any moment. I need this day to be over quickly. When all of the pictures are done, I happily report back to Lindsey's peaceful bride room to await the start of the ceremony.

When it's time, the bridal party leads the way for Lindsey down the steps and toward the sanctuary. She looks strikingly beautiful in her Princess gown, and her genuine elation and anticipation of marrying my brother is evident to anyone around. The music starts and we all line up with our color-coordinated partners. To say that I'm disappointed with my match would be a massive understatement.

"Man, do I owe Jack. May I escort you, Ms. Jennings?" Shawn Edwards asks, offering me his arm.

"What did I do to my brother to deserve this?" I joke, when in reality, Lindsey and Jack matched me with exactly the right person. Conversation won't be an issue with Shawn and there definitely won't be any relationship drama.

"You must have done something really awesome," Shawn says, winking at me. The entire bridal party stares at us, and I get the feeling that we need to stop talking. I'm not immune to the fact that both Trent and Gabe continue to stare at us way longer than the others.

"Seriously, I just don't get it," Caroline sneers behind us. Since she is the maid of honor, she is walking down the aisle by herself.

"What?" Shawn asks, turning to face her.

"What is so fucking great about her?" She motions her head my way.

Shawn looks over at me, shocked that she would say that, and then he manages to shock me with his response.

"Because she's fucking awesome and has a sweet little body to boot." He turns back around, winking at me. I grace him with a huge smile for being my hero from the evil red head.

Soon, all the couples start their march down the aisle and when it's our turn. Shawn leans over and whispers, "Let's do this." He squeezes my hand and we both look at each other, nodding our heads.

I walk down the aisle, smiling at friends and family before glancing up at Jack. His lips are spread wide and I don't know if I have ever seen him this happy. He winks at me with a smirk, before turning his attention to where my soon-to-be sister-in-law will join him at the altar.

The ceremony goes off without a hitch, and when the pastor announces Mr. and Mrs. Jackson Jennings, everyone applauds and the wedding party begins to exit. We all stand in the receiving line as the guests file out and I hug friends and family members, all who tell me how beautiful I look and that they can't wait to catch up with me at the reception. I smile reflexively, but feel no real emotion. All I can think of is that I have less than twenty-four hours before I am back in New York, far away from Belcrest and the Basso brothers.

"Honey, you look stunning." Ian wraps his arms around me, pulling me close. "Try to enjoy yourself. Your fake smile isn't fooling me," he whispers in my ear.

Before I can respond, he is already moving down the line, greeting Shawn.

Once all of the guests have made it through the line, the wedding party files into the limos, and I am both upset and relieved when I see Gabe and Trent hop in the opposite one from me. Through the open window, I see that Trent is saying something to Gabe and Gabe is nodding his head in agreement. It could be my imagination, but Shawn looks my way at the same exact moment and his eyes seem sorrowful.

Two glasses of champagne later, we pull up to the reception hall. The trip wasn't that bad since Shawn had us all laughing the entire time, finally distracting me from thoughts of Gabe. Exiting the limo, Shawn holds his hand out for mine to help me out. I see Gabe and Trent doing the same for their partners, and I cringe when I see Gabe continue to escort his, wishing it were me. Twenty-three hours, I tell myself.

Chapter 27 – Present Day Reception

During the cocktail hour, I stay close to Ian and Shawn since Kenna is busy taking candid shots of the crowd and Bryan is trailing her, making sure she doesn't overdo it.

Trent smiles over at me a few times, but he is enjoying the time with his family and friends. Gabe, on the other hand, never glances my way at all, standing alongside Trent but never really joining in on the conversations.

When the dinner bells rings, the guests file into a large banquet room. It is decorated beautifully, each with a white cloth-covered table and a vase of multi-colored roses in the center, surrounded by small votive candles. Every table also has a different colored sash tied to the chairs, and the little tulle packages we previously prepared have been placed in front of each guest's seat.

I walk along the head table, which has been reserved for the wedding party, trying to find where I am seated. I am relieved to see that Shawn and I are seated next to each other, but a nervous feeling flows through me when I see Gabe's name next to mine. Something must have slipped through Lindsey's careful planning for her to put me next to him for the entire meal.

I take my seat and minutes later, Shawn and the rest of the wedding party joins me, but the seat to my left remains empty. Just as I think he must have already noticed the arrangements and isn't going to show, I see Gabe walking across the room. I haven't seen him smile once today, except in the pictures and even that look forced. His shoulders are slumped over and he stares at the ground as he walks toward us. After a quick glance down at Trent who is staring at the two of us, Gabe sits down but continues to remain silent.

Soon after everyone is seated, the speeches begin, which have everyone roaring with laughter. Well, almost everyone. Immediately after, the soup arrives and I can't take the silence anymore.

"Gabe," I whisper to him.

He turns his expressionless face my way, saying nothing.

"Can we talk?" I ask.

"There is nothing to say, Maddy. You got what you wanted; Trent and I are okay again." He places his spoon down next to the untouched bowl of soup.

"So, why are you being like this?" I ask.

"What way am I being?" he asks, raising his eyebrows.

"You haven't said anything to me the whole day. You've barely looked at me."

"I can't talk about this. Not now and not here, Maddy," he says, his voice cold.

"So when?" I impatiently probe. I notice Trent's eyes glancing back and forth between his soup and us.

"I don't know. I don't really feel like there is anything to talk about. It's over." He shrugs his shoulders.

"Are you serious? That's it, you aren't going to talk to me ever again?" I ask, my voice rising uncontrollably.

"Hey Jennings, quiet down a bit," Shawn says softly in my ear.

The look I give him could probably stop a train in its tracks.

"Or not," he says with a shrug and a smirk.

"So Gabe, is that it?" I repeat my question.

"I told you, not here," Gabe says through clenched teeth. Unable to take it anymore, I rush down the steps and out of the hall.

"Maddy, wait!" I hear Gabe call after me, but I don't turn around. I refuse to make a scene at my brother's wedding.

There's an atrium area to the right surrounded by cement benches and flowerpots around a beautiful fountain. Twinkle lights illuminate the trees and shrubs, making it a picture-perfect romantic setting. Fortunately, I find a bench that is hidden in the back of the porch area that conceals me.

I slowly wipe the tears from my eyes before they become so uncontrollable I can't catch them all. I wanted him and Trent to patch things up. That was the whole point. Didn't he know it was killing me being away from him? That I can't breathe when I think of a future without him?

"Maddy," his voice calls, "where are you?" Gabe comes around the corner and sees me sitting on the bench. So much for my hiding spot.

"Just go away, Gabe," I say.

"You know I won't," he says, sitting next to me.

"We only have a few more hours and then we don't have to see one another anymore, and then you can go back to your girlfriend in Florida."

"What the hell are you talking about? What girlfriend?" He finally turns to me, confused.

"Come on, Gabe, I'm not stupid. The phone calls. Something you have to take care of in Florida..." I say, trying to jog his memory.

"Again, Maddy, you don't get it. Those phone calls were for work. We had a situation with a house, and Grady and Rich wanted my input. It's as simple as that," he responds angrily.

"Then why did you tell Caroline you had a girlfriend?" I spat back.

"I lied because she wasn't getting the hint. Do you actually think I would have a girlfriend and still chase you?" he asks, looking hurt.

"No...I don't know," I stutter, regretting bringing this up in the first place.

"I am madly in love with you. Do you have any idea what it's like to not be able to get someone out of your head? There is no way I could have a girlfriend when all I dream about is you," he says, turning back away from me.

"I know exactly what it's like. When I told you at Great Adventures that I picked you, I meant it. You are it for me. Trent and I will always share something; I can't change that. But you hold my whole heart, Gabe. It is completely yours if you want it," I tell him.

"Are you really asking me if I want you?" Gabe asks, leaning in closer.

"Yes," I answer with a lump in my throat, unsure of his answer.

"You've got to be kidding me? I've wanted you since the day I broke down that door at Cooper Sears' party." He closes in on me and I arch my body toward him reflexively.

"I thought I was always Little Jennings to you?"

"Never, but that didn't mean you weren't unattainable. I could only admire you from afar, no matter how much I wanted more," he reveals.

"And now?" I ask.

"Now…" He kisses my shoulder. "You," he says, his lips moving to my neck. "Are," he kisses my jaw. "Mine." His lips capture mine and he presses his body into mine on the bench.

In return, I wrap my arms around his neck, pulling him closer. His lips are desperate and pleading, and his tongue plunges directly into my mouth. God, he feels good. Suddenly, he pushes away from the bench, grabbing my hand.

"Come on, let's go." Before I can protest, he drags me around the corner to a private hallway. Pulling us into a bathroom, he locks the door.

His lips are back on me in an instant. "Maddy, did I tell you how incredible you look tonight? You wanted to know why I couldn't look at you. This dress has been driving me crazy," he says, moving his hands to the hem while inching it up my legs. He reaches under it, pulling me up by my ass and I wrap my legs around him.

"Oh…Gabe," I moan, feeling his sizeable bulge pressed against me.

"I can't tell you how long I have imagined doing this." He pulls one side of my dress down, exposing my bra. His lips capture my already pebbled nipple through my pink satin bra, sucking it into his mouth.

He props his leg between mine so he can raise me higher against the wall and pulls my bra down, revealing my breast. He licks my nipple in slow circles before taking it into his mouth.

"Gabe…" I moan again.

"Relax, Maddy, I'm just getting started," he says, moving his hands up my dress between the two of us.

The anticipation of his fingers touching my swollen clit has me on edge. I'm afraid I might come at the slightest touch. He gradually slides his hand under my already-wet panties, inserting one finger and then another.

"Jesus, Gabe," I rasp, holding onto him with my arms clasped around his neck and my legs firmly squeezing his hips.

"You are so warm…so ready," he whispers, circling my clit with his thumb.

"I can't hold it much longer. I'm going to come," I divulge, my voice breathless and strained.

"Go ahead, I want to watch you," he says, thrusting his fingers into me deeper and moving his thumb faster.

I open my eyes for a second, relishing the fact that it is Gabe pleasuring me, and when my eyes see the fire in his, it's my undoing. I moan out his name when my body finally reaches that moment of pure ecstasy.

"You're even more beautiful when you come," Gabe whispers in my ear, removing his fingers from me while capturing my lips in a soft, loving kiss.

He holds me for a few moments until I unwrap my legs from around his body and try to make myself presentable again.

"Can I have you tonight?" he whispers hopefully.

"And every night after," I happily confirm, kissing him again.

We start to leave the bathroom when Gabe stops abruptly and I run straight into his back.

"Can I talk to you two?" Trent asks, and there is surprisingly no sign of rage in his voice or on his face.

"What about?" Gabe looks at me and I nod my head.

"Please, just follow me out," Trent says, leading us to the lobby.

"What's going on Trent?" I ask, noticing that most of the guests have left.

"I want to apologize to you both," Trent says.

"Really?" Gabe asks with obvious disbelief.

"Yes, really." Trent sounds annoyed. "Maddy, I never realized how badly I treated you before now. You have always been there when I needed you, but I was too blind to see what you wanted. I don't know if I didn't want to see it or if I was that egotistical to think you would only want me," Trent admits honestly. "I know I have said that I'm sorry a million times, so I am hoping my actions tonight will show you how regretful I am for everything."

"What are you doing tonight?" I ask hesitantly.

"Just wait." He pauses, looking over at Gabe. "She's always so impatient." A smirk spreads across Gabe's lips.

"Glad you two can come to solid ground when it comes to that," I say and Gabe smirks down to me.

"Gabe, I blamed you for coming between me and Maddy, when in reality, it was me that came between you two. I let Maddy go when we left high school, hell, maybe even before that. I had no right to keep you two apart and make you promise me to stay away from her," he confesses.

"Don't get me wrong, I don't regret a single second I have had with Maddy," he says to me, a loving expression on his face. "You have to understand that. I should have let you go a long time ago, but that has nothing to do with how much our time together has meant to me."

A tear rolls down his check, and I know how hard this is for him to say. But I also know that it's way overdue.

"Until Maddy told me how much she loves you, Gabe, I honestly thought you two had some kind of physical attraction that would pass. I have pushed away your happiness in order to fulfill my own. I have to be the one to step aside and let two people I love have the happy ending they deserve. I'm sorry I interfered."

He steps up to Gabe and holds out his hand. "Thank you, Gabe."

"For what?" Gabe chokes out, speaking for the first time.

"For taking care of her when I didn't. For always making sure she was okay. For giving her a shoulder to cry on when she needed it. For picking her up when she was down." He releases a breath. "For being everything I wasn't. She deserves the best and that's you, brother." They shake hands and then embrace in a tight hug. I can hear them murmuring to each other, but I can't make out what they're saying.

Then Trent comes over to me, wrapping his arms around my waist and pulling me into a bear hug. "Take care of him," he says, kissing my cheek and positioning me next to Gabe. He then walks away, leaving Gabe and I alone once again. We look at each other, not believing what just happened.

"Who would have thought?" I ask, wrapping my arms around Gabe's neck.

"Definitely not me," he laughs, grabbing my waist and pulling me into him. "But I'm not going to waste any time thinking about it."

"So...what do we do now?" I ask him, placing small kisses on his chin.

"Well, I have a few ideas…" He motions with his head to the elevators.

"You read my mind," I say, starting to walk toward them.

"Hey wait up, Madgirl." Gabe walks swiftly to catch up to me.

"For you…always," I say, placing my hand on his cheek and bringing his head down to mine. "I love you, Gabe Basso."

"I love *you*, Madeline Jennings."

Epilogue

Gabe convinced me to move to Florida, although it didn't take much for me to agree. Personally and professionally, there is no place I'd rather be. The company that Gabe and his friends own have been needing an interior designer to pick out color schemes involving paint colors, tiles, and carpeting. He tried to pay me an absurdly high salary, but after some very steamy negotiation sessions, I convinced him that it was in the best interest of his business to pay me the going rate for designers.

To say Ian was upset was an understatement. We promised each other we would visit often, but I was still sad that I wouldn't see him every day. We drove down to Florida in another monster SUV, except this one was white. We took our time, stopping frequently because we couldn't keep our hands off each other.

Because neither of us wanted to be apart another minute, I moved into his two-bedroom condo on the ocean. I love kissing him goodnight and waking up to him every morning. We go for long walks on the beach and most days we have quiet dinners at home.

After what I'm sure was a hot and heavy honeymoon, Jack and Lindsey are happily married and living in Belcrest. I imagine I will receive news of being an aunt soon.

My mom and Mitch eloped in Hawaii, sending us all a picture of their rings to announce it. I was disappointed at not being there to see how happy she was, but I was ecstatic for her nonetheless. Our relationship has definitely come a long way. I talk to her at least three times a week, and she and Mitch are looking at properties down here to be closer to Gabe and me.

Trent left the wedding that night after talking with us, and we didn't hear from him again for a month. We both tried to call him numerous times, but he never answered our phone calls or texts.

Gabe's parents let us know that he needed some time before he could talk to either of us, but he still meant what he said and knew he made the right decision. So we both gave him space and let him be the one to reach out when he was ready. Now Gabe talks to Trent a couple times a week and I talk to him too, but not as often.

Trent's ankle is healed and doing better, but right now, he isn't the star he was before. Chicago didn't make it to the Soccer National League cup this year, but they did re-sign him for one more year, which he was happy about. He pushes himself every day to make sure he ends up on top again, and I have faith that he will get there one day.

He isn't dating anyone, at least not seriously. According to the online gossip that Ian sends me constantly and I try not to read, he is with a different woman every night. I know that isn't entirely true, but I am sure that his bed is a little bit of a revolving door nowadays.

He is supposed to come down to see us after the season is over, along with Gabe's parents, and Doug and his family.

Sometimes it surprises me how it all turned out, that I have Gabe next to me and still have a friendship with Trent.

Mackenna, Bryan, and baby Josey are coming down next week. We haven't seen them since Josey was born and she is already three months old. Pictures just don't cut it; I need my baby fix. I'm staring at the latest picture Kenna sent me when I feel Gabe's arms wrap around me from behind.

"What do you think?" he asks, kissing my shoulder.

"It's a little artsy, but I guess when your mom's a photographer..."

"No," he says, kissing my earlobe, "what do you think about having a baby?"

"Didn't we miss a step somewhere?" I ask, smiling up at him.

"Details," he answers. "Plus, you never know, it might take a while. We probably better practice." He grabs my hand, pulling me to the bedroom.

As Gabe leads me into our bedroom, I kiss my hand, placing it on the picture frame hanging just inside. The MASH prediction that Mackenna made for me when we were eleven serves as a reminder to us that you never know when a game of chance *can* reveal your future.

352

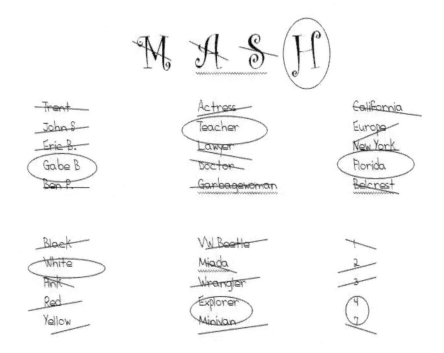

Number: 6
What a great life. You live in a house with your amazing husband
Gabe Basso in Florida with your four kids. You are a teacher and drive
a white explorer. I am forever jealous.
Love you Maddy!
MacKenna
BFF

Dear Readers,

Thank You! I truly appreciate you taking a chance on a new indie author and I hope you enjoyed *Love Me Back.*

Please reach out.

Michelle Lynn

www.michellelynnbooks.com
Facebook - https://www.facebook.com/pages/Michelle-Lynn/413280762102448?ref=hl
Goodreads - http://www.goodreads.com/author/show/7065829.Michelle_Lynn
Twitter - @michellelynnbks
E-Mail – michellelynnbooks@gmail.com

S.G. Thomas (Editor)
www.perfectproofandpolish.com
perfectproofandpolish@gmail.com

Turn the page to take a sneak peak at Michelle Lynn's upcoming novel Don't Let Go, released in Fall 2013

Don't Let Go
Coming FALL 2013

Chapter 1 – Four Months Ago Drayton University

He slams me against the door, his lips meeting mine urgently. His hands search my body and I wrap my right leg up around his, moving my dress higher up my thighs.

His lips move to my tear-stricken cheeks, where lines of mascara still cover them. He makes his way to my neck and then my ear, lightly nibbling around my earlobe and I know at that moment, I need this.

"Make me forget," I whisper.

"Oh believe me, you will forget your name when I am done with you," he says, grabbing my ass, forcing my legs to wrap around his torso.

He carries me across the room, his lips on my mine, thrusting his tongue deeper in my mouth with every step. My arms are tight against him, keeping him close. The feeling of safety is what I crave.

He throws me on the bed, our eyes never leaving one another. Pulling on my legs, he brings me to the edge of the bed and takes off my heels. His hands inch up my legs until his fingers are wrapped around each side of my black thong. He slides it down my legs, tossing the tiny piece of material onto the floor before returning to push my dress up, exposing me to him. I hear the breath hitch in his throat before he starts unzipping his dress slacks and pushing them down. He shuffles over to the nightstand and seconds later he is on top of me.

"I have been waiting so long to have you," he says, entering me hard and rushed. "Oh...so worth the wait."

I remain quiet, trying to push all thoughts out of my head. When his hands reach my ass, pulling me harder against him, the pleasure increases and everything disappears. He thrusts forcefully into me, whispering how good I feel. He may not have as many moves as others and he talks too much for my liking, but I am enjoying how well-endowed he is.

The feeling builds inside of me; I love this part. All I feel is his touch while he pumps into me. As sweat starts slicking between us, I flip him over, straddling his body. I can no longer wait for him, he is going way too slow and I crave my release. Isn't this what it's all about?

"That's what I'm talking about!" he says and smirks as I slide him back into me. I want to stick a sock in his throat. His talking is making it harder for me to find my relief.

He grabs my hips, trying to move me to his rhythm, but I pick up his hands and place them on my breasts so I can control the speed and rhythm. Five minutes later, my body shudder and I sink down on top of him.

"Fuck, Sadie. You're awesome." He moves to kiss me, but I climb off his body, pulling my dress back down.

I stand up to put my heels back on, but he grabs me from behind, bringing me closer to him. "Stay with me tonight," he says, wrapping his arms around my waist.

"Okay," I agree, crawling back on the bed. It is better than being alone. I hate being alone; it only makes me relive my mistakes.

He wraps his arms around me and I can smell the alcohol on his breath as his mouth rests close to my neck. The feeling of safety surrounds me and I drift off to sleep.

The next morning the light streams into the small room, waking me up where I find myself alone in a strange bed. I look around, trying to remember where I am and what I did. The dirty clothes overflowing in the hamper and the sports team paraphernalia on the wall tell me that I am most likely in a frat house…again.

I tip toe to get my shoes, hooking them in my hands. I slowly open the door, peering right and left down the hall. I see no one, so I quietly make my way down the stairs. It seems like the front door is a mile away and I can't get through it fast enough. Just as my hand reaches the knob, I hear talking in the next room.

"I wouldn't brag, Soren, I had her last week." A deep voice laughs. "Actually, you might be the last to have her."

"She a great lay though," Jeff Soren says in return.

"I told you she was," the other male agrees. "Ever since…the incident, she has become the college slut."

"I know. It's kind of sad though." Jeff's voice actually sounds concerned. "I wish…"

"Dude. You can't save girls like that, you just enjoy what they give you," the other voice replies back.

I close my eyes, taking a deep breath. I catch a glimpse of myself in the mirror. Mascara is stained in long lines down my face and my long honey-colored hair looks like a bird made its home in it. My lips are swollen red, and I can't help but think I resemble a hooker on the corner waiting for her next trick.

I turn the knob to the door slowly, hoping Jeff and his friend don't hear me. I sneak out, walking across the street to my sorority house. I am happy to find that everyone is either still asleep or out. When I crash into my bed, I take the picture out of my drawer that's been hidden away since last year. I clutch it hard against my chest, while sobs escape my mouth. Curling up into the fetal position on my twin bed, I can't help but think how I have disappointed him. I need to change the direction of my life. Make him proud of me.

4575095R00200

Printed in Great Britain
by Amazon.co.uk, Ltd.,
Marston Gate.